There
Will Be
Consequences

A Biographical Novel of Old New Mexico

Loretta Miles Tollefson

PALO FLECHADO PRESS

ISBN: 978-1-952026-05-8
Library of Congress Control Number: 2021920790

This novel uses only historical characters and strives to provide an accurate depiction of past events as far as they are
known. However, the thoughts, words, and motivations of the
people portrayed in this book are products of the author's imag-
ination and interpretation of the historical materials. This book
is a work of fiction. References in it to historical events, real
people, or real places are used fictitiously.

Palo Flechado Press
Santa Fe, New Mexico

Other Books by Loretta Miles Tollefson

Old New Mexico Fiction
Not Just Any Man
Not My Father's House
No Secret Too Small
The Pain and The Sorrow
Old One Eye Pete (short stories)
Valley of the Eagles (micro fiction)

Other Fiction
The Ticket
The Streets of Seattle

Poetry
But Still My Child

ACKNOWLEDGEMENTS

A special thanks to my early readers, Ellen McBee, John McDermott, Olga Núñez Miret, and María Rinaldi.

CONTENTS

Foreword

In early August 1837, rebellion broke out in New Mexico, thirty miles north of the capital at Santa Fe. The insurrection was triggered by the impending implementation of a Federal sales tax as well as changes to the Mexican Constitution, modifications that moved power from individual communities and placed it more firmly in the hands of the federal government, President Antonio López de Santa Anna, and New Mexico Governor Albino Pérez.

The situation in New Mexico quickly turned deadly. By August 10, 1837, Pérez and over a dozen administration officials and military personnel were dead and José Angel Gonzales, a rebel of Native descent, occupied the governor's office. It was the beginning of a tumultuous period that wouldn't end until late January 1838, with the rebels dispersed and Gonzales himself executed.

Because there are so many different aspects of and perspectives on this story, I have chosen to tell it in twelve separate but linked sequential narratives, each chapter from a different person's point of view as the tale unfolds. All of the characters in this book are based as closely as possible on what I have been able to discover about them from historical sources. A short biographical sketch for each person is provided at the end of the novel.

Because this book is set in New Mexico in the late 1830s, I've striven to use Spanish that reflects the local dialect at that time. This was a unique combination of the language of the conquistadors, indigenous vocabulary, and terms that had filtered in with French and American trappers and traders. I've tried to represent the resulting mixture as faithfully as possible. My primary sources of information were Rubén Cobos's excellent books, *Refranes, Southwestern Spanish Proverbs* and *A Dictionary of New Mexico and Southern Colorado Spanish*. Any errors in spelling, usage, or definition are solely my responsibility. A vocabulary list is included at the end of the book.

I have also striven to portray what is today called the Palace of the Governors as accurately as possible. If you've visited the Palace, you'll notice that it no longer looks the way I've described it. That's because it was renovated extensively following American occupation in 1846. I've based my description on material published in the *New Mexico Historical Review* and by the Museum of New Mexico press. Again, any errors in fact or interpretation are solely my responsibility.

Researching and writing this novel has reminded me once again that our human desires and motivations are very similar, no matter how much distance or time separates us. I hope you will find the events and people of New Mexico in 1837/38 as fascinating as I do.

EPIGRAPH

Como siembras, segarás: As you plant, so you will harvest.
Southwestern Spanish Proverbs, Rubén Cobos

There
Will Be
Consequences

A Biographical Novel of Old New Mexico

Loretta Miles Tollefson

CHAPTER 1

Dec. 1836–March 1837: A Grave Offense
(The Montoya Family)

When Dolores enters the room, Antonio Abad is still pacing back and forth in front of the adobe fireplace in the corner and waving Governor Pérez's letter in the air. His brother Desiderio sits in the oak armchair puffing his ridiculous pipe.

Dolores sniffs to get their attention, but they're engrossed in their conversation. She shoves the door closed with her hip and lugs her armload of shaggy churro fleece across the room to the wood-plank table.

"The man seems to think we're all illiterate peones," her husband says for the twentieth time in the past week. His booted foot scrapes the edge of the hearth. Dolores scowls at him. There's already a scuff on the plastered wall beside it.

"But how can we refuse him?" Desiderio asks. He runs his fingers through his curly black shoulder-length hair. "Though I'm sure you're right, that it's a loan we'll never see repaid." He shrugs. "En el mejor paño cae la mancha."

Antonio Abad raises an eyebrow. "The stain falls on the best cloth?"

Desiderio taps his pipe on the arm of the chair. He's only twenty and thinks smoking it makes him look more mature. "I'm sure we aren't the only ricos who've received a letter demanding funds." He shrugs again. "We have more money than most. We have to pay more than most."

"Then he should say so instead of asking for a loan!"

Dolores's lips thin. What an idiot. She looks away before she says something she'll regret and spreads the fleece out on the table. It's thick and relatively clean. It should bring a good price. She runs her fingers through it, letting the lanolin soothe her hand.

But it can't soothe her heart or her irritation when her husband starts in again. "And Pérez doesn't even have the courtesy to write himself!" he says. "The letter is from his aide, not the governor." He turns the missive toward the fire-light and glances down at it. "Requesting the pleasure of a small loan from Don Antonio Abad Montoya and his illustri-ous brother Desiderio," he reads aloud. His handsome mouth twists in disgust. "At least he deigned to call me 'Don,' though I'd rather have some kind of guarantee that we'll be repaid."

He turns and starts pacing again. "It's a damn tax, that's what it is! And in addition to the new sales tax that's com-ing!" He scowls at Desiderio. "Remember what I said in April, when Francisco Sarracino was replaced as treasurer? By Manuel Armijo, of all people? I knew we'd be asked for more money!"

Dolores raises her head. She's said it before, but he clear-ly needs to hear it again. "Armijo's only the interim treasurer until the charges against Sarracino are proven to be the falsehood they are. Besides, you have no evidence that Armi-jo is taking funds that don't belong to him. This is simply a loan, and it's for a good cause. If the presidio troops and lo-cal militiamen don't go out every year to remind the Navajo who's in charge in Nuevo México, they'll continue their raids until none of us have anything left."

2

Antonio Abad scowls at her. "We're safe enough here in the valley of the río del Santa Cruz."

"We won't be if the Navajo aren't pushed back a little."

His scowl deepens. "It's Pérez's own fault that he has no money to pay the troops. He's short on funds because he's been spending on other things. Remember that ridiculous independence day celebration in Santa Fe last year?" He waves the letter in the air, emphasizing his words. "Twenty-one gun salutes. Three days of parades and dances, along with a bullfight in the middle of the plaza! It must have cost a fortune! Why couldn't he just give a speech?"

Desiderio takes his pipe out of his mouth. "A celebration on the Santa Fe plaza is safer than going out against los indios bárbaros." He uses his free hand to push his hair away from his face. "Pérez may be a colonel from Vera Cruz, but he'd never fought the Navajo before he arrived here last year."

His brother nods abstractly and glances at the letter again. "Everyone who's received one of these should band together and refuse to pay."

This is new. Something quivers in Dolores's chest. "You can't refuse."

He glares at her. "I'm a free man with lands and animals. I can do as I like with what is mine!"

Desiderio's chin lifts. "As can I."

She gives him a withering look and faces him, her hands on her hips. "And what then? You'll be arrested!"

He waves an impatient hand. "You don't understand." He turns to Desiderio. "If we all stand firm, nothing will happen. Pérez can't throw every propertied man in Nuevo México in jail." Then he grins. "Besides, the local officials will be on

3

our side, not his. It's useful to have relatives in the right places and a governor unfamiliar with our customs. Our good alcalde won't be able to find me or Desiderio, and Pérez will never realize he isn't actually looking."

Dolores's lips tighten. "Antonio Abad Montoya, that's the stupidest thing I've ever heard you say."

He swings toward her, his dark brown eyes mere slits in his handsome face. "You watch your tongue, woman."

She glares back at him. "You may be the oldest of your family and therefore its head because your parents have died, but that doesn't make you the holder of all knowledge."

The door opens just then. Seven-year-old Ygnacia slips in. She pauses on the threshold and looks from one parent to the other with apprehensive hazel-green eyes.

"Come inside," her mother says impatiently. "We're only talking."

The girl's forehead creases with anxiety, but she obeys. She moves to the far corner of the room and drops onto a low stool, where she fiddles with the tendrils that have escaped her black braids and watches the adults.

Dolores turns back to her husband. She jerks her head sideways toward Ygnacia. "She's the reason you should send Pérez the money. If you won't think of the consequences to yourself or me, think of her. What kind of life will she have when her father is known throughout Nuevo México as a man who doesn't support the authorities? Or when you've been exiled for your foolishness?"

He turns away from her. "No one's going to be exiled." He looks at his brother. "We are free men in a nation of free men. We have constitutional guarantees!"

Desiderio stirs uneasily. He fingers his pipe. "We did have guarantees. But remember, the Congress in la Ciudad de México is still modifying the national constitution. The plan is to give the governor more power than the men who came before him. Which I expect he will enjoy. After all, he disbanded the Santa Cruz de la Cañada Council simply because the members were related to each other."

"I don't believe he had the right to do that, either," Antonio Abad snaps. "Or good reason! What fool thinks a group of people with common ancestors will agree on every issue? The man takes too much on himself!"

"He was enforcing the new law," Dolores says.

He begins pacing again, slapping the letter against his leg. "Or so he says. Have you read this law that gives him such authority? I haven't! I've never seen a copy of it! Is what we've been told about events in Mexico City even true? We have no way of knowing! This talk of reducing the number of councils, limiting who can vote, and all the rest of it. How much can we believe?" He waves the letter in the air. "Or is it all simply a ploy to wring more money from us? Pérez should be extracting funds from rich mine owners like that Sonoran José Francisco Ortiz, not us!"

Dolores presses her lips together and turns back to the table and her fleece. There's no point in continuing the discussion. He won't listen. Maybe her brother Juan can talk some sense into him. Or Catarina, who's the oldest of Antonio Abad's two sisters and married to Juan. They'll be here tomorrow to help with the annual hog slaughter the day after. Her brothers sometimes listen to her.

Dolores turns to Ygnacia, who's watching her father with wide eyes. "Come, child. While your father complains about

5

something he can't control, we have work to do to prepare for your aunt and uncle's arrival." She can only hope her brother can talk some sense into the man.

However, when Juan and Catarina arrive the next day, they also carry a letter from the governor, and Juan's almost as aggravated about the demand for a loan as Antonio Abad is. His brother has brought a guest, a distant Montoya cousin named Pablo who's from Taos. He and others there have also received letters. The following day, as more people arrive for the matanza and subsequent feast, it becomes clear that every propertied family in the region has been tapped for funds. And the men are universally angry about it.

Which makes Dolores even more uneasy and irritable. "These stupid men, with their talk and their plans," she mutters to her sister-in-law. "As if keeping their families fed and clothed isn't enough to occupy them. They should just pay the loans!"

But none of the men see it that way. By the time the butchering is over, the feasting done, the pork fat rendered, and the remaining meat distributed according to need and participation, all the men present are determined to ignore Governor Pérez's demands.

"No good will come of it," Dolores says grimly the next afternoon as the wagon carrying Juan and Catarina rumbles out of the adobe-walled yard, Pablo riding his horse beside them.

Antonio Abad closes the big gate and drops the wooden bar into place. "It's time those newcomers in Santa Fe remember that we of the people are the true basis of power."

She shakes her head. "We of the people? We don't live in the United States of America, we live in México."

"Los Estados Unidos Mexicanos. Where all men are equal. We decided that in 1824, remember?"

She snorts impatiently and turns toward the house. "That may be so, but saying it won't keep the soldiers from coming for you."

"There is strength in numbers," he says as he follows her inside.

She doesn't answer. It will do no good. But she shivers a little as she moves to the fire to check the bubbling stew.

~ ~ ~ ~

And then, in spite of her fears, nothing happens. Dolores goes about her daily tasks and completes her preparations for winter. The corn is dried and stored, the chiles threaded onto heavy string and hung from the rafters, the rosehips collected and tucked away into their clay pot.

Activity like this always makes her feel better. She's smiling with contentment as she carries a fleece in from the storeroom one chilly morning. After she's finished cleaning this one, she'll have only two more to do and can begin combing and spinning.

As she enters the sala, there's a loud knock on the outer door. Ygnacia, beside the hearth, drops her cornhusk doll onto a chair. "I'll answer it!"

Dolores's smile deepens as she watches the little girl cross the room. She's getting so big. So grown-up. Time passes so quickly.

Then the door swings open and time stands still. José Esquibel, the local alcalde, is poised on the threshold, two soldiers behind him. The magistrate's lips smile at her over Ygnacia's head, but his eyes are anxious.

"¡Entre por favor!" the child says, dropping him a curtsy.

His gaze drops to her face and he nods absently, then turns back to Dolores.

She has to swallow hard before she can speak. Even then, her invitation to enter is hesitant, unlike her usual demeanor.

The alcalde moves into the room. The two soldiers follow. Then a tall broad-shouldered man ducks through the door. It's Donaciano Vigil, dressed in his presidio sergeant uniform, his long oval face slightly paler than usual.

"Cousin!" Dolores says. "Buenos días." She turns to the others. "Please, have a seat. Would you like something to eat? To drink?" Perhaps it's only a social visit. If she treats them as guests, surely nothing bad can happen. She forces her lips into a mischievous smile. "Or something stronger, perhaps?"

The magistrate glances at the soldiers. "Not today."

"In fact, we need to speak to your husband," Donaciano says gravely. He takes off his flat-brimmed black hat and studies it for a long moment before he looks up at her and pushes his wavy black hair from his brow. "I'm afraid we're here on official business."

Dolores swallows past the dry spot in her throat and turns to Ygnacia. "Go find your father."

The child's eyes are large in her small face. She looks at her mother, then each of the men, and crosses quietly to the door.

Dolores turns to the alcalde and gestures toward the massive oak chair beside the fire. She moves to it, collects

Ygnacia's doll, and says, "Please, seat yourself," a little too heartily.

Then she turns away and sinks onto the banco, the seat built into the adobe wall beside the fireplace. She focuses on her cousin. "Primo, how is your family? Your mother is well? And your wife and the little ones?"

His tone is polite as he answers her, but she's not sure what he says. There's a thrumming sound in her ears and a sour feeling in her stomach.

Then Antonio Abad comes through the door, Ygnacia behind him.

"Welcome, Alcalde Esquibel," he says formally.

"Buenos días, Don Antonio Abad," the magistrate says politely. Then his face contracts. He glances at the sergeant. "I'm afraid we have a slight problem."

Vigil nods, his eyes on Antonio Abad's face. "I have been directed by His Excellency the Governor to take you into custody." There's no apology in his voice, but neither is there pleasure. As he speaks, the two soldiers step forward. He gives them a warning glance and they stop where they are.

"And you had to bring soldiers with you?" Antonio Abad asks. "Were you afraid I might knock you down and run away?" He spreads his hands. "Do you not know that I am a God-fearing man?"

Esquibel chuckles nervously.

He swings toward the alcalde with a scowl, then refocuses on the sergeant. "Did the governor truly think soldiers were necessary? Does he know so little of me that he believes me capable of disobeying a directive from my alcalde?" His chin lifts. "I am a law-abiding citizen."

"A citizen who refused to pay the loan requested of him and who encouraged his neighbors to do likewise," Vigil observes mildly.

"Ah, so that is the charge, is it?" Antonio Abad turns to the alcalde. "And for that I am to be arrested?"

Esquibel nods unhappily.

"Well then, let us be on our way." He looks at the banco. His face doesn't soften at the look of fear in Dolores's eyes, the way her fingers clutch Ygnacia's doll. "Fetch me a blanket and a parcel of food."

Any other time, she would have dropped the toy, jumped to her feet, and told him what to do with his orders. But she's too frightened to quarrel with him just now. She places the doll gently on the banco, rises, and goes into the storeroom for bedding and some white cotton fabric in which to place the food.

By the time she's returned, she's breathing again. And she's had time to become angry. At the alcalde, at her cousin, at her husband. She pushes the shaggy fleece aside, drops the rolled-up wool blanket onto the table, then flings the cloth down beside it. She brushes past the men to the cupboard for bread and dried meat, returns to the table, slaps the food into the middle of the cloth, and shoves its corners into two rough knots.

"You and your mouth," she says as she thrusts the resulting bundle into Antonio Abad's hands.

He scowls at her. "I have a right to speak my mind."

"You have a responsibility toward me and your child!"

Alcalde Esquibel steps forward. He puts a hand on her arm. "It is a small thing, Doña Dolores. I'm sure it will be resolved quickly."

One of the soldiers snorts. She scowls at him and he glances at the sergeant.

Donaciano frowns at him and looks at Antonio Abad, then Dolores. "The governor calls it a grave offense," he says reluctantly.

Her husband's jaw tightens. "The man's an—"

"Don't say it!" she shouts. She glares at him, her hands on her hips. "Whatever you think, don't say it!"

Vigil, the magistrate, and even the soldiers take a step back, their faces wary. Her husband merely chuckles, reaches for the blanket roll, and heads toward the door.

"You stupid pig!" she shrieks as the other men follow him. "You fool! You think only of yourself and your damnable pride!"

The door thuds shut behind them. Dolores drops into the chair by the fire, covers her face with her hands, and weeps.

On the stool in the corner, Ygnacia blinks slowly. Her little chin trembles but she doesn't speak.

The fire has burned low on the hearth before Dolores stops sobbing. Finally, she lifts her head, wipes her wet cheeks, and stares at the glowing coals.

Then her jaw tightens and she jerks to her feet. She turns to the girl. "Come," she says. "There is work to be done." She goes to the fire, bends, and tosses in a log. Sparks fly up. She moves to the table and lifts the fleece into her arms. "Go to the stables," she says over her shoulder. "Find someone to send a message to your uncles. Both Desiderio and my brother."

By the time Ygnacia returns, Dolores has taken the fleece back to the storeroom, swept the house, and begun preparations for the evening meal. She gives terse orders to the workmen who follow Ygnacia into the house, but says little else. The evening meal is a silent one.

~ ~ ~ ~

Early the next morning, Dolores places more provisions into a bundle and sets out for the Santa Cruz de la Cañada jail. When she arrives, she has to wait for Alcalde Esquibel to be called, so he can examine what she's brought. She stands ramrod straight in front of the table while he pokes half-heartedly at its contents. "None of this is to my liking, Doña Dolores," he says.

She glares at him.

"I tried to keep it from happening." He pushes the bundle aside and spreads his hands palms up, expressing his helplessness. "When the governor sent word the first time, I lost the message. I thought he would think better of the order and be glad when I didn't obey." He smiles ruefully. "Instead, he sent word again." He shrugs. "Again, I misplaced the message."

Then his black eyes darken. "But the third time, Pérez sent Sargento Donaciano Vigil and two men to ensure his order was carried out. There was nothing I could do then but obey." He eyes her, looking for sympathy.

She reaches for the bundle and begins retying its knots.

"You know how much I like your husband," the alcalde goes on. A pleading note enters his voice. "We grew up together. He is mi primo. In fact, we are closer than many cousins." He peers into her face. "I did the best I could."

"Water that's gone won't turn the mill," she says irritably. She lifts the bundle from the table. "Are you going to let me take this to him myself or is that not allowed?"

He heaves a self-pitying sigh and pushes away from the table. "I'll tell him you're here."

She isn't her husband's only visitor. Desiderio sits on the single chair, facing Antonio Abad, who's lounging on a cot on the other side of the narrow room. At the end opposite the door, her big scar-faced cousin Juan Vigil, the one they all call "El Quemado," leans against the wall below a small wood-barred window.

They stop talking as she enters. Desiderio glances up at her, then away. All three have the look of boys who've been caught doing something they shouldn't have but aren't sorry for.

Dolores's jaw tightens. Stupid men. She thrusts the food at Antonio Abad. "This should keep you going for a week or so, until you and the governor can come to some kind of arrangement."

He chuckles as he takes the bundle and drops it beside him onto the bed. "I won't be speaking to Pérez any time soon. He's gone with his militia and troops to fight the Navajo." He nods toward her cousin, whose old burn scar is suddenly very shiny and red against his brown skin. "El Quemado here says it will be at least forty-five days before they return, and probably as many as sixty."

"Forty-five days?"

"Probably sixty."

He sounds so pleased with himself. As if he wants to be here in this tiny room instead of at home doing his duty. Her fingers twitch. Only the other men's presence keeps her hands at her sides. Then she frowns. "But that's Christmas and all of January. The holy days and the very worst of the winter!" She looks at El Quemado. "Surely you misunderstood."

"No, Doña Dolores." He has the grace to sound sorrowful.

But her husband's face isn't sorry. She narrows her eyes at him. "And you would rather be in jail than at home caring for our animals and ensuring the well-being of your family?"

He glances at his brother. "Desiderio will assist you." He leans back against the adobe wall and puts his hands behind his head. "I have other tasks to accomplish."

"What tasks?" She glances at the dusty room, the tiny window. The only decoration is a roughly carved statue of a saint in a cobwebby niche in the wall beside Desiderio's chair. She turns back to her husband. "What can you possibly accomplish in this place?"

"I am setting an example of solidarity with mis amigos y vecinos. I am demonstrating how to stand up for one's rights."

"An example of how to get oneself thrown into jail!"

"They can't throw everyone in el calabozo." He smiles smugly. "His Excellency believes me to be a leader in my community. He thinks making an example of me will quell the spirit of the others. I will show him just what a leader I am."

"And how do you know what Governor Pérez thinks?"

He glances at El Quemado.

Her cousin's burn scar twists across his right cheek as he smiles at her. "We have our sources."

She glares at him, then her husband. "So you plan to be here until February. And I will have to manage alone. The animals, the laborers, the house."

"I will help you," Desiderio says.

She softens a little as she looks at him. He's a good man, although he looks like such a boy. And acts like one, following her stubborn, unthinking husband in whatever he does. She gives Antonio Abad a withering look. "He shouldn't have to."

His hands drop to the cot. "You don't understand."

She snorts derisively and sweeps out of the room without another word.

~ ~ ~ ~

As the days pass, Dolores's stony silence continues. Desiderio appears at the hacienda every few days to make sure the laborers are doing their work and that there's wood for the fire and meat in the house. Dolores goes to the Santa Cruz jail once a week with food and other essentials. While she's there, she speaks only to remind her husband that when he pays what he owes, he can come home.

Right from the beginning, Antonio Abad refuses to listen. Instead, he tells her to bring Ygnacia with her next time. Dolores obeys unwillingly. The child shouldn't have to experience the degradation of her father's incarceration. And she suspects that, though he may want to see the girl, he's also using her presence as a shield against Dolores's opinion.

This goes on through Christmas and all of January, a month of hellish cold wind and icy snow. Early in February, Dolores and Ygnacia arrive at the jail to find El Quemado there again. His bulky body overwhelms the little chair as he watches Antonio Abad pace from window to door, his forehead furrowed with thought.

Dolores stops just inside the door. "What's the matter?"

He looks up. "The governor has returned, but he refuses to hear my petition. He says my case must go south to México City."

El Quemado's eyes drift toward her. "You'll need to hire at least one abogado. Maybe two."

"A lawyer? We can't afford that!"

He nods and refocuses on Antonio Abad, who's standing under the window now and peering up to catch a glimpse of the sky.

"It's still gray," she says. "We'll be lucky to get home before it begins snowing again."

He sighs, runs his hands through his dirty black hair, and turns. "Ygnacia, niña de mis ojos. Come and give me a kiss."

The little girl goes to him and he crouches to hug her. She looks so tiny in his arms. There's something between a lump of pain and a stab of worry in Dolores's throat. She coughs it away. "What will you do?"

Antonio Abad kisses Ygnacia's forehead and looks up. The tender moment is gone. His eyes are mischievous now, a look Dolores has had six years to learn to dread. "Oh, something will come up."

The words turn her worry into bitter anger. She crosses to the cot, drops the bundle of supplies onto it, and holds out a hand to Ygnacia. "Come," she says. "Let us go before the storm arrives." She shoots her husband, then El Quemado, a disgusted look. "Your father and his advisor have important matters to address."

16

As she and the child reenter the outer room, Alcalde Esquibel rises from his table.

"Keep him well observed," Dolores says grimly. "Or he's going to do something stupid that you and I will both live to regret."

He smiles at her blandly, almost smugly.

Her jaw tightens. They're in this together, the lot of them. "You're all a bunch of idiots!" she mutters as she stomps out the door.

~ ~ ~ ~

The weather warms slightly in the next week, as it often does in February in Nuevo México. Then, after a fortnight of sunshine, another snowstorm hits, this one a real ventisca. Blizzard winds howl around the adobe hacienda and topple the wood in the walled courtyard. Dolores is focused on her spinning, trying to ignore it all, when there's a thudding sound at the base of the outer door.

Ygnacia looks up from her doll. "What was that?"

"That wood pile is unstable," Dolores grumbles. "A piece must have fallen and landed on the doorstep. Without a man around the place, the laborers are getting careless. They left the courtyard gate open, too, but I'm not going out to close it."

There's another thud, louder this time and higher up. The wood planks move a little under the pressure. "No, that!" Ygnacia says.

Dolores frowns and half-rises from her seat. She peers toward the door, confirming that the inner bar is wedged tightly into place. There's another dull thud from the other

17

side, then a whole rain of blows, slamming the boards. Fear claws Dolores's chest. That's not from a random chunk of wood. But who would be out in this weather? Not anyone with good intentions. "Those pendejos should have shut that gate," she mutters. She turns to Ygnacia. "Get me the machete."

The child's hazel eyes are round as plates. She runs from the room but returns more slowly, holding the big wood-handled field knife sideways like a platter. It's almost as long as she is tall.

Dolores takes the weapon and jerks her chin toward the door. "Lift the bar just enough to crack the door open," she says. "And stay well behind it."

The wind is pushing the boards so hard that the little girl has to brace her hip against them to give the crossbar enough room to move, but she manages to lift it out of the way. As the brace slips aside, the door pushes toward her, but she shoves back with both hands, blocking it from opening more than a crack.

Dolores hefts the machete. "Who's there?" she demands.

"Your husband!" Antonio's voice yells above the storm. "Let me in, woman!"

The machete hits the floor with a thud. Dolores springs to pull Ygnacia out of the way as Antonio sweeps inside in a whirl of snow. He pulls a blanket from his head and shoulders, sending more cold whiteness onto the floor.

"¡Papá!" Ygnacia runs to him and he swings her into the air.

"What are you doing here?" Dolores asks as she shuts the door and shoves the crossbar back into place.

He laughs at her, his frustration forgotten, and sets the child on her feet. "What kind of a welcome is that?" He pushes his curly black hair back from his face. It's almost as long as Desiderio's now.

Dolores wants to touch it, but instead she tucks her hands into her skirts. "Did the governor release you?"

Antonio's lips twitch in amusement. "Not precisely. He has other things on his mind at the moment and seems to have forgotten all about me." His smile widens. "Alcalde Esquibel and I came to a mutually beneficial arrangement." He reaches for Ygnacia and swings her into his arms. "And so here I am!"

Dolores stares at him for a long moment. Her hands drop to her side as a great wave of weariness sweeps over her. "And so, here you are," she agrees. "Whatever the outcome, here you are."

CHAPTER 2
Spring 1837: In All Fairness
(Víctor Sánchez)

"I paid their customs fees for them," Víctor Sánchez says again. He gestures toward the paperwork on the table between him and the seated Santa Cruz de la Cañada alcalde. "The amount is there, in the documents signed by the Chihuahua official. One hundred pesos."

Alcalde Esquibel glances toward the back of the room, where two men stand watching, hats in their hands. "They say they sold you their goods," he says. "In that case, the fees were your responsibility, not theirs."

The merchant from Arroyo Seco shakes his head. "As I explained before, I took responsibility for their goods only long enough to complete the paperwork and pay what they owed." He glances at the men behind him. "They were not aware of the duties charged in Chihuahua and had not prepared accordingly. I offered to assist them. They were to repay me once they'd sold their merchandise."

"But you saw no reason to wait until they had done so. You returned home as if your account with them was settled."

Sánchez suppresses his irritation. "I returned home because I had sold my own goods and wanted to get home as quickly as possible."

"To your wife."

He nods, unwilling to go into it again.

20

"Because it was near June and she would be anxious for your return. The anniversary of your child's death upsets her." It's hard to tell if the alcalde enjoys reminding the merchant of the great sorrow in his life or is mocking him for coddling his wife.

Even as the memory of his loss stabs Víctor's heart and irritation with the magistrate stiffens his spine, he tries to be fair. The pompous little alcalde made a point earlier of referring to his own half-dozen children and several grandchildren. How could the man know the pain of losing one's only child before the poor baby has even begun to crawl?

Esquibel's chair scrapes the floor as he stands. "Whatever your purported rationale for leaving Chihuahua City, the fact remains that you did so without making an effort to collect what you say you were owed." He puffs his chest out and raps the table with officious knuckles. "In this matter, I find no evidence that these men owe you a debt of any kind. I hereby declare them under no obligation to pay what you demand."

Sánchez's jaw clenches. He points at the documents on the table. "The evidence is there." He glances toward the back of the room. One of the men studies the floor while the other stares at him belligerently. "If you question these two more closely, you will realize their story is untrue."

"I have known them both since they were boys," the alcalde says stiffly. "I know they do not make a habit of lying."

Víctor reaches for his paperwork, but Esquibel pulls it toward himself. "These must be duplicated and the copies placed in the town archives before they are returned to you.

It will take time for my scribe to complete the work. Perhaps three days."

Sánchez frowns. "Three days while my affairs at home remain untended."

Esquibel's eyes crinkle in feigned amusement. "Ah, but you are a wealthy man, a merchant in Don Fernando de Taos with a house and land three leagues north at Arroyo Seco. Surely you have the funds to remain here in Santa Cruz a few days while the formalities in this matter are accomplished." His fingertips drum the forms filled out by the customs official at Chihuahua. The only documentation Sánchez has. There's nothing to do but acquiesce.

For the time being. Even as he nods his agreement, Víctor Sánchez vows to continue his fight for justice.

~ ~ ~ ~

He settles in to wait his three days. They are long ones. He knows few people in Santa Cruz de la Cañada, this hot little town on the hill above its overly green river valley.

He scolds himself for this thought. It's unfair to dislike an entire region because of one man's decision. But he can't shake the bad feeling. The feeling that, if he himself had been born here, had known the alcalde as a boy, the outcome of his suit might have been very different. Not even the massive adobe walls of the big church on the west side of the plaza can charm him out of his irritation.

Finally, he's able to head home. It's still warm and sultry as he moves north beside the greening fields along the río del Norte. Only when the river's course narrows and its bed becomes rocky and turbulent, does the air become markedly cooler. Víctor camps among the rocks, then the next day takes the road up to the stony slopes above the stream and on towards home.

It's another day before he comes within sight of the great gash in the earth that bisects the flatness that is the Taos Valley. Víctor's spine seems to lengthen and his breath deepen as he rides out of the mountains and into its eastern expanse, past the green-blushed pastures, the fields waiting to be planted. Perhaps it's only because this is his valley, but the very air seems brighter.

He reaches Don Fernando by late afternoon. He doesn't stop to check on events at the store. He's anxious to get home and eager to savor those last nine miles. Although he traverses the distance between Arroyo Seco and the larger village almost every day of the week, they're still the most pleasant part of his journey. Especially as the setting sun casts long purple shadows across the land, the way it's doing today.

Then at last his village comes into view in the valley of the río Lucero. Its newly furrowed fields, stretching east toward the towering crag of El Salto, seem to breathe a welcome. The newly built church in the village center, symbol not only of his religion but of his community, sends a finger of peace into his heart.

Arroyo Seco isn't ancient like Taos Pueblo to the southeast. It's not even as old as Don Fernando. And it's certainly smaller than either of them. But this little valley is his place. His people. He knows that if someone from outside tried to cheat a citizen of Arroyo Seco or even of Don Fernando, he would do his best to protect them. Just as the Santa Cruz alcalde endeavors to protect those of his own community.

Víctor frowns. But the magistrate made no effort to be fair. "I would not be so quick to decision," he mutters. "I would at least make an attempt to see justice done." He sighs. In all fairness, perhaps it's difficult for an official to be truly unbiased if he knows only some of the persons involved in a dispute. Has grown up with them.

When he proposes this idea to Ana María later that night, her eyes twinkle. "Mi querido," she says. She smooths a tiny garment over her knees and shakes her head at it.

His eyes drop to her hands. His breathing stops. Could it be? After almost three years?

She looks up and sees his expression. A shadow crosses her face. "It is for my Martínez godchild," she says gently. "Little José Agapito. A new shirt for the first anniversary of his birth."

"Severino's child? The Severino not related to Padre Martínez?"

"Sí."

He looks away. She is stronger than he is. Once upon a time he too loved being asked to be a godparent, relished choosing gifts for them. Now he can barely look at a newborn.

"What will do you about this debt?" she asks, changing the subject.

Víctor stares into space, trying to fight his way back from the memories to the subject at hand. When he looks again at his wife, the little garment has been folded away into her work basket and she's knitting a stocking. The slim needles flash in the firelight.

"I should just let it go," he says slowly.

Ana María smiles at her work.

"But it's not right to allow wrongdoing to remain unpunished."

She raises an eyebrow but keeps her eyes on her needles.

"It is possible that justice would be more properly served by the administration in Santa Fe," he says thoughtfully. "Governor Pérez has no relatives in Nuevo México. Many of his officials also have few connections here. In Santa Cruz de la Cañada, at any rate. They may be able to see the evidence more clearly."

She glances up at him. "It will cost you. There will be the expense of the journey as well as the necessary payments and recording fees and so forth."

"It's the principle of the thing."

She chuckles and shakes her head at her work. "When do you expect to leave?"

He waits a few days before he makes a final decision, taking some time to tend his animals and fields, and discuss the matter with his brothers. One of them thinks he should stay home. The other two encourage him to protest the Santa Cruz alcalde's decision, regardless of the cost.

He sets out in early May, he and his sturdy brown pony. It's an easy trip and a pleasant one in the late spring sunshine. He plans to be back well before the June 6 anniversary of the baby's death. He will spend the night at the church, as he does every year, praying for the little one and for himself and Ana María, his brave esposa, his dove.

His thoughts are tender as he and the pony move south again on the road above the río del Norte, then drop into the tiny villages beside the river, with their green fields and blossoming fruit trees.

25

Then the track turns west and through the plaza of Santa Cruz de la Cañada. Víctor is tempted to stop and pray in the adobe church there. It would be good to kneel before an altar for a moment, to ask for help with his task. But if he lingers in the town, he may give in to the urge to find Alcalde Esquibel and try to persuade him to change his decision.

The merchant smiles, remembering Ana María's wry glance, hearing his brothers' voices in his head. Even the one who didn't advise him to appeal thought the magistrate was unlikely to change his mind. Víctor nudges his mount with his heels and hurries himself away from Santa Cruz and temptation.

~ ~ ~ ~

He follows the old route instead of the more direct one to Santa Fe. It's a more pleasant, greener road which trends east toward río del Norte then, before it reaches the floodplain, curves south past the black hulk of La Mesilla, the outcropping that towers above the surrounding land and the nearby pueblos of Santa Clara and San Ildefonso.

The mesa is sacred to many of the pueblos in the Río Arriba, the region upriver from Santa Fe. As Víctor camps among the tumbled boulders at its base, he reflects on the stories the rocky crag holds. Not only tales of spirits and magic, but of Indians fighting off the Spanish during the 1690s reoccupation, rocks crashing down from the flat top onto the helmeted men below. He stares up at the ridge, dark against the star-filled sky. It has an indomitable quality, a solid stubbornness that breathes strength into his spine.

He takes the feeling with him the next morning as he follows the road east toward the pueblo of Pojoaque, then south through the various other Native settlements. This track was here before his own ancestors arrived, but of course they gave it a name of their own, called it the royal road, the Camino Real de Tierra Adentro. He and his vecinos still call it that, even though it's been sixteen years since México became independent of Spain and the route was relabeled El Camino Nacional.

Víctor ponders the changes that have and have not happened since independence in 1821, when he was not quite twenty. Certainly, the men of his village have more legal rights now. But then, Arroyo Seco is so far north that it and the other outlying settlements have always operated somewhat independently. There's little time to consult with Santa Fe when Comanches are filtering through the mountains toward you or when disagreements erupt over which vecino should be the first to move water from the acequias onto their crops. The community members protect each other and look to their respected elders to resolve their differences. This has been the way since his forebears arrived in this land.

Although some things did change when the country became the United Mexican States. The group of respected elders who made decisions was replaced by an elected council. Víctor chuckles. The same men under a different title. The only difference was the process for identifying them.

Then he sobers. In recent months there have been rumors that more changes are coming. The Congress in Mexico City has decided to call Nuevo México a department instead of a state and to eliminate the elected village councils. Víctor shrugs. At least in Arroyo Seco, the community will simply return to the old ways. They're too far away from Santa Fe to do anything very differently.

In any event, custom has always allowed for appeals to the governor when local politics overwhelm good sense. That's why he's on his way to the capital. Of course, many resent the fact that His Excellency Albino Pérez is from Vera Cruz— Or is it Mexico City? However, sometimes an outsider's perspective on internal squabbles can be a good thing. Víctor grins wryly. In his particular case, at any rate. He certainly hopes so.

He'll find out soon enough. As he tops the juniper-and-piñon-strewn hills north of Santa Fe, he glimpses buildings and fields beyond. The city is large compared to Arroyo Seco. But then, even Don Fernando de Taos is large compared to his village. Víctor braces himself a little as he rides out of the hills, past the old guardhouse on the east side of the road, and into Santa Fe's adobe-walled streets.

The dusty plaza is quiet in the afternoon sun. Víctor locates a well, draws water for the pony, tethers it to a narrowleaf cottonwood in the plaza's northeast corner, then returns to the well to take a drink of his own and wash the dust from his face.

As he swipes the moisture away from his eyes, he studies his surroundings more carefully. The north side of the big square is taken up by a long adobe building that would look like a fortress if it didn't have so many doors in it and a covered porch over them. Most of the doors are in the section to the left of a massive wooden gate which breaks the building in half and is large enough for wagons to pass through into the courtyard beyond. The rest of the building has fewer doors, only two or three, but they look bigger than the others, more important. All of them are shut tight against outsiders.

Víctor frowns slightly, then turns to consider the rest of the plaza. On the south side is a series of houses. Some of the adobe walls connect to others, some don't. Maybe it's simply the dryness and heat, but even the buildings with porches look unapproachable.

Except for the bright blue door of a small chapel. Marble bas-reliefs are set into the adobe above its entrance. A wooden cross rises from its flat roof. Víctor suppresses the urge to cross to it, examine the carvings, enter, and pray.

The square's east and west sides contain more buildings. There's another chapel on the west side, facing a long, low, tired looking building on the east. The larger building has only one door and a series of tiny windows just under the flat roof. It looks like it's a community structure no one is truly responsible for. Scattered nearby are a couple mercantiles and several cantinas.

Víctor turns again toward the long building with the portal and doors. This must be the governor's palacio where he'll will need to make his case. He notices for the first time that there's a man with a weapon sitting on a bench under the portal just to the right of the gate. As Víctor watches, the man looks up, catches his eye, and stands, gun to his shoulder. A guard for the governor.

Víctor's throat is suddenly dry, but not with thirst. He slaps at his clothes, beating the dust off as best he can. When he feels he's ready, he straightens, pulls his shoulders back, and moves firmly forward.

The portal is blessedly cool. Víctor hesitates, trying to decide how to explain what he wants, but before he opens his mouth, the guard looks away, towards a tall portly man in brilliant white sleeves and an embroidered waistcoat who has just stepped out of one of the doors farther down the portal. The soldier salutes and the newcomer smiles at him benevolently.

"Ah, I'm not your commander anymore," the big man says jovially. He slaps the guard on his back. "We're all friends here, aren't we?" Then he turns to Víctor. "But I see you have company!"

They both smile at Víctor, the guard a little guiltily, the newcomer with a small smile on his lips. There's an edge to it, an expectation that the guard will know who this stranger is, what he wants.

Víctor looks back and forth between them, not sure who to address. "Forgive me," he says. "I have not yet introduced myself. My name is José Víctor Sánchez. I live in Arroyo Seco and operate a mercantile business in Don Fernando de Taos. I have come to present a petition to His Excellency, Governor Albino Pérez."

"Ah," the other man says. He flashes a smile at the guard. "This is more my province than yours, is it not?" Then he turns to Víctor and bows slightly from the waist. "Permit me to introduce myself. You see before you Don Manuel Armijo, former governor of Nuevo México and currently serving as secretary of its treasury."

Víctor blinks in surprise. He had expected to talk to an underling, not someone important.

Don Manuel frowns slightly. He seems to have expected a different response. "If you would like to explain the purpose of your petition to his excellency, I may be able to be of some assistance," he adds. There's a hint of impatience in his tone.

"I apologize," the merchant says awkwardly. "I had assumed I would present my petition to a clerk or a scribe of some sort."

Armijo smiles, apparently pleased at Sánchez's discomfort, but still a little impatient. "Perhaps I can facilitate this petition of yours." His lips twist a little. "That is, if it's not about the forthcoming sales tax. Although some of our citizens don't appear to believe so, there is truly no recourse to be had at this time regarding that issue."

Now Víctor feels even more stupid. He nods, shaking himself mentally. All the words he'd planned to use to explain his problem have escaped him.

"And your request?" Armijo leans forward a little, peering into Víctor's face, then rocks back onto his heels. "If you have taken the trouble to travel all the way from Arroyo Seco, your petition must be of some value."

When Víctor looks at him blankly, the former governor cocks his head. His fingers drum lightly against his leg. Then he seems to make a decision. He waves toward the building. "But come, come. Let us repair indoors, out of this heat, and discuss the situation in comfort." He turns to the guard and gives him a mock salute. "Carry on, soldier."

The man gives him a half-smile, nods, salutes, and takes a step away, as if returning to his duties. Armijo motions to Víctor, gesturing him to precede him up the porch. They pass two doors and several carved cottonwood benches before the former governor moves forward, lifts a latch, and ushers the merchant inside.

The space is cool and dark and confusing. Víctor follows Armijo through a series of doors and into a small but cozy and well-appointed room. There's a carved wooden desk at the far end and two leather-upholstered armchairs near a fireplace halfway down the whitewashed adobe wall. Armijo waves the merchant into a chair and bustles about, pulling food and drink from a mahogany sideboard.

He puts a plate of bizcochitos on a low table between the chairs, hands Víctor a small goblet of red wine, and settles himself opposite. He rubs his left thigh. "My old wound is aching a little, so it is good to obtain some sustenance and comfort before we begin."

"I believe I have heard of this wound," Víctor says politely. "You received it fighting los indios bárbaros, did you not?"

The other man's chest puffs a little as he nods. "It has been many years ago now, but the injury still pains me from time to time, particularly when I'm here in Santa Fe." He sips his wine, then sets the goblet aside, leans back, and puts the tips of his fingers together. "However, I'm quite certain you didn't travel all this distance to inquire as to the condition of my old combat injuries. Please speak to me of the events which bring you to our illustrious capital."

So Víctor tells him: The journey to Chihuahua with his goods, the same type of merchandise he's carried there in the past. The two men from Santa Cruz, on their first trip and unsure about procedures and costs. His offer to assist them, the Chihuahua paperwork, the hurry to return.

Armijo's eyebrows contract sympathetically when Víctor explains why he wanted to be home by early June. His eyes sharpen as the merchant describes waiting for the debtors to send what was owed or come themselves with their payment and he nods his agreement with Víctor's decision to seek redress.

"And so in due course you presented your case to the good alcalde of Santa Cruz de la Cañada, the magistrate to whom such concerns should be presented, since they pertain to men of his constituency," Armijo says.

"Sí." Víctor grimaces. "I suppose he has reason to believe the word of men he knows over that of someone he has never met. However, he didn't appear to examine my claim closely or consider it very seriously."

Armijo chuckles, then sobers. He reaches for his wine. "And now you desire to appeal the alcalde's decision to His Excellency, Governor Albino Pérez?"

"Sí."

The former governor sips thoughtfully. "Such a procedure will, of course, involve certain inevitable expenses. Fees of sundry types to various individuals."

Víctor's lips twitch in amusement and he starts to nod, then he catches himself. He must be careful not to appear too willing to spend. "I am aware that some costs are necessary," he says slowly. "However, there is no point in laying out more than the debt is worth."

Armijo nods. "Certainly." His free hand smooths the edge of his waistcoat. "I quite understand your concern. However, if you wish to see the matter through, some expenditure will be required."

"How much?"

Armijo blinks, a little startled at the abruptness. Víctor catches himself again. This is clearly a man who likes words and the webs they can spin. He will appreciate the ability of a man whose language can slip around bald truths.

"That is, I must be careful not to overextend myself," Víctor explains. "Before I decide my next steps, I would like to gather some sense of the type of outlay I might reasonably expect to make."

Armijo smiles and nods. Now he's more comfortable. He takes another sip of wine, places the goblet on the little table, and leans back in his chair. "The typical fee for such a case is approximately ten percent of the value of the goods or other property in dispute," he says. "This is the sum generally required to assure the issue in question is properly recorded and then processed in a timely manner. Of course, prior to that event, there will also be the necessity of acquiring the Federally approved forms and the services of a scribe trained to express appropriately the particulars of the case prior to its presentation to His Excellency the Governor." He pauses. "And there may be other expenses as well." He spreads his hands, palms upward. "It can be difficult to foretell just what complications might arise."

"Of course." In spite of the flowery language, the man's meaning is clear enough. "I appreciate your assistance with my petition, Don Manuel," Víctor says humbly. "I hope to be able to offer you a small gift as well, in appreciation for your friendship. The wheat crop in Arroyo Seco is expected to be especially healthy this year. Perhaps a portion or two from the fall harvest?"

The former governor smiles at him benevolently. "I believe we understand each other." Then his face falls and he shakes his head. "Unfortunately, we may be unable to approach the matter quite as expeditiously as you might prefer."

He leans toward the table and takes a cinnamon-flavored cookie. Crumbs fall onto his waistcoat as he nibbles at it. He carefully brushes them off the glossy embroidery, then squints at Víctor. "His Excellency the Governor is preoccupied at the moment with the deficiencies in the funds for the presidio troops. He returned from the Navajo campaign to an inadequate treasury and is not in the best of spirits."

Víctor nods. "I understand. Although in my village we suffer more from Comanche depredations than Navajo, I gladly provided the loan requested of me late last year. However, I know some of mis vecinos were not enthusiastic in their response to His Excellency's letter."

Armijo nods morosely. "The situation has placed my role as interim treasurer in a precarious and complex position. Nuevo México's resources simply do not extend as far as one could wish." Then he pushes himself to his feet. "But come, come! What one cannot change one must bear and in the meantime I will introduce you to a skilled scribe who is experienced in the arrangement of petitions into the proper forms and then we will speak to those responsible for scheduling interviews with His Excellency."

~ ~ ~ ~

It's another three days before Víctor Sánchez meets with Governor Pérez. While he waits, his appeal is written up with the proper flourishes and seals and he spends his evenings listening to the gossip at the inn near the parish church.

All is not well in the capital. Fees were imposed last summer on dances, woodcutters, and flocks passing through town. People are not happy. Some are also upset about the new edict that they send their children to school. It wouldn't hurt so much if they weren't also required to pay for said education.

And the threat of the new federal sales tax looms over all. Why should Nuevo México pay a tax they've been exempted from for so long? After all, the government in la Ciudad de México isn't sending more troops to guard the frontier against los indios bárbaros. They should continue the exemption in exchange for the defensive line New Mexico provides!

There's also a pervading personal dislike of the governor. A disapproval of the fact that his housekeeper warms his bed at night as well as tidying his rooms and seeing to his meals. In fact, she's borne him a child, a little boy. Also, Pérez has apparently borrowed more than money from Nuevo México's biggest landowners—everything from mirrors to bureaus and the candlesticks that top them.

The complaints seem a little petty to Víctor. After all, a governor has a certain standard of living to uphold. And if the woman wishes to share his bed and take the risk of childbirth outside of marriage, that's a private matter.

Then the time comes to meet the man. The merchant joins Don Manuel on the portal early in the forenoon and takes wine in Armijo's office. Afterward, the acting secretary of New Mexico's Treasury Department marches ahead of him back onto the porch and into the next door. There's another maze of rooms, then finally they halt in front of a thick oak door with flower designs carved into it. Armijo turns to

Víctor, puts a quieting finger to his lips, then raps smartly on the wood.

"Come!" a voice snaps from the other side.

Armijo opens the door with a flourish and ushers Víctor inside. "Your Excellency," he says. "This is the gentleman of whom I spoke, the merchant from the Taos valley who has requested you to consider his appeal of a decision made by the alcalde of Santa Cruz de la Cañada."

"Ah yes." A very straight, thin man of average height and wearing a red satin waistcoat stands at the end of a long whitewashed and mirror-lined room behind a large oak desk. A throne-like chair of the same wood is positioned behind him. The man is handsome in a cold narrow-nosed way. As Armijo and Víctor move toward him, he looks Víctor up and down appraisingly with gold-flecked brown eyes. The merchant fights a sudden urge to swipe his dusty shoes on the back of his trousers.

Governor Pérez sinks into his chair and places his hands on its armrests. "I have received the affidavit with the details of your request," he says formally. "However, I always prefer to hear accounts such as yours in the petitioner's own words."

Víctor suppresses a flash of irritation. He's already told the story to Armijo, the scribe, and the governor's private secretary. The affidavit to the governor lays it out as well, in excruciating detail. However, if receiving justice requires that he explain what happened a dozen times more, he will do so.

He licks his lips, opens his mouth, and begins his story once again.

CHAPTER 3

July 1837: Arrogances
(Juan José Esquibel)

The alcalde of Santa Cruz de la Cañada, does not rise when Prefect Ramón Abreú enters the main room of his casa. He has a little girl on each knee and is laughing at something a slightly older boy, who's standing by the fire, has just said. Esquibel nods at Abreú with a friendly expression but doesn't speak.

Although it's mid-July, the fire is still pleasant in the morning coolness. Abreú stands watching the little group in front of it with an uncomfortable look on his narrow face. Esquibel finds the fair-haired man's emotion satisfying, even though he knows he shouldn't.

The youngest girl leans back against his chest and he kisses the top of her head and pats the other girl's shoulder. Then he smiles companionably at the boy. "All right, chamacos," he says. "Go see what your grandma and aunties are doing in the kitchen."

The children scamper off. Abreú gives them a wistful look as they pass.

Esquibel rises and crosses to him. "Forgive me, prefect," he says unapologetically. "Until you have grandchildren of your own, you will not understand how time-consuming they are." The man doesn't need to know that two of the children are actually the alcalde's niece and nephew. Let him be impressed.

The prefect smiles slightly. "Since my own son is not yet six, it will be some time before I can appreciate your dilemma."

Esquibel knows all about Abreú's family situation, but he still says, "Only one son?" as he ushers his visitor to a cottonwood armchair by the fire. "By the time I was your age, I had four boys and a daughter besides." He settles himself into the seat opposite and smiles at the other man. "But it's not too late for you. I had two more sons after that. Although I must say that providing for them all does keep me busy."

Ramón Abreú smiles slightly. "And of course, you also have your work as alcalde."

Esquibel nods warily. "Yes, my position does take up a good deal of my time." He smiles, finding the right note. "But then, as prefect of the district of Río Arriba, you can fully understand the complexities and dilemmas that confront me on a regular basis."

Abreú doesn't smile back. "The case Víctor Sánchez of Arroyo Seco brought you some time ago does not appear to the governor to be very complex."

Esquibel raises an eyebrow. "And to which governor do you refer? As I'm sure you know, we have many here in Nuevo México. For example, there is a governor of the pueblo of Taos, then the one at San Ildefonso, and the one south of Santa Fe at Santo Domingo, as well as all those in between. Pojoaque and Tesuque and so on."

Abreú stirs in his chair, as if trying to suppress his impatience. "Those are mere titles. The man with authority over them all as well as yourself and me is His Excellency Governor Albino Pérez."

Esquibel's eyes narrow. It isn't true. His authority doesn't arise from Pérez, who's an appointee from la Ciudad de México with no real knowledge or understanding of the people of Nuevo México. An alcalde's power comes from his neighbors, the ones who agreed to his leadership.

However, it would be foolish to say so. He forces his shoulders to relax and says smoothly, "The petition of the merchant Víctor Sánchez was more complex than it might appear. I am not acquainted with the man or his relatives. It is possible he and this supposed official in Chihuahua worked together to defraud men who were unfamiliar with the customs and practices of the southern trade."

"Ah." Abreú nods and looks away. He studies the fire for a long moment before he turns back to the alcalde. "I will inform His Excellency of the rationale for your decision."

Esquibel rises from his seat. "Well, that was easily settled. May I offer you something to drink?" He moves to a side table. "I have an excellent wine made with wild plums from the bosque of the río del Santa Cruz." He turns to smile at the younger man. "And, if you would like, I can share my tips for producing fine sons." He grins mischievously. "My wife and I started a little later than many, but we made up for lost time quickly enough."

The prefect stiffens, then smiles slightly, giving in to the familiarity. "How old were you when you married?"

The alcalde chuckles and returns to the fire. He hands Abreú a goblet of wine and settles back into his chair. "I was 22, which isn't that old for a man, but my wife, María Rafaela Martín, was older than me by nine months. She'd been of marriageable age for almost ten years." His eyes crinkle at the corners. "However, once we decided to wed, we didn't waste any time. We were married in early December 1810 and our first child was born ten months later." His white teeth flash mischievously. "You know what they say: Donde hay yeguas, potros nacen."

The prefect makes a choking sound. "Where there are mares, colts will be born?"

Esquibel grins. "And we kept on from there."

Abreú smiles politely, then puts his drink to one side. "There is another issue here in Santa Cruz which has caused His Excellency some concern."

A stillness settles in the alcalde's chest. He looks down at his wine, then up again, his face carefully noncommittal.

Abreú's gaze is steady, his voice deliberate. "It is this matter of Antonio Abad Montoya. The governor has learned that Montoya is no longer incarcerated in the Santa Cruz de la Cañada jail. In fact, rumor has reached the capital that his release was facilitated by the exchange of funds or goods of some sort."

Esquibel straightens in his chair. "That is pure slander!"

The prefect raises his hand, stopping him. "I am simply reporting what is said. Governor Pérez is loath to believe that any official under his jurisdiction would go so far as to use his position to enrich himself."

Esquibel jerks from his seat, crosses to the table, and lifts the carafe of wine, then thinks better of it and sets it down with a clink. He places his goblet beside it and turns to face Abreú. His hands clench and unclench at his sides. There are so many things he would like to say, and none of them wise.

The prefect again holds up a hand. "I am not accusing you. However, it will be a simple matter to prove the injustice of these accusations, if you wish to do so." His eyes are fixed on Esquibel's face. "Governor Pérez suggests that Señor Montoya be returned promptly to the Santa Cruz calabozo. If Montoya then initiates the appeal he sought earlier this year, his whereabouts during the past few months will be of no importance."

Esquibel stiffens. "Don Antonio Abad will not agree to such a procedure. He has many friends and much influence here. If I try to arrest him and return him to jail, there will be trouble and it won't come only from the Montoya hacienda."

Abreú frowns. "Montoya's agreement is unnecessary. You are the alcalde. You have the authority to do what is required."

The man simply doesn't understand. Esquibel tries to keep his voice even. "My authority rests in the people. When Don Antonio was arrested last year and then left to sit in jail for two months while the governor was on campaign, los vecinos didn't like it. The man had simply spoken his mind, as is his right. The punishment far outweighed the perceived infraction. When the governor ruled that Montoya's appeal must go to la Ciudad de México, many people came to me and demanded that he be released. They felt my actions had been heavy-handed and unnecessary."

Abreú frowns. "You jailed him on His Excellency's orders."

"And it cost me. In the eyes of my community, it was an unjust order and should not have been carried out. The responsibility for doing so rests on my shoulders." He pauses. Should he say it?

Then irritation at Abreú's lack of comprehension surges through him. He plunges on. "If the governor wishes law and order to prevail in the valley of el río del Santa Cruz, he would do well to remember that here in Nuevo México we follow men we know and respect and have agreed to follow, not strangers who've been appointed from beyond our borders and know nothing of our customs."

Abreú stiffens in his chair, his eyes mere slits in his thin face. Then his body relaxes and he says drily, "You may temporarily lose the respect of your neighbors if you return Señor Antonio Abad Montoya to jail, but if you do not, it will cost you a fine of at least 50 pesos."

"And if I don't pay?"

"There will be consequences."

Esquibel snorts. "And how is His Excellency going to enforce those consequences? His coffers are so empty he's had to send all the presidio soldiers home without pay."

Abreú stirs uneasily. "They're still in Santa Fe, for the most part."

"But they aren't receiving their salaries. I suspect you'll have trouble finding anyone willing to help you enforce the governor's so-called consequences."

"Francisco Sarracino has been reinstated as treasurer. He and His Excellency Governor Pérez are working diligently to acquire the necessary funds."

Esquibel chuckles. "That should take a while. I doubt the governor will have the resources to send anyone north any time soon."

The prefect shakes his head but Esquibel's smile only broadens. It's true. Nuevo México's finances are in especially bad condition right now. Pérez and Abreú can make as many threats as they like but they have no funds to pay anyone to enforce them.

But anything is possible and there will be resources eventually. It's unwise to be too recalcitrant. The alcalde drops his smile. "I'm afraid it will be impossible for me to return Don Antonio to jail or to gather the funds to pay the fine you have named. I have children to support and grandchildren to think of."

Abreú's face twitches in irritation, but he nods and rises from his seat. Esquibel accompanies him to the door. As he opens it for his guest, he says, "I hear the Navajo are raiding again west of el río del Norte, even up around Abiquiu."

Abreú nods. "It is a concern, although the raids have been intermittent and only a few sheep have been lost."

Esquibel slides him a sideways glance. That isn't what he's heard. But there's no reason to continue the discussion. He's made his point: The governor would do well to focus on the Navajo problem instead of who is or is not sitting in the Santa Cruz calabozo.

Abreú steps into the courtyard and puts on his hat. The alcalde smiles with satisfaction as he closes the door behind him. He's done a good day's work and has asserted the right of his people to see to their own business. They don't need outsiders telling them what to do. They're quite able to govern their own crops, flocks, families, and finances.

He catches himself and makes the sign of the cross. They can do all those things only with the help of El Dios and His saints. In fact, the village of Chimayó's feast of Santiago, the one the americanos call Saint James, is only a month away. He needs to consult with the leading men and women there about the preparations for the festivities.

~ ~ ~ ~

44

The day of the feast dawns bright and clear. Antonio Abad is out of jail and Prefect Abreú hasn't returned to the valley of el río del Santa Cruz. The alcalde and his family climb the hill to Chimayó the afternoon before the feast and spend the night with a cousin of his wife.

The house is crowded and Esquibel escapes it and its bustling women at first light. He pauses on the doorsill and looks around. The joined walls of the single-story flat-roofed homes that enclose the plaza present a unified front to the world. Each door is painted a different color, to identify the family within. The big rectangle they face contains neatly fenced garden plots and a road straight through the center, from the eastern mountains west toward Santa Cruz.

It is a good place. It has a safe feeling to it. It makes him feel reverential, somehow. Perhaps that's because today is the feast day of Santiago, the village's patron saint. The alcalde inhales the morning air, faintly scented with mint, and moves toward the chapel on the western end of the plaza to pay his respects.

When he's done with his prayers, he takes a leisurely stroll through the gardens. As the sun rises, other men drift outside. The alcalde perks up a little and begins to move among them in an official capacity, patting some jovially on the back, speaking a quiet word to others in support or discouragement of one project or another, inserting a word of caution or commendation about personal behavior where needed.

A few of the men mention the new federal sales tax to him, but he waves them off. This is not a day for intense emotions. It's a time for community leaders like himself to cement relationships, build goodwill, and renew community bonds. Families from throughout the Río Arriba have come to venerate the saint, give thanks for the harvest, and enjoy the feast. Tomorrow, some of them will continue up the valley to the sanctuary of Jesús Esquipulas to anoint themselves with holy dirt and pray for healing of one kind or another. It is a time of thoughtfulness and holy petition, not politics.

In the meantime, the square fills with more people and the Santa Cruz de la Cañada alcalde moves from group to group basking in the respect of his neighbors and smiling benevolently at the children who pop in and out of the house doors, some carrying platters or bowls of food, others playing tag. A black-clad woman bends over a beehive-shaped adobe oven and pulls out a batch of newly baked bread. The alcalde's stomach quivers.

Not everyone has stayed the night in the village. Clusters of vecinos climb toward it from the surrounding countryside, many of them singing hymns of praise. They all carry contributions to the feast.

Except the men on horseback, whose steeds are glorious with silver-ornamented saddles, bridles, and other trappings. Esquibel grins. These are the young men who will participate in the rooster race this afternoon, a competition that's as much about showing off to the marriageable girls as it is about racing for a rooster.

Then another group of riders enters the village from the road to Santa Cruz and the alcalde's smile fades. "What is he doing here?" someone behind him mutters.

The lead horse carries Prefect Ramón Abreú, his back stiff. A small contingent of blue-jacketed presidio soldiers rides behind him. The prefect pulls his tall brown gelding to a stop and stares over the suddenly silent crowd without acknowledging them.

Then a tiny white-haired old lady appears in a doorway on the south side of the plaza. "¡El Prefect Abreú!" she exclaims. Her voice is loud in the stillness. She doesn't speak again until she's standing beside his horse, peering up at him. "You honor us, prefect."

The gelding turns his head to sniff at her hair and she bats its muzzle away. "Although you should teach this beast better manners," she says with a smile. Then she makes a welcoming gesture with both hands. "But come! Come! You can't feast on the back of a horse! Besides, he should rest up for the rooster race!"

On the other side of the square, Esquibel chuckles in spite of the anxiety in his stomach. It's hard to imagine the stiffly correct prefect in the rough-and-tumble of the corrida del gallo.

"Honor us indeed," a voice behind him growls. "The man infects us with his federal poison. Sales taxes now and what else tomorrow?"

Esquibel turns and raises an eyebrow. The man scowls, then, recognizing him, bows slightly. "Señor alcalde," he says. "Permit me to make myself known to you. My name is José Angel Gonzales."

Esquibel's eyes crinkle in amusement as he nods. "You are the buffalo hunter from Don Fernando who married Ramona Bernal in December of last year." His smile broadens. "They call you 'Angelito'."

The other man smiles deprecatingly as he nods. He isn't a tall man, but there's a thickness in his chest and neck that gives him an aura of quiet power. He opens his mouth to speak, but just then the sound of singing erupts from the little chapel near the plaza's western entrance. Both men turn toward it. Gonzales takes off his hat and holds it over his heart.

Then there's sudden movement from the other direction. The crowd swings toward the eastern entrance. A man on a white horse parades through it and down the road toward the chapel door, his horse tossing its braided and blue-ribboned mane.

The man is also decorated. Silver buttons run down the side of his pantalones and his short fitted coat gleams with embroidered silk flowers. He moves past the prefect and his men and reins in outside the chapel.

The door opens and two men appear, walking carefully sideways and carrying the brightly painted and clothed wooden statue of the saint between them. They're followed by a cluster of singers, who are repeating the lines of the hymn they began inside. Behind them, three men strum guitars.

The people in the square join in the singing as the saint is reverently held out to the horse's rider. He takes it and cradles the statue against his chest with one arm. Then he clicks his tongue and moves the reins to one side with his other hand. The white horse tosses its head, then turns to face the road to the fields below. But it doesn't move forward. Instead, man and animal look over their shoulders toward the eastern entrance.

More riders enter the square. The prefect and his men are forced to one side as they approach. They halt in the road just before the chapel. The man with the statue waits until all the riders are still, then speaks to his mount. The big white switches its tail proudly and moves regally into the road, to head the procession.

There's a long, waiting pause. José Angel Gonzales gives Alcalde Esquibel a questioning look. "You are the magistrate," he says. "You should be leading us."

But Esquibel has already decided he'd rather stay with the crowd. As he shakes his head, Ramón Abreú moves his horse forward. The alcalde half smiles at Gonzales and jerks his head toward the prefect. "That one will have the honored position today."

Gonzales grimaces, shrugs, and nods. A low mutter spreads across the square as Abreú, Donaciano Vigil just behind him, heads toward the white horse. The prefect nods to the rider as if authorizing him to begin.

Somewhere to Esquibel's left, a man growls, "As if he is giving permission to the saint!"

Gonzales turns toward the voice. "He isn't from here," he says quietly.

"That's the problem," the man replies.

"One of many," someone else adds.

Esquibel chuckles. The crowd moves forward and the singing starts up again. He joins in.

Even though he's not in his rightful place near the saint, the alcalde is still filled with the reverent joy this particular ceremony always creates in him. He's surrounded by his vecinos, singing the old hymns brought by their ancestors from Spain. A solemn peacefulness fills his chest.

He loves all religious observances, but especially this one, with the hand-carved bulto of Santiago clothed so lovingly by the women of the plaza and held so carefully by the rider who leads the way to the fields. Santiago, the patron of horses and Chimayó, as well as of soldiers, is the saint who legend says helped the Spanish push the infidels out of Spain. A deep sense of reverence fills the alcalde's heart.

The feeling is mixed with a deep love for the land that spreads out before him. Below el cerro de Chimayó, the neat fields of maíz stretch richly toward río del Santa Cruz. Along the river banks, the heart-shaped leaves of giant gnarled cottonwoods sparkle in the late July sunlight as they twist in a breeze no one else can feel.

It is his land and a good one. Contentment fills him as he and his comrades slowly follow the statue and its attendants and share in the words of the blessings for the fields and the harvest they contain.

Two hours later, as the crowd moves back toward the plaza, Antonio Abad Montoya's younger brother edges toward him. "It is said that the prefect is here for more than the feast," he mutters in Esquibel's ear. The alcalde's head jerks, his reflective mood broken.

Desiderio's eyes are anxious. "He caught a glimpse of my brother and spoke of a fine that is not yet paid." He frowns. "Antonio Abad says the prefect was speaking of you, not himself."

José Angel Gonzales moves forward until he's at the alcalde's elbow. "The prefect would profane Chimayó's holy day with talk of secular things?" His quiet demeanor has transformed into a bristling anger made more intense by the fact that he hasn't raised his voice. An anger that draws the attention of others.

"More than talk, I think," Esquibel says. However, the best way to avoid trouble is to diminish it. He shrugs and gives the men around him a confident smile. He allows a glimmer of mischief to touch his eyes. "But there's a large crowd here today and I believe the prefect is supping with cousins of my wife, who will keep him well entertained. I and my family will be eating with good friends on the opposite side of the plaza." He opens his arms in a calming gesture. "Santiago will protect us on his day."

Then he makes a flapping motion, gesturing the men toward the hilltop and the waiting tables inside its homes. "Let us not profane his holy day with talk of secular things. Let us enjoy our feast."

And the feast is a pleasurable one, perhaps made more tasty by the sense of danger outwitted. The alcalde thoroughly enjoys the talk, the comradeship, and the good food. María Rafaela, pleasantly harried and distracted by gossip with the other women, has never looked quite so lovely to him as she does at this moment.

After the eating comes the preparations for the rooster race, the corrida del gallo. Esquibel is not especially fond of this portion of the traditional Santiago feast day festivities. Just prior to the race, a wooden peg will be pounded into the ground and a rooster tethered to it by one leg. The contestants will race to reach the bird and swoop to snatch him up, stick and all. The organizers usually choose a wily old fowl who knows how to fight, but eventually one of the more experienced riders will succeed.

Then the real race will begin, the part the alcalde prefers not to watch. One contestant after another will attempt to grab the rooster for himself. Feathers will fly. The squawking fowl will be dropped and nabbed again, repeatedly swept up before it can be trampled by the horses as it frantically tries to escape. If the rooster is lucky, someone will miss the catch and a descending hoof will end the poor bird's trauma before it collapses from fear or is literally torn to pieces by reaching hands.

Esquibel has done his best to discourage his own sons from participating in the race over the years. The game is barbaric and seems out of keeping with the day's earlier observances. If he could, he would ban it. But he was elected by his neighbors to keep the peace, not to innovate.

He's on his horse at the edge of the group of men tasked with refereeing the race, bending down to shake yet another hand, when Prefect Abreú's horse reenters the plaza from the direction of Santa Cruz. The blue-jacketed presidio soldiers ride behind him, sargento Vigil bringing up the rear. Abreú's thin jaw is tight with determination. The feasting is over and he's clearly not here for the corrida del gallo.

The plaza falls silent. The only sound is the dull thud of horses' hooves on the dirt road. As the prefect comes nearer, the men around the alcalde move their mounts aside and he braces himself.

Abreú reins in, facing Esquibel.

Even though the alcalde is certain he knows what is about to happen, he can't help himself. In spite of his better judgment, his official demeanor kicks in. "Good afternoon, Excellency," he says. "I hope you enjoyed the bounty of our feast."

"It was well enough," Abreú says. Someone behind Esquibel growls with irritation at the slight but the prefect doesn't seem to hear it. His mouth is flattened into a thin line. "Señor Esquibel, you are hereby under arrest." He glances pointedly at the soldiers behind him, then sweeps his gaze around the crowded plaza. "It would be best if you came quietly."

Esquibel feels a sudden urge to laugh. Abreú's sergeant and soldiers may have weapons, but it's highly unlikely that they'll use them. Most of them are related to people in the crowd.

The prefect waves a commanding hand. "Take him into custody."

The soldiers' horses twitch, but no one moves forward.

The prefect scowls. "I said, take him into custody!"

Still no one moves. Then Donaciano Vigil maneuvers his mount around the others, edges past Abreú, and reins in alongside Esquibel. "Excuse me, my friend," he says, making no effort to keep his voice down. "We have come to place you in safekeeping until the events leading to your decisions in recent months can be investigated and addressed."

The alcalde's eyes narrow. Decisions? So there's more to this than Antonio Abad's release from jail. His horse's head jerks sideways as his hands tighten on the reins.

However, if he tries to run or resist, there'll be a fight. There are women and children in the plaza and his vecinos have no weapons to hand. After all, it's the day of the feast. They didn't come prepared for a physical confrontation. "We have knives," someone behind him says quietly, as if for his ears alone. Gonzales?

But it's too risky. Esquibel looks toward the door of his wife's cousin's home. María Rafaela stands on the sill. She's clutching a cloth in her hand and staring at him with fear in her eyes.

He turns to Prefect Abreú, who glares back at him. The man would like nothing better than a physical altercation.

The alcalde looks at Vigil, who meets his gaze calmly. There's no malice in his eyes. Watchfulness, but not malice.

The alcalde shakes his head. "Safekeeping, you say?" Then he smiles slightly and lets his eyes twinkle. "Ah, amigo, you have a rare gift for words. It's too bad you persist in working for men who know so little of honor."

The prefect's scowl deepens. "I said, arrest him!"

Esquibel's eyes are still locked on Vigil's face. The sergeant glances around the plaza, then turns back to the alcalde. "I believe it would be best if you came with us quietly, mi amigo," he says gently.

Esquibel nods abruptly, moves his horse past Abreú's, and heads toward the western end of the plaza. Just before he reaches the chapel, he spies a friend of Antonio Abad standing with a small group beside the road. The alcalde leans toward him. "Get word to the Montoyas."

"Silence from the prisoner!" Abreú shouts. He spurs his horse into action, careless of bystanders, and gallops past the soldiers, then Esquibel, and down the hill toward Santa Cruz.

Esquibel and the others follow more slowly. Vigil moves forward to ride beside the alcalde, who gives him an apologetic look. "I'm sorry you had to participate in this," he says. "To make a choice between your friends and your duty." Then he raises an eyebrow. "However, I was surprised to see you here. I thought the governor had no funds for presidio salaries."

The big sergeant chuckles. "He has money for the tasks he deems essential. I'm wearing the uniform today, but not necessarily next week. Then I'll be back at my wife's cousin's mercantile." He shrugs. "But we all do what we must." Then he brightens. "Did you hear that I have a new son?"

Esquibel's laughter rings out over the corn fields below. On the road ahead, Ramón Abreú turns and glares, but both men ignore him as they plunge into a discussion of children, cousins, and other family matters.

~ ~ ~ ~

However, once he's locked up in the Santa Cruz calabozo and the prefect and presidio soldiers have left for Santa Fe, the alcalde's smile fades.

The room is narrow and contains only a small cot, a chair, an old pot for his bodily excretions, and a tiny open-air window at the far end. There's a niche in the adobe wall opposite the bed. A roughly carved bulto of Santiago is perched inside.

Esquibel drops to the bed and stares at the little statue. There's a cobweb behind it. He must remember to reprimand the woman who comes in to clean.

Then he catches himself. He's a prisoner here, not the person in charge.

Ironically, it's the same prison space Antonio Abad Montoya occupied earlier this year. Esquibel glances at the window. He pushes up from the cot and moves to it, then paces to the door. He hadn't realized how small this space is. How long will he have to remain here before the governor sees reason?

Just before sunset, María Rafaela arrives with food and blankets. She says the community is divided on the issue of his incarceration. Some believe he should pay the fine. Others say Antonio Abad should take his place. No one is happy that he's inside the jail he usually supervises. He's their chosen magistrate. Confining him is an insult to their own dignity as well as his. And to their right to choose him.

As the sky darkens outside, he gently tells her to go home. Then he sinks onto the cot and gazes at the little saint in the niche. Santiago is also the patron of travelers. Esquibel shakes his head. This particular bulto seems a poor choice for this room. A statue of Santo Niño de Atocha, the patron of prisoners as well as wayfarers, would be more appropriate.

Though that would remind those incarcerated here of their lack of ability to visit El Niño's shrine in the valley southwest of Chimayó. He would give much to visit there himself. It's such a comforting place.

He sighs and looks up at the window. The moon's pale light glints on the carved wooden bars. The day's heat is dissipating rapidly. Tendrils of coolness slip across the room and sink to the floor, chilling his feet. He slips off his shoes, stretches out on the cot, pulls a blanket over his legs, and stares into the darkness. He hasn't been this alone since the night before his marriage over thirty-six years ago. It's a strange feeling.

The feeling continues. He has visitors, and his wife comes or sends someone daily with food and supplies, but there are still long stretches of silence. At home there would be the grandchildren and María Rafaela's nieces and nephews, their mothers bustling in and out, laborers seeking direction, and constituents with requests of one kind or another. Here there are only four dusty adobe walls, a tiny window, and the saint.

The alcalde has never been one for looking inward, but he has nothing else to do. He stares at the little statue, which gazes back at him. One hand clutches a staff while the other holds out a small seashell.

It's an actual shell, and represents the pilgrimage to Saint James's sanctuary in Spain and the sacrifices one must make to reach such a holy place. Someone has gone to the trouble of trading for a shell from the faraway ocean and donating it to this particular bulto.

The action is typical of his vecinos, so devout and willing to sacrifice what little they have to create an object that honors God and gives comfort to others. He feels a sudden surge of affection for the people of his valley and beyond—all those who inhabit el Río Arriba, this land north of Santa Fe that stretches along the upper río del Norte.

Santa Fe. Esquibel scowls, his good feelings replaced by sullen disgust. The capital contains everything that's wrong with Nuevo México. Officials who know nothing of the people, who slap taxes on families already struggling to survive. Men not from here or whose fathers were born elsewhere and think that fact somehow makes them superior to los paisanos. Men like Ramón Abreú, who believe their secular role gives them the right to order a holy procession to stay or move forward.

Though the prefect isn't the only official with a lack of proper religious feeling or respect for morality or custom. Pérez flaunts himself and his gaudy possessions everywhere. There's even a rumor that he's made a concubine of his housekeeper and that she's borne him a child.

Esquibel scowls. Surely the governor is old enough to restrain himself or rich enough to bring his wife into the country with him. There's no excuse for such profligacy. He himself had great urgings as a young man, he knows what it's like. But after he wed, he kept his holy acts for his wife alone. He didn't spread his seed where it wasn't authorized.

He twitches. The thought of the governor with the young housekeeper makes him yearn for María Rafaela's sweet plumpness. However, to pleasure oneself is a sin. He crosses the room in two steps, kneels before the saint, and begins to pray. Is it wrong to say the Hail Mary in front of Santiago? He doesn't know, but it's better than burning. "Dios te salve, María, llena eres de gracia, El Señor es contigo—" he begins.

The prayer soothes him. The next day he finds himself kneeling before the little statue more than once. The following day, he rises from it only to receive and eat the food his wife has sent.

Then it is Sunday. She arrives after mass, bringing gossip along with provisions. The community is swinging behind him. There's less criticism of him now and more muttering against Abreú and Pérez. The sales tax was bad enough, but throwing community leaders in jail isn't the way a Christian nation should act toward its people. Is the administration actively trying to pit neighbor against neighbor?

Esquibel smiles at María Rafaela's report but doesn't press her for details. Something has shifted inside him. A deep stillness nothing can unsettle. Even as she talks, his eyes drift to the bulto in the niche. He loves his wife dearly, but he wants only to kneel again before the saint and resume his prayers. Feel the rhythm of the words and the quietness they create in his soul.

When she finally leaves, he returns to his devotions. The next day, she sends a servant with the food and Esquibel is guiltily thankful she didn't bring it. As he eats the fresh bread, he gazes out the cell's little window. Thick blue-black clouds darken the sky. The air is heavy with heat and suppressed moisture. It will rain tonight.

After his meal, the alcalde returns to his place in front of the bulto. The sky darkens further and the wind picks up. Thunder crashes overhead, but he hardly notices. The words of the prayer pour from his lips, over and over, building and building, then suddenly dropping into a great silence.

His mind is a mountain lake, its waters strangely still. An image of his village slips into the quietness. The dusty plaza, the church, the people kneeling in reverent silence. A holy affection fills him, untinged by personal ambition. "Oh my people," he murmurs.

The image of Ramón Abreú's narrow face enters his mind, overshadowing the worshipping vecinos. Then Governor Pérez's visage appears. Strangely, Esquibel feels no anger toward either of them. But he does have a strange compulsion to push them away. His hands move outward, safeguarding his people. "It must stop," he whispers.

Then his hands drop to his sides and his eyes open. He knows what he must do. A shudder runs down his spine. He glances toward the window. Rain slaps against the wooden bars and spits past them into the room.

But the storm isn't the cause of his chill. The alcalde's gaze moves again to the bulto. Santiago, patron of travelers but also of warriors. "Help me, Santiago," he whispers. "Help me in the battle that must come."

He begins again to pray the Hail Mary, his voice a mere thread against the storm.

Then the rain slows to a mere patter. Outside the window, someone calls his name. Another voice repeats it. A curious stillness hovers in Esquibel's chest. Somehow, he knew they would come.

He stares at the little bulto, which gazes solemnly back at him. "It is time," the alcalde whispers. Then he crosses himself, rises, and goes to speak to his vecinos.

CHAPTER 4

August 8, 1837: Everybody's Cousin
(Donaciano Vigil)

Colonel Manuel Aponte is waiting for Donaciano Vigil when the sergeant enters the governor's palacio. "Those cousins of yours in Santa Cruz have finally gone too far," Aponte says grimly.

Vigil frowns and takes off his hat. "Which cousins are those?"

"Those Montoyas in Santa Cruz. Antonio Abad and his brother." Aponte turns and leads the way to Pérez's office. "His Excellency is not happy."

"I and the Montoyas are only distantly related," Vigil says mildly.

"That may be sergeant, but you're still the most likely person to help us understand what they're doing up there." Aponte knocks on the carved door to the governor's room.

"Come!" a voice bellows.

The two men outside exchange an anxious look, all difference in rank forgotten. The governor is clearly furious. The colonel pushes through the door, the sergeant right behind.

Governor Pérez is standing behind his desk, ramrod straight and glaring at the prefect of Río Arriba, who's facing him, fists clenched at his sides. Pérez acknowledges Aponte with a jerk of his head, then spies Vigil. "Those cousins of yours!" he spits. "Those Montoyas!"

The sergeant hesitates, then says politely, "We are cousins by marriage only. Antonio Abad and his sister Catarina are wed to my cousins María Dolores Vigil and José Ramón Vigil."

"Everyone in New Mexico is related by blood at some level!" the governor snarls. "Marriages here are positively incestuous!"

Donaciano looks down at the flat-brimmed black hat in his hands. There are times when he wishes he'd never enlisted in the presidio troop. He glances at Colonel Aponte, then focuses politely on the governor. "How can I be of service?"

His Excellency sinks into the big oak chair behind the desk. "You can explain why the Montoya brothers thought it wise or even advisable to break the alcalde of that hell hole Santa Cruz de la Cañada out of jail on Monday night." He shoves at a piece of paper on the desk. "And why, after I ordered him back to jail, the said alcalde saw fit to issue this so-called proclamation instead."

Vigil's forehead wrinkles. "Proclamation?"

The governor scowls. "Calling for unity, of all things. In New Mexico, of all places." He snorts. "The most godforsaken part of the entire country." He leans forward and reads out the words on the page without touching it. "Long live God and the nation and the faith of Jesus Christ, for the most important issues they stand for are the following—"

He looks up. "What does that even mean? Who is 'they' for God's sake?" He waves an impatient hand at the document, jerks out of his chair, and begins pacing between the desk and the nearest wall. "The rest of it is somewhat clearer. In short, they don't want to pay the new federal sales tax." He sniffs derisively. "It's all about money."

Vigil's forehead wrinkles further. If the governor knows what the proclamation is about, why has he summoned him?

"They've formed a council of twelve," Ramón Abreú tells him. The prefect looks uneasily at Pérez. "A kind of substitute government for the people of Río Arriba."

"A direct rejection of my authority!" The governor turns and glares at the proclamation as if it were Antonio Abad Montoya himself. Or Alcalde Esquibel.

He moves back to the desk and leans forward, peering down at the proclamation. His voice rises as he reads another section aloud. "To defend our country even to shedding the last drop of blood in order to secure the Víctory intended. Not to admit the Departmental Plan." He scowls and turns away. "So now they're rejecting the actions of Congress."

Then he turns back to the desk. "Also, no taxes." He bends toward the paper again. "And this, of all things. 'Not to admit the disorder of those who are trying to effect it.'" He lifts his head, his eyes snapping at Donaciano. "What the hell does that even mean?"

The sergeant wets his lips with his tongue and speaks carefully. "They seem to be saying that someone is trying to divide the members of their community against each other and create dissension."

The governor's face reddens. "They're the ones creating dissension!" He jerks toward Colonel Aponte. "Have the messengers left yet?"

"Yes, Your Excellency. However, it is my considered opinion—"

Pérez holds up his hand, stopping Aponte's words. "I will not flee," he says flatly. "There is no real danger. Esquibel is an ignorant rabble rouser."

He moves behind the desk, picks up the proclamation, and places it on top of a stack of other papers on his left. Then he begins shuffling the entire batch, aligning their edges. He looks up at Ramón Abreú. "Esquibel doesn't know what he's doing and the rest of them are simply in it for the fun of causing mischief. They can't seriously suppose I'll give up you and your brother Santiago for execution."

Donaciano's head jerks toward the colonel.

"It's only a rumor," Aponte says quietly. He turns to the governor. "The militia should arrive from Bernalillo and Alburquerque in a few days, as will the warriors from the pueblos. A few have already come north from Santo Domingo."

Vigil stiffens. They've asked the pueblos to rally against the men of Río Arriba? How do they know the Native communities will side with the governor in this matter? He opens his mouth, then closes it again. It's not his place to question his superior officers. None of them are looking at him, anyway. They haven't registered his reaction.

In fact, they seem to have forgotten he's in the room. Pérez frowns at the colonel. "In a few days? I want to march out tomorrow! The sooner we squelch this nonsense, the better."

Aponte shakes his head. "We don't have enough men yet. We should be ready by Saturday or Sunday."

Abreú frowns. "Marching on Sunday will cause even more trouble. It'll be seen as an affront to the church."

"Monday then."

Pérez nods, his equilibrium restored. "I want you to head up the men that go with me."

Aponte hesitates, then says, "As you wish, Excellency."

"With a brevet commission of lieutenant colonel."

A glimmer of satisfaction crosses the colonel's face. He salutes, turns sharply, and goes out. The governor turns to Ramón Abreú. Donaciano coughs softly to get their attention.

Pérez looks at him in surprise. Then his face twists contemptuously. "No explanation or advice?"

"I wonder if a quiet discussion with Alcalde Esquibel would be helpful."

The governor stiffens. "He disobeyed my direct orders, both to return Antonio Abad Montoya to jail and to disperse his constituents back to their homes. The only discussion I plan to have with him will be a public one, with a wall of presidio soldiers, militia, and Pueblo warriors behind me."

Vigil nods noncommittally and, when Abreú leaves a few minutes later, follows him out.

~ ~ ~ ~

The following Monday morning, the sergeant notes that the governor has achieved at least part of his goal. The men marching out of Santa Fe include presidio soldiers, community militia from as far south as Belén, and over three hundred Pueblo warriors. There are enough men under arms to allow Pérez to order a large portion of the presidio garrison to stay behind and still have a sufficient crew for the two cannon he's assigned Donaciano to superintend.

The governor has even found the means to pay them all. As the government forces stream past the old guardhouse on the road to Santa Cruz de la Cañada in the brilliant August morning, there's a sense of hopefulness in the air, despite the fact that no one knows exactly what awaits them. Perhaps it's the people scattered along the road, bidding them farewell. Or the knowledge that Santa Fe will be well defended by the troops who've stayed behind.

Or perhaps it's all the officials who ride beside the governor's big brown-spotted appaloosa. There are two Santa Fe alcaldes, Treasurer Sarracino, former governor and current Judge Santiago Abreú, and the judge's two brothers—the Río Arriba Prefect and Marcelino, the Tomé schoolmaster. The presence of all these civilians implies that His Excellency expects to do more talking than fighting. Donaciano certainly hopes so.

Or maybe his own sense of well-being is the result of the row upon row of blue-coated militia behind the presidio soldiers. Or the Pueblo warriors massed in the rear, obsidian-pointed spears in their hands, bare chests gleaming. Their headdresses alone, which range from feather-rich plains-style bonnets to shaggy buffalo heads, horns still attached, inspire confidence.

Or maybe it's simply the turquoise-blue of the clear sky, the sun gleaming from the Sangre de Cristo peaks on the right, and the hazy blue Jemez range lining the western horizon. It's a glorious Nuevo México day, the kind that makes the heart sing.

Also, the government forces aren't likely to meet the insurgents any time today or even tomorrow. Perhaps the whole issue will resolve itself by the time they reach Santa Cruz de la Cañada. The rebels will decide a direct confrontation isn't the wisest way to deal with their issues, or this display of united strength will bring them to their senses.

They camp that night in the sand hills just south of the pueblo of Pojoaque, then Pérez leads them west along the Camino Real's old route toward the río del Norte.

Sargento Vigil, riding beside his cannon and crew, isn't sure why the governor has chosen this road. It will take longer than the newer route through Pojoaque. However, he isn't complaining. The delay will give the rebels more time to reflect on the size of the force coming to meet them.

And the group of officials. He contemplates Colonel Aponte's thickset shoulders, Pérez's slim stiff back, and the broader one of Sarracino beside him. Perhaps cooler heads will prevail and they can all have a good meal together and then go home.

Up ahead of the officials, the road swings north toward the black bulk of La Mesilla. Sparsely grassed sand-and-rock hills half again as tall as a man border the dirt track. The mesa's flat black top looms overhead, ominous against the bright sky. A chill runs down Donaciano's spine. His horse's head jerks as if agreeing with him.

But then one of the mules pulling the nearest gun carriage stumbles and the sergeant focuses on his work. When the wheels are stable and rolling again, he glances at the forces behind. The presidio horses are looking a little dusty, but they and the militia are in good order, each troop with its own flag. The Pueblo warriors follow steadily behind. The tips of their lances flash in the light as Vigil stretches his neck, trying to see to the back of the phalanx.

Then his attention is jerked toward the front of the column. The men ahead have stopped, sending a recoil back through the lines. The gun carriage mules toss their heads in protest. The cannons grind to a standstill as Corporal Tomás Martín, riding beside the other one, snaps a command.

Donaciano leans forward. A bend in the road hides Governor Pérez and the others from sight. La Mesilla looms overhead. The governor's contingent must be almost directly beneath it. The sergeant squints up at the massive outcropping, blinks, then looks again. Are those people standing on its flat top? Around the bend, there's the blast of a trumpet, then the governor's voice. "My people!" he calls.

Tomás Martín looks across the cannon at the sergeant, a question in his face. Donaciano shakes his head to indicate he doesn't know what's happening, then nudges his mount forward just enough to see around the curve in the road. His spine stiffens. "¡Maldición!" he whispers.

Beyond the governor and his entourage, the foot of La Mesilla is crowded with men. They stand with their backs to the black outcropping, in front of and between the tumbled boulders at the mesa's base. They all have weapons in their hands. Spears, notched arrows, and guns: ancient flintlocks, carbines, and American long rifles.

A flash of light overhead catches his eye. There are more men wedged into the niches in La Mesilla's cliff-like sides. And more above, lining the rim. All armed and ominously silent.

The governor turns his head toward Aponte and says something Vigil can't hear. As the colonel wheels his mount and trots toward Donaciano, Pérez refocuses on the rebels. He raises an arm. "My people!" he cries again. "Countrymen! Hear me!"

"Hear you?" a voice bellows from the side of the mesa. "¡Predicas, pero no aplicas!"

Donaciano winces. Telling the governor 'you preach, but do not practice' may be apropos, but it's not the best way to get him to listen.

His Excellency raises himself in his stirrups and lifts his arm, signaling a response, but Donaciano doesn't hear what he says. Aponte's horse is suddenly crowding his and the colonel is leaning anxiously forward.

Aponte jerks a thumb toward the sharp angle of the rock-and-sand slope on the left side of the road. "Move the cannon back and get them up onto that hill. We don't have much time." He nods toward the troops behind the cannon. "They'll spread—" Then he stops. "What the devil?"

Vigil turns to follow the colonel's gaze. Air hisses through his teeth. The presidio soldiers are still there, but there are few militia. And no Pueblo warriors. As he and Aponte watch, more men slip out of the remaining ranks and between the hills on either side. The colonel yanks his horse's reins, turning toward the governor. Vigil yells to Martín to get the guns onto the slope, then follows Aponte. He pulls up behind Ramón Abreú and peers past the officials to La Mesilla.

The space at the foot of the mesa is black with insurrectos, militia, and warriors. Some of them have climbed onto the boulder-sized rocks at its base. They all gaze silently at the governor and what's left of his men. Sunlight glints from buffalo headdresses and the tips of spears. The Pueblan faces seem sharper now, more fierce than they did marching out of Santa Fe yesterday morning.

Vigil wheels his horse back toward the cannon and their unwieldy carriages. Tomás Martín stares at him, an uncertain look on his face. "Onto the hill!" the sergeant barks. "Quick-ly!"

Behind him, the governor's voice has turned angry as he bellows at the massed rebels, alternating between promises and threats. Donaciano gestures the remaining troops backwards so the guns will have room to maneuver. The gun crew helps, pushing at the carriage wheels until the mules are beside the shallowest point of the slope on the left. They make an awkward half turn in the narrow roadbed and angle gingerly onto the sandy dirt.

The sergeant leads the first gun up the hill, maneuvering between the largest of the rocks, while Corporal Martín gets the second one into position on the road below.

It's not an easy climb. The loose soil slips underfoot, revealing rocks the size of a man's skull just below the surface. The mules toss their heads and strain upward, hooves slipping in the dirt. Finally, the gun carriage reaches a bit of flatness at the top of the hill. As the mules swing into position, Donaciano looks back. The second cannon is having a tougher time because of the damage the first one did to the slope.

And there's no possibility of surprising the rebels. The men on the mesa have had plenty of time to spot the guns. As the first cannon's barrel settles into place, a shout goes up. There's a distant popping sound. The man nearest Vigil looks up nervously, but the sergeant waves him back to work. "They're not serious yet," he says. "If they were, we'd hear more noise than that."

But the single shot is enough to get Governor Pérez and his entourage out of the mesa's range. Their horses pound down the road and up the little hill past the second cannon, whose mules are still struggling in the loose soil.

The governor is pale with rage. "Those damn Indians!" he growls. "Traitors! We're outnumbered three to one!"

Donaciano looks at the black crag. The rebels don't seem to have realized yet what the cannon are capable of. A solid mass of men remains at the base. Sergeant Vigil looks at his crew. The gunner nods to him. "Ready to fire, sergeant!"

Vigil turns to Colonel Aponte, who looks at the governor. Pérez glares back at him. "Well, what are you waiting for?" he demands.

The colonel nods to Vigil, who turns to his men. They lean toward the gun, then pause and look at him as if for final confirmation. The hesitation in their eyes isn't fear. It's something worse. They may have cousins among the men below. Or even brothers-in-law. Or brothers. Donaciano pushes the knot in his belly out of the way, stiffens his shoulders, and barks the order. His men turn to their task.

The shot falls short of the rebel crowd and a jeer goes up from the men below the mesa. However, someone among them realizes that the next shell is likely to find its mark. By the time the cannon is reloaded and its aim adjusted, the crowd has thinned and spread sideways and backwards, farther into the tumbled rocks. A few men climb into the crevices in the mesa's side, but then they turn to face outward, silent and waiting, weapons still in hand.

Vigil's eyes narrow. Another volley won't produce much effect. Behind him, the governor yells something incomprehensible but clearly furious. The sergeant nods to the gunner. The shell pounds through the air and slaps into the dirt at the mesa's base, digging a boulder-sized hole and sending two men flying.

Suddenly the insurrectos are no longer silent or still. They scream in fury as they erupt from the black rock and run towards the little hill. "Fire at will!" Vigil yells. The cannon roars once, pauses, then pounds the cliff itself. Rock tumbles from its side.

But he needs more firepower. Where is Tomás with the second gun? He turns—and sees rebels. He's been so focused on the mesa that he hasn't understood what the governor has already realized. The hill is surrounded and being rapidly overrun. The only part not swarming with insurrectos is the sharp drop to his right, straight to the road.

But being surrounded doesn't mean defeat. Colonel Aponte is on foot and a third of the way toward the second cannon, his sword swinging steadily. Governor Pérez is on his appaloosa below and to the right, his face a mask of pure fury as he empties his pistols at anyone who moves toward him with a weapon, then reloads at lightning speed.

The two Santa Fe alcaldes, also still on horseback, flank the governor, slashing at anyone within reach. The three Abreú brothers have dismounted and are trying to coax their mounts and Aponte's into a dip in the hilltop between the cannon and the break to the road.

Sarracino edges his horse toward Donaciano and the first cannon. He slips from the saddle and whacks the animal on the rump. As it skitters toward the bank above the road and disappears over the edge, he leans toward the sergeant. "We need to get His Excellency away from here!" he shouts. "He shouldn't be fighting! He's going to get himself killed!"

Vigil nods but doesn't answer. He's too busy firing his handgun, reloading, and firing again. The cannon is useless now except as a rallying point or a kind of breastwork. But the big guns are still his primary responsibility. He peers down the hill, trying to spot Tomás Martín.

Colonel Aponte blocks his view. He and a thick-set insurrecto with a burn-scarred face are battling hand-to-hand. The rebel has no proper armor, just heavy Chimayó plaid wool secured to his body with row upon row of heavy cord. He dances away from Aponte's slashing sword, then lunges forward, swinging a machete as if it's a hatchet and howling with fury. The colonel sidesteps and charges, blade flashing in the sun.

Then he disappears from view as Santo Domingo warriors flood up the hill. Donaciano fires his pistols, but there's no time to reload. He pulls out his long knife. The gunner appears beside him, his own blade in hand. Sarracino is beyond him, then the other men, ranged in a half circle around the cannon, braced for what's coming.

The melee that follows is short but fierce. Vigil loses track of everything but the nearest rebel. Finally, the attackers pull back, allowing a breathing space. The Abreú brothers appear, leading the horses. The governor and his appaloosa have reached the hilltop again. His chest heaves as he looks down at Colonel Aponte, who's bent over and clutching his right side. Blood oozes from between his fingers.

The governor bends toward him. "Colonel?" he asks. "Lieutenant Colonel?"

Aponte nods, then looks up. "Forgive me, Excellency," he gasps. "My wound—" Then he shudders and collapses to the ground.

The governor's horse steps nervously back. "Sergeant!" Pérez bellows.

Donaciano moves down the hill. "Get him on his horse!" the governor cries. "We're getting out of here!" As he wheels the appaloosa away, he spies Sarracino, who's leaning against the cannon at the top of the hill, one hand on a blood-stained shoulder. "Don't let them get the artillery!" Pérez yells.

"With my life!" the other man responds. He lifts his hand in salute as a bellow of triumph echoes from the direction of the second cannon.

They all jerk toward the sound. The gun is now on its side, carriage wheel in the air and barrel jammed into the dirt. Tomás Martín sprawls face down beside it. A man wearing a buffalo headdress is doing an impromptu dance around them both. A cluster of insurrectos howls in delight. The burn-scarred man, then others, fall in behind the dancer and mimic his movements.

"Savages!" Governor Pérez growls. But he doesn't move toward the disabled gun. Instead, he glares at Donaciano. "Get the colonel on his horse!"

The sergeant nods and turns toward the Abreús. Marcelino comes forward with Aponte's horse and drops the reins into Vigil's hands. Donaciano strokes the animal's neck. It flares its nostrils and shakes its head, but follows him to the colonel and stands quietly enough while the sergeant helps Aponte into the saddle. The colonel clings to the high silver-decorated pommel with one hand and presses his wounded side with the other.

The prefect moves his own horse forward and the sergeant hands him Aponte's reins. Abreú barely glances at him as he turns to follow the governor and his brothers, who are already halfway down the bank to the road. On the hilltop, the Santa Fe alcaldes have pulled their horses alongside Sarracino and are bending toward him with urgent faces.

Donaciano glances toward the road. The governor's big horse has reached the track and is galloping full tilt toward the curve to Pojoaque and Santa Fe, the three Abreús right behind. A handful of militia men filter through the sandy hills after them. It's impossible to tell whether they're fleeing loyalists or pursuing rebels.

However, he has no time to speculate. The bulk of the insurrectos have regrouped. They ring the base of the little hilltop, looking upward. They want the cannon. Or Sarracino and the Santa Fe officials. The two alcaldes peer down the slope, see what's happened, slide off their animals, and slap the beasts' rumps, sending them away.

As the horses scramble down the hill, Vigil and the others reload their handguns. They don't waste words, but they do form a circle with their backs to the gun carriage as the rebels begin to move up the hill.

The ammunition doesn't last long. Sarracino draws his sword and the others reach for their knives. Donaciano has lost his. He looks around wildly. There's a gap between the combatants and he spies a dropped spear beside a rebel who's sprawled facedown a few feet from Tomás Martín.

As the sergeant darts toward the weapon, more rebels boil up the slope. Someone tackles Donaciano from the side and he's knocked sideways, onto the corporal. He has only a moment to register Martín's grunt of pain before his own arms are wrenched behind his back. A rope twists around his wrists, then a hand grabs his shoulder and he's jerked to his feet.

"Well, well." Antonio Abad Montoya grins at him, his eyes crinkling in amusement. "Cousin. How good to see you again." One sleeve is torn, but otherwise Montoya looks as if he's having the time of his life. "I thought that was you up here on the hill." He looks down at Tomás Martín, who's pushing himself up from the dirt, his face twisted with pain. "And you brought a friend." He looks up the slope. "A number of friends, as a matter of fact. Excelentisimo."

Then he turns and waves an arm at someone further down the hill. "General Gonzales!" he bellows. "We have prisoners!"

CHAPTER 5

August 8–9, 1837: In The Name Of Mercy
(Albino Pérez)

Governor Albino Pérez, still in the dusty uniform he wore to the morning's battle, scrabbles through the documents on his desk. He pulls out a sheet here, a notarized invoice there, and tosses them into a loose pile on the seat of the big chair behind it. Pérez's plumed bicorne hat hangs from the back of the chair. A small rifle with delicately engraved silver fittings leans beside it.

The governor's aide, Lieutenant Joaquín Hurtado, kneels on the floor beside the chair. He removes the papers one at a time, sorts them into small stacks on the floor, then ties them into neat bundles and slips them into an embossed leather satchel. Light flickers from the candles in the sconces on the whitewashed adobe walls. On a mahogany side table below two large gilt-frame mirrors, a clock strikes the hour. Pérez's hands freeze. He turns and stares at the brass numbers. It's half past nine o'clock.

His head snaps toward Hurtado. "Hurry up! The others will be here in less than an hour. We must escape while we can!"

Skirts rustle in the doorway at the other end of the room. The two men turn toward the sound. Trinidad Trujillo stands framed in the entrance.

The slender young woman with the enormous eyes has never looked much like a housekeeper and now she seems even less like one. She's wrapped in a finely woven black cloak. The blanket-swathed baby is just visible beneath it. She also carries a leather satchel. She drops it at her feet, tucks the infant closer, and drops her chin slightly as her luminous brown eyes meet the governor's. "I'm ready," she says.

Pérez shakes his head. "You'll only slow us down. I've sold the carriage back to the merchant and there's no other way to transport you."

She takes a step into the room. "I can ride a horse if I need to."

"Not with a child in your arms. You wouldn't be able to keep up."

"But I can't remain in Santa Fe." Her voice rises. "There is no safe place for me here. The rebels—" She pauses and looks down at the sleeping child. When she looks up again, her chin is trembling and there are tears in her eyes. "Los insurrectos call me a whore because of our son. What will they do to me if I am no longer under your protection?"

She's beautiful when she pleads with him. It's how she first caught his attention that day she asked for the role of housekeeper. He makes a small gesture with his hand, pushing the memory aside. He can't take her with him. It's him and his men now. His band of brothers. There was no place for women on the battlefield earlier today and there won't be in the days to come.

He stiffens his spine and roughens his voice. "These rebellious peones are your people, not mine. You certainly tried to explain them to me often enough." He snorts impatiently and looks down at the papers on his desk. "Not that your explanations and pleas have been of much use to me."

She murmurs something and he glances up at her. "What was that?"

She's not pleading now. There's only reproach in her beautiful eyes. "You didn't believe me when I tried to express the danger of the new fees and taxes. You think we all have bags of gold tucked away in the vigas."

He glances at the ceiling of stripped aspen poles, the smaller pieces above them holding back the flat soil roof. "There's certainly plenty of dirt above them in which to hide things," he says sourly. His mouth twists as he looks around the room. "Adobe mud walls for the governor's house. It's a travesty." He refocuses on her and scowls impatiently. "You're from here. You'll be safe enough."

She shifts the sleeping child in her arms and the cloak moves to one side. The pale blue blanket the baby's wrapped in is of finely woven wool and is edged with satin that exactly matches the cloth. "And little Demetrio?" she asks. "What of him?"

The governor's face softens in spite of his resolve. He moves down the room to her and lifts a corner of the blanket away from the infant's face. The long dark lashes flutter open, then close again.

"He's a beauty," Pérez says wistfully. Then he drops the cloth and steps back. "However, I can't take either of you with me. It's too dangerous."

She opens her lips to protest and he lifts a hand to stop her. "Besides, this rebellion is a temporary misunderstanding. It will all blow over and then I'll return and teach those Río Arriba troublemakers a lesson they won't forget." He smiles at her beguilingly. "And then we'll have a most tender reunion, you and I."

Her lips twitch in amusement and she looks at him seductively through her lashes. His groin stirs. If Hurtado wasn't here, he'd take her right now.

But the others will be arriving soon. He turns abruptly away, crosses to the side table, and opens the elaborately carved wooden box that sits beside the brass clock. He pulls out a lumpy leather bag and carries it to her. "Take this."

She frowns slightly and holds out a reluctant hand. When he wraps her slender fingers around the bag, the coins shift. "This will be enough to tide you over until I return."

She nods, then lifts her eyes, giving him her most trusting expression. "I will wait for you."

But he's already halfway to his desk and doesn't respond. He reaches for another stack of documents, then looks back at her. She's tucked the money away and stands watching him, as still as a Madonna. A young and fragile Madonna. Even down the length of the room, she pulls at his heart.

"Go to your mother," he says gently. "Find a place away from the capital where you can stay until I return and send for you."

She shifts the baby slightly and something twists in his chest. She must flee. Now. Before it's too late. "When the insurrectos arrive, they will look for the child," he says. "At best, they will hold him hostage, hoping for ransom. At worst—"

But her eyes are huge now, tears swimming behind the terror. He doesn't need to say more. "We would be safer with you," she chokes, but he shakes his head grimly.

She stares at him for a long painful moment, then looks down at the child, tucks him back inside her cloak, and bends to scoop up the satchel with her other hand. She gives Pérez another long look, then turns and is gone, lost in the palacio's black depths.

His chest constricts as he stares at the empty doorway. Behind him, Hurtado moves, bringing him back to his senses. This is no time to appear weak. The governor's shoulders straighten and he turns back to the desk. He picks up another sheaf of papers. "That's one way to get rid of a mistress," he says dryly. "I can thank los insurrectos for that, at any rate."

The lieutenant, still on the floor, chuckles and drops another neat bundle into the satchel. "Anything else?" he asks.

Pérez looks at the papers in his hands, then at the clock. Ten minutes to ten. Beyond the palacio's thick adobe walls, it will be full dark. The new quarter moon will make the road south just visible enough to travel but not so bright that travelers can be seen from a distance.

Cloth rustles in the doorway again, but this time it's four men, with more hurrying in behind them. "Your Excellency?" Prefect Ramón Abreú asks politely. "We are at your service." He and his brothers doff their hats. Ensign Diego Sáenz, who serves as Santiago's aide, hovers at his elbow. A cluster of soldiers remain in the space behind them.

Pérez nods his greeting and moves behind the desk. As the others watch, he opens a drawer, removes a flat wooden box, and lifts the lid. Inside are two long-barrel pistols with finely carved grips. He loads them, tucks them into the sash at his waist, then turns, retrieves his hat, and settles it onto his head. He gestures to Hurtado to bring the satchel and rifle, then moves toward his officials and escape.

~ ~ ~ ~

As Pérez and his men ride southwest out of Santa Fe, the heat of the day is replaced by a small breeze. They stay on the Camino Real through the sleeping hamlet of Agua Fría and the fields beyond, then move onto a smaller track that trends west toward Las Golondrinas. They stop short of the hacienda there, on the edges of the hamlet of El Álamo, and camp among the gnarled cottonwoods that line its creek bed.

Pérez lies with his back to a downed branch and listens to the leaves rustling in the darkness as he considers his options. The río del Norte isn't far. The river won't be deep this time of year, though this section does flow through a steep-sided canyon. If they can find a way down to the water and then up the other side, they can reach the Jemez mountains.

And Navajo country beyond. The indios bárbaros who've continued to raid Nuevo México's villages and farms the last two years, despite Pérez's best efforts. They're an elusive people, coming and going at will. Knowing them, this is when they'll choose to make an appearance.

No, the only escape is south along the Camino Real, the very road he travelled so proudly to reach this benighted land after he received his appointment as its governor. His teeth grind as he thinks of it, then he forces his mind to the business at hand. What should he do?

There's safety to the south, in Bernalillo and then Alburquerque and the rich farmlands of the ricos there and farther down river. If the insurrectos can't be brought to heel from that position, he'll go on to México, the land of sanity where the lower classes know their place.

And then come back with reinforcements. The thought of revenge swells his chest, then he turns back to consider his next move. Between the ricos of Bernalillo and where he now rests is La Bajada, the basalt escarpment that divides the lower and upper rivers and marks the descent from the plains of Santa Fe. Santo Domingo lies beyond.

His eyes narrow. That pueblo of traitors. That viperish nest. If he had his way, he'd make a blanket of their hides and drape his horse in it. He smiles at the thought. Somehow, he'll get past them and on to reinforcements. Santiago Abreú has a hacienda in that area. He'll know a route. The governor settles into sleep.

He wakes to the sound of the heart-shaped cottonwood leaves still whispering. The morning light slips through the green leaves and touches the old gray trunks with fresh strength. The air is cool and clean.

Hope surges through his chest. Surely news of yesterday's disaster, of the way those sneaking Pueblo devils who call themselves warriors deserted him, will have reached Bernalillo and Alburquerque by now. Every Spanish-blood militiaman available there will be racing north to his assistance, to prove that the rabble who went over to the insurrectos do not represent the best of their communities.

In fact, Don Antonito Chávez of the Alburquerque militia should be on his way north with his troop by now. A good man, Don Antonito. Sensible. Able to read the political winds. He'll know that reward lies in hastening to his governor's aid. And, with what Sarracino has scrounged and the money Pérez borrowed from the americano merchants late yesterday, he has the funds to reward Chávez handsomely. The bit he gave Trinidad is a small portion of what he has on hand.

Money and men. He has one. Soon he'll have the other. Pérez nods to himself and heads to his horse. El Buen Amigo's ears tilt forward and he nickers softly as the governor approaches. Pérez strokes the brown-spotted neck. "Ah, my good friend," he says. "Are you ready for this day? We will meet our reinforcements and then we will return to Santa Fe and send those insurrectos back into the rat holes from which they emerged."

The appaloosa nudges Pérez's shoulder as if to hurry him along and the governor laughs. "Let's go then!" He turns toward the campfire, where the Abreú brothers are standing in a small knot, and lifts his voice. "My horse is ready! Are you?"

~ ~ ~ ~

With hopefulness and the thought of the Alburquerque militia has come the decision to return to the Camino Real and the most direct route south. Two hours later, a troop of blue-coated militia come into view with Antonito Chávez at its head. He raises a gloved hand and his men rein to a stop as the governor's party rides up.

"Ah, Don Antonito," Pérez says. "You have received word of yesterday's events. I congratulate you on the rapidity of your response."

"Your Excellency," Chávez replies. But he doesn't remove his hat as a token of respect and his eyes sweep coldly over the men whose mounts cluster behind the governor's. He nods to Ramón and Santiago Abreú, then refocuses on Pérez. "You have left Santa Fe undefended?" There's a slight accusation in his tone, inappropriate for a man who is merely a commander of militia.

Pérez's eyes narrow. "The presidio troops are there to defend it. As is their duty. My responsibility as governor is to rally the countryside and gather reinforcements." He gestures toward the men around him. "With these and the men you have brought, we will lift our strong right arm and crush that rabble as they deserve."

Don Antonito's gaze shifts to the governor's entourage. Something flashes across his face. Contempt? Pérez is suddenly aware that his little band doesn't present a very martial appearance. Only four of them are soldiers and one of those merely a militiaman.

Chávez's eyes return to the governor. He doesn't blink. "I beg your pardon most sincerely, Your Excellency," he says unapologetically. "I'm afraid I must refuse the honor of your company and that of your—" He glances behind Pérez again. "Your men."

Then he turns his head and barks an order. He and his men step their horses into the rocky soil beside the road and file past the governor and his band, moving toward Santa Fe.

Joaquín Hurtado is near the back of Pérez's band. "And what are we to do instead?" he asks as Chávez comes level with him.

Chávez reins in and gives the lieutenant a pitying look. "Find somewhere to hide for a few days. But don't go directly south. We camped this side of Santo Domingo last night. They are gearing for war, women and children as well as men. I wouldn't advise trying to cross their land." He jerks his head toward Santiago Abreú and his two brothers. "Especially with them with you."

Abreú scowls at him. "Dog!" he spits. "How dare you speak of us in that way!"

Chávez's lips quirk in amusement. "I don't know about your siblings, but I do know that the people of Santo Domingo have more than one score to settle with you as former governor. Face them at your peril."

His eyes skim over the rest of Pérez's little group, then his mouth twists sardonically. "Though you may well survive. After all, you have His Excellency's strong right arm to aid you." He lifts his hand in a small salute, spurs his horse and is gone, his troop cantering after him. A cloud of dust rises behind them.

Santiago Abréu waves his hand in front of his face, clearing the haze. "I don't know what the Santo Domingans might have against me," he grumbles. "Every leader must make difficult decisions." He looks at Pérez, but the governor is staring at the road south. The Santo Domingos are formidable warriors. And they proved yesterday that they have no sense of honor. At least los insurrectos have some Spanish blood in their veins.

Pérez lifts his plumed bicorne hat away from his forehead and stares into its crown. It's no use. There's no safety southward. He must turn and fight.

He puts his hat back on his head and looks at the Abréu brothers, then Hurtado. "We will return to the capital," he says grimly. "And when this is over, I will have that bastard Antonito Chávez court-martialed and sent to Mexico City in chains. He hasn't seen the last of my strong right arm!"

He wheels toward Santa Fe and the others follow. He keeps them at a steady trot. There's no point in raising a plume of dust that can be seen for miles. His dander may be up, but he's still cautious. Who knows where the Pueblo warriors might be or what they might do?

The steady pace gives him time to feel the sun, soak in the deep blue of the sky. To the east, a handful of fluffy white clouds drifts over the peaks of the Sangre de Cristos. Even with all its faults, Nuevo México is still a majestic land. Under different circumstances, this would be a quite pleasant ride.

An hour later, the clouds have darkened and billowed upward into thunderheads that obscure the pine-covered eastern slope. The air is hot and so thick with moisture that Pérez can hardly breathe. Drops form under his armpits. At this rate, his coat will be ruined.

But then there's a sudden movement just behind him and to his right, where Prefect Abreú is riding. One of the soldiers has trotted forward. He leans forward and speaks in a low, urgent voice, then Abreú's mount moves up beside El Buen Amigo.

The other horse is dragging its head, already weary from the heat and the pace the appaloosa has set. Even in the anxiety of the moment, Pérez notes the difference between the two animals with satisfaction.

"Your Excellency," the prefect says. His mouth twists nervously and the skin around his hazel eyes is white with strain.

Pérez nods for him to go on.

"There seems to be a small party of men following us."

"Following?"

Abreú nods, raises his arm to point at a low grassy ridge to the left, then abruptly drops his hand, and jerks his head in that direction instead. "Out there."

The governor starts to turn, then checks himself. "Who are they?"

Abreú wets his lip with his tongue and looks away. He's either afraid of the news he's about to give or of how the governor will react to it. He turns back to Pérez. "They appear to be warriors from Santo Domingo."

Pérez frowns. "How can you tell?" People from the pueblos all look alike to him.

Abreú shrugs. "It's what the soldiers are saying." His family are newcomers too, though they've lived here longer than Pérez. "There are signs, ways of knowing."

The governor nods and slows his horse to a walk. He considers his men. They're all tired from yesterday's events and their horses are not fresh. He eyes the landscape, which is devoid of anything but thin, drying grass, rocky sand, and a few scattered bushes. There's no good location here to stage a defense and Santa Fe is still a good three or four leagues away. Staying together will give the warriors a larger target. Better to split up and give them more to track.

He glances toward the ridge. From a distance, it barely seems like any kind of rise, but this country has a way of doing that. And it could be the edge of an arroyo deep enough to hide a man on horseback.

His gaze moves to the other side of the road. He's suddenly aware of every cluster of man-tall chamiso bush and rounded hillock sprinkled with autumn-dry grass. Any of them could hide a warrior. Or two. Even three.

Something moves off to the left, on the edge of his vision. His hands tighten on the reins as he tries to see it without twisting all the way around. It's just a small solitary tree tossed by a gust of wind. He forces his breathing to slow and looks up at the clouds.

They're blacker now and moving steadily from east to west. They haven't completely covered the sky yet, but they'll be topping the Jemez mountains within another hour, lidding the space between them and the Sangre de Cristos. There will be rain before the day is over. Which will be a blessed relief from this heat.

Then he brings himself back to the matter at hand. He turns to Ramón Abreú. "You're certain we're being followed?"

The prefect nods unhappily.

The governor reins to a stop. His men draw up around him. Their shoulders droop, beaten down by heat, dust, and worry.

Their exhaustion gives him new energy. His spine straightens. "Divide et impera," he says abruptly.

They blink at him like confused owls. Pérez smiles contemptuously. "We must divide in order to rule," he translates. "We'll split up and give those so-called warriors of Santo Domingo too many trails to take at once. I will continue on to Santa Fe, but each of you should choose the best location for yourself over the next few days." He looks down at El Buen Amigo with a twinge of regret. "Though we must go on foot, to make it more difficult for them to spot us from a distance."

He swings out of the silver-mounted saddle and hands the appaloosa's reins to the nearest soldier. "Take good care of my friend here and you will be rewarded accordingly," he tells him. There's an unexpected knot in his throat. He gives the horse's neck a sharp pat, then moves to his brown-spotted flank and rummages in the saddle bags for his rifle and ammunition.

When he turns away from the horse, only Santiago Abreú and his aide are still astride. "I would advise you to walk," Pérez says. "You'll be more easily spotted on horseback."

Diego Sáenz looks questioningly at Abreú, but the former governor shakes his head. "My hacienda is south of here," he tells Pérez. "If we ride swiftly we have a chance of reaching it ahead of the warriors." Then his chin lifts. "I know this part of New Mexico like the palms of my hands. We can avoid them."

Pérez shrugs. "As you wish." His right hand tightens on his rifle as his left touches the pistols at his waist. He turns, studying his men. The Abreú brothers, the soldiers. Their eyes drop before his, but none of them move. They are unwilling to go until he does.

His gaze lands on Hurtado. "With your permission, Excellency," the lieutenant says. "I will be pleased to accompany you." The satchel of Pérez's papers is slung over his shoulder. He pats the strap. "I would like to return these to your desk as soon as possible."

A chuckle runs through the men. Pérez steps toward Hurtado and claps his shoulder. "That's the spirit!" Then he looks at the satchel. There are papers in it which will be difficult to explain if they fall into rebel hands.

Pérez looks into Hurtado's face. "It is better that we separate and that what you carry is safely guarded."

Hurtado nods obediently. "I will go east into the mountains and return by the traders' road from Missouri," he says.

Pérez nods his approval, then turns in a slow half circle, casting his gaze over his officials and the others, then raises his hand in a farewell salute. He settles the little rifle against his shoulder. "Until we meet again, gentlemen." He gives them one last nod, turns away, and walks firmly north, up the dusty road toward his capital. He glances back once, to confirm that the others have dispersed, then trudges on.

~ ~ ~ ~

It's a dreary way to travel, this walking. Within a quarter of a league, Pérez's black boots are coated with dust. But he was right to dismount. The road is a series of gentle undulations, its dips just deep enough to effectively hide a man on foot from view. The tops of the little hills are another matter. As he reaches them, Pérez's shoulders hunch instinctively and he pulls his little rifle closer to his thigh, as if doing so will reduce his profile against the horizon.

Eventually, he raises his head enough to take in his surroundings, the road behind. No one there. Except a bare-chested man beside a bush half a mile back. He frowns. Did one of his men follow after all?

He blinks, trying to see more clearly, but then the shape disappears. Had he imagined it? The governor hurries forward into the safety of the next dip in the road.

There are no trees beside the camino. The sun peers through the gaps in the clouds and beats onto Pérez's back. His hair is damp with sweat in spite of the protection of his hat.

His hat. He stops in his tracks, his free hand going to the bicorne with its white plume, the symbol of his rank, floating jauntily above his head for anyone to see. He places the rifle butt-end on the ground and leaning against his leg, and yanks the hat from his head. He wrenches the feather from its crown, then stands with it pinched between his fingers.

Think. He must think. If only Hurtado was here, or Santiago Abreú. They know this land better than he ever will. He needs to find somewhere to hide, as that bastard Antonito Chávez recommended.

Anger boils in his chest. Chávez and his insolence. Strong right arm, indeed. When this is over, the man will pay tenfold. Then Pérez abruptly drops the feather and reaches again for the gun. This is not the time to plan retribution, however well deserved. He needs to leave the road. He's too easy to spot here. Also, his bladder is suddenly aching. He steps off the track.

While he relieves himself into a small yellow-flowered bush, his eyes wander the landscape, looking for options.

To his right is el río Santa Fe. It parallels this section of the camino in a miniature valley so deep that the crowns of the old cottonwoods along its banks are level with the surrounding countryside.

The space between the trees is actually a very private place. He took Trini to the river for a picnic just two weeks ago and made love to her under the trees. His thoughts linger for a moment on the smoothness of her belly, then he forces his mind back to his predicament.

The grass and brush along the río are kept down by clusters of goats and sheep herded by small boys. So there is a chance he'll be spotted. However, on the other hand, there's more cover there than here on the road.

The other problem is that the channel the river has carved over time meanders a good deal. If he follows its course, he won't reach the safety of the palacio until well after dark.

Yet he needs to do something. And soon. Involuntarily, he glances south. Small hills block his view. There's almost certainly at least one warrior behind him. Probably more. Do others lie waiting beside the road ahead?

The thought pushes him off the road and toward the treetops. The dry soil slips under his feet, slowing his pace, but he plunges on, and scrambles down the crumbling bank into the safety of the gnarled, thick-barked cottonwoods.

As he reaches them, the sun ducks behind a cloud and Pérez is suddenly cold. His shoulders hunch as he hurries forward, trying not to imagine who might have seen him drop out of sight.

Not that it should matter who saw him. He is, after all, governor of all Nuevo México, sent to bring the rule of constitutional law to this forsaken frontier of los Estados Unidos Mexicanos. He scowls and shoves his shorn hat back onto his head. Yet here he is, slipping along the river bank because it's too dangerous to show himself. This is how the idiot peones who inhabit this barrenness thank him for his work.

A small wind picks up and rattles the leaves overhead. Pérez stumbles against a rock half buried in the dirt. ¡Maldición! He scowls and continues to plunge forward. The grass is starting to die back and it lies sideways, slick under his feet. Just when he's adjusted to that, his boots drop into patches of dry, slick river silt as deep as his ankles.

He grits his teeth and keeps moving. He won't be deterred by this or anything else. He doesn't deserve the way the people here turned against him. As if he's personally responsible for the taxes the national legislature decreed. As if his salary is coming directly from the workers' dirty pockets.

He knows there aren't many coins in those pockets. Trini certainly reminded him of that fact often enough. However, it's not his fault the tax exemption New Mexico's enjoyed these last fourteen years has expired. And he didn't stand in the way of the petition the ricos drew up asking for the exception to be reinstated. Once they got their request into the proper form, he sent it on to Mexico City.

Yes, he didn't send it right away. But he did send it. You'd think these pendejos would be grateful for what he's done. Instead, they take up arms against him. They'd like to relieve him of his position and probably his head.

He snorts derisively, straightens his shoulders, and readjusts his rifle against his shoulder. It's an elegant thing but, as light as it is, he's beginning to feel its weight against his epaulets.

His coat feels heavy, too. He should take it off, but then he'd have to carry it. He could stash it somewhere and come back for it later. He looks around as he walks, considering possible hiding places. Then his chin lifts defiantly. These epaulets are a sign of his rank. He's earned them and he's not leaving them behind for some goat boy to play with. He's a man who leads troops into battle.

He winces. Not yesterday. However, that farce can hardly be described as a battle. He'd had almost no troops left after the treacherous Santo Domingans and their allies went over to the other side.

It doesn't bear thinking of. He turns his thoughts firmly toward Santa Fe. The presidio troops are still there. When he arrives, he'll gather them together, clap Antonito Chávez into jail, then rally the loyal militia and crush those rebels once and for all, damn them.

They're all traitors and villains, the men from Santa Cruz and the so-called warriors of Santo Domingo and the other pueblos. Sneaking insurrectos, lying in wait among the rocks of that hulk they call La Mesilla. Skulking among the rocks like animals instead of meeting him in the open and fighting like men.

Pérez's scowl deepens. He adjusts the rifle to a more comfortable position on his shoulder. The rebels are a lot of fools who believe they can turn against their lawfully appointed rulers with impunity. They'll pay for their crimes and he'll wear this coat the day he watches them hang. Or fall under a hail of executioners' bullets. Or have their throats cut like the pigs they are. His eyes narrow. Which would be more appropriate?

He's still debating this issue when the sides of the channel flatten out and the trees at the bottom move farther apart. Pérez stops and stares at the river. The water is shallow here, but it's a muddy ooze that reaches from bank to bank. The hooves of cattle, sheep, and who knows what else have not only broken down the sides of the little valley, they've turned the water into a sucking mass sure to pull a man's boots right off his feet.

The governor's lips curl in disgust. He looks farther up river. The channel seems to be much narrower from this point on. He can't continue to follow it. He either has to cross here or go back to where he left the road and follow it to the nearest bridge.

If there is a bridge. He doesn't remember one last night. There was a muddy patch. Was this it? He was riding then, not walking. He grimaces, bends to remove his boots, and steps into the muck. On the other side, he moves cautiously to the only bit of grass in sight, wipes off his feet as best he can, replaces his boots, then laboriously climbs the broken-down bank.

At the top, he crouches behind a large bush with feathery flowers and studies the lay of the land ahead. There are corn-fields now and, beyond them, the brown walls of adobe houses and outbuildings. This must be the hamlet of Agua Fría, the one he and his men passed through last night. It seems like a century ago.

He studies the nearest fields. Because it's early August, the stalks of maíz are taller than he is and still contain ears waiting for harvest. But most of the once-lush green leaves have shrunk into straggly brown wisps that rattle in the breeze. They won't provide much cover.

His shoulders twitch. He glances anxiously behind him. After the protection of the river and its trees, the sense of ex-posure is acute. He needs to keep moving.

He looks again toward the village. The few walls he can see look thick and secure. Long rows of corn lie parallel to them, blocking the way. The tall plants are strangely menac-ing in the shadow of the now-black clouds overhead. The wind has died down. Nothing moves.

The governor shifts onto his haunches, considering the best way to proceed. The plants are dry and bound to rattle if anything touches them. However, if he tries to stay outside the long rows and go around, he'll be visible to the entire countryside. And it will take him longer. His shoulders twitch again. He needs to move before someone spots him.

He squints at the field. If he's careful and moves slowly, he should be able to keep the noise to a minimum. Maneuver down the rows to the end of the field and then head for the closest building. He's thinner than those hulking Santo

Domingans. If they try to follow him through the corn, he'll hear them coming. When he reaches Agua Fría, he'll be safe enough. Anyone following him won't dare to attack in the middle of the village.

All he needs to do is cross the field. He takes a steadying breath, moves away from the safety of the bush, runs half crouching to the rows of maíz, and plunges in.

He realizes immediately that he's miscalculated. The dry leaves rattle sharply and he can't make himself small enough to avoid them. His only hope is to get through the field as quickly as possible. He peers past the dying stalks toward the nearest house, takes a deep breath, and pushes through the corn.

Long brown leaves grab at the corners of his hat as he passes, skewing it sideways and over his eyes. The strands that are still green are no better. Their sharp edges slice at his chin. He lowers his head, using the twisted hat as a kind of shield, and elbows the stalks aside, forcing a path.

He's so focused on fighting the maíz that he doesn't realize how close he is to the edge of the field until he stumbles past the last row and into the shallow disused irrigation ditch alongside it. The sudden drop brings Pérez to his knees and his rifle flies out of his hands and into the dirt beyond.

The governor pushes himself to his knees, wipes his sweaty face with his sleeve, then looks down at the fine wool in disgust. The coat was already streaked with dust and bits of corn leaf. Now it's stained dark with moisture from his face. Trinidad will have a fine time getting it clean.

Trini. The governor closes his eyes. He didn't treat her the way a well-bred man ought to deal with a woman. He wipes his face with his sleeve again. But then, gentlemen are not

97

often reduced to walking instead of riding, slipping across country to escape skulking Pueblo warriors, or experiencing defeat at the hands of an illiterate rabble.

He forces himself to his feet and bends to brush the dirt from his trousers. The ones she made him, her hands moving steadily over the cloth as she looked into his face with those luminous eyes. Her hands smoothing the fabric over his thighs as she checked the fit—

Enough. He straightens, adjusts his hat and epaulets, and looks around. To his left are more cornfields. On the right, a scatter of goats grazes a field of wheat rubble. A small boy stands among them and stares at the governor, his hands on his hips. The sky behind him is ominously dark.

Pérez turns away. Directly ahead is a long warm-brown adobe wall, perhaps six feet high. It extends to his right, then bends around a curve. There's a bit of roadway beyond and more walls to the right. Agua Fría. The north end. His breath comes more easily now. He bends to pick up his rifle, examines it carefully, wipes the dirt off the silver inlay as best he can, then faces the wall, looking for an opening.

There's nothing. Not so much as a shuttered window. He hurries forward, then follows the structure within touching distance, hunting a way inside. The sky darkens further. Fat drops of rain begin to slap the dirt around him and spot the adobe, turning it a deep warm, mocking brown.

Then the darkness tightens. Thunder cracks and rain slams down in a rush, soaking the governor's coat and pouring from the corners of his hat. He dashes along the wall. Dear God, there must be some sort of entrance.

He rounds the corner to the road and spies a blue-painted door set deep in the thick adobe and shut firmly against the weather. He rushes to it and slams the wood with a closed fist. "Open up!" he cries. "Open up!"

He pauses, gathering his breath, striving for calm. Movement flickers to his right. Pérez freezes in place, then slowly turns.

An impassive brown face gazes back at him from the shelter of the next house.

Then another warrior materializes on the far side of the road.

They carry spears, the black obsidian points darker than the rain. There's more movement on his left, in the middle of the Camino Real.

He turns back to the door and slams it furiously. "¡Por favor!" the governor of Nuevo México cries. "In the name of all mercy! Open up!"

CHAPTER 6

August 9–10, 1837: Santa Fe Women
(Gertrudis Barceló)

"Oh, Tules," Gertrudis Barceló's mother says fretfully from one of the two settees by the fire. "I wish your brother was here."

Gertrudis looks up from her list of monte bank earnings for July. "So do I," she says, "Although I'm also glad he's in Sonora right now. It's safer there than it is here."

"We need a man to deal with this. To bring us news."

Gertrudis has already returned to her work. "I learned long ago that, other than my brother, most men are pretty much useless," she says absently as she begins to tally the debts she still needs to collect.

"The men are the ones who started this," Gertrudis's foster daughter Petra says bitterly. She's pacing the length of the room, her arms wrapped around her fourteen-year-old belly.

Eleven-year-old Refugio, who's playing with her fair-haired doll in the corner, looks up. "Is your stomach bothering you again?"

Petra nods without speaking.

"If I didn't know better, I would think you were pregnant," Gertrudis's mother says.

Petra turns away and continues to pace.

Gertrudis's head jerks up. Her eyes narrow. "You and James Giddings did seem to have a good deal to say to each other before he left for Missouri in June," she says slowly.

Petra doesn't answer. But when she paces past the table again, she keeps her eyes carefully turned away.

Gertrudis's lips tighten. She slaps her pencil onto the table. "María Petra Gutierrez—" she begins.

She's interrupted by a knock at the street door. Gertrudis's anger turns to a clutch of cold fear. Petra moves toward the sound, but Gertrudis lifts a warning hand. "We don't know who it is,."

The girl nods, but she doesn't retreat into the center of the room. Gertrudis's lips tighten further. The child has no fear. And her hand is still on her stomach.

However, this isn't the time to be worrying about a recalcitrant fourteen-year-old. Gertrudis rises, crosses to the door, and opens the tiny window in the center plank. A thin pale face swathed in black gazes anxiously back at her.

"Pelegrina!" Gertrudis peers past her, trying to see up and down the street. "Is there anyone with you?"

The head moves from side to side. Gertrudis fumbles for the latch.

The tall thin figure of María Pelegrina Domíngues, wife of Prefect Ramón Abreú, pushes a towheaded six-year-old boy through the door before it's completely open, then stops just inside the room. Her eyes are wide with fear and she sways slightly and tangles her hands together as if she's forcing herself to stay upright.

As Gertrudis shuts the door, her mother rises from the settee. "What is it?"

"He's been captured." Pelegrina's voice is a mere hiss of sound. As if she can't bear to speak the words, can hardly believe she's saying them.

Gertrudis takes her arm and guides her to the fire. "Bring wine," she says over her shoulder and, for once, Petra obeys without question.

Gertrudis's mother leads the little boy to the other settee chair and sits, her arm around his waist. He stands beside her and watches his mother.

Even in her anxiety, she reminds him of his manners. "Luis my love, say hello to Doña Tules," she says.

The child smiles shyly at Gertrudis, then turns to the old lady. "Buenos días, Doña Dolores," he says bashfully.

Gertrudis's mother smiles into his eyes and strokes his head. "Such an obedient and polite little one." She looks at Pelegrina. "With this fair hair, he looks remarkably like his father."

Pelegrina nods and tries to smile, but covers her face with her hands instead.

Petra appears at her elbow with the wine. Pelegrina's lips tremble as she takes it. Gertrudis looks at Luis, whose gaze is still fixed on his mother.

Dolores is also watching her. "So it is true?" she asks. "He has been taken?"

Gertrudis glances at the boy, then her mother. "Las paderes tienen oídos," she says mildly.

Dolores leans to peer into the child's face. "This wall certainly does have ears," she agrees. She gestures to Petra. "Put the wine on the table and take him into the kitchen. There are still bizcochitos in the tin."

The girl's jaw juts out. She wants to hear the news, too. She looks at Gertrudis, who says, "Take Refugio with you."

There's a little sigh from the corner, then Refugio puts her doll down and comes forward to take Luis's hand. He pulls away and stares at his mother. "¿Mamá?" he asks.

She reaches out to him and he moves toward her. She smooths his hair from his thin face. "Go," she says soothingly. "I must speak with las señoras."

He bites his lips but turns to Refugio and takes her hand. Together, they follow Petra down the long room to the kitchen.

The door thuds behind them before Pelegrina's gaze returns to Gertrudis and Dolores. "Forgive me for bringing my sorrows to you." She shudders. "I am so afraid."

"Was your husband the only one taken?" Doña Dolores asks.

Pelegrina shakes her head. She glances toward the kitchen as if to make sure the door is truly closed. "The man who brought the news said there were others, but he wouldn't tell me who they were." She closes her eyes. "Though the way he said it frightened me. I know Ramón and his brothers will stay together if they possibly can."

There's a long silence. It's hard to tell whether she's lost in her thoughts or simply can't bring herself to put words to her fear.

Gertrudis suppresses a twist of impatience. "And that's all you know?"

Pelegrina looks down at her hands. "They took them to the rebel camp west of town, on that empty land in front of the Rosario chapel."

"And the governor?"

She looks up in surprise. "He didn't escape south?"

"We were told that he's trying to return to the city."

Pelegrina's brow furrows. "Why?"

Gertrudis shrugs. "Who knows the thoughts of men?"

It's something she says often and a glimmer of habitual amusement flashes across Pelegrina's face. Then her shoulders tighten. "What will they do with them?"

Doña Dolores leans forward. "When did you last eat?"

Pelegrina looks at her blankly. "I prepared something for Luis earlier this evening, but I couldn't—"

"You need to keep up your strength. And that child should have something besides cookies in his stomach before he sleeps tonight." The old lady pushes herself out of the chair and heads toward the kitchen.

"Who can sleep?" Pelegrina asks. She turns to Gertrudis. "I thought perhaps you had heard something. That someone would bring you news."

Gertrudis shakes her head. "I have heard only that Manuel Aponte was captured."

Pelegrina nods. "When Ramón came back from the battle yesterday afternoon, he said the colonel was wounded and so couldn't escape south with the governor and the others. He planned to go into hiding."

"He did. He hid here in Santa Fe, in the house of a friend." Gertrudis's face darkens. "The insurrectos tracked him down and demanded his release. His friends gave him up to them."

Pelegrina stares at her in horror. "It is a sacred duty to protect those under your roof!"

"I suppose he wasn't under their roof when the rebels did what they did to him."

"He's dead?"

"I don't know." Her lip curls in disgust. "There are men in my sala almost every day, gambling and drinking and spending their money. But not today. Today, they were too intent on rebellion and war."

Pelegrina's knuckles are white as she grips the goblet of barely touched wine. "What do you—"

There's another thud on the door, this one louder and more insistent. Both women start and turn toward it. The knock comes again. Gertrudis gulps back her fear as she rises and moves toward it.

When she opens the little window, she almost sobs in relief. "Juana Prada! How you startled me!" She fumbles for the latch.

The other woman's rebozo is off her plump braid-crowned head almost before she's in the house. "There is news," she gasps. "They have captured—" Then she sees Pelegrina in the chair beside the fire, her thin face turned toward the door and stops moving. "You have heard?"

"No, that's why I came here. I thought La Tules would know, if anyone did." Pelegrina rises from her seat, moves to the table, sets the goblet on it, and braces herself on the smooth wood beside it. "What do you know?"

"There is talk—" Juana glances at Gertrudis, who's leaning with her back against the closed door, her eyes shut.

Then Gertrudis gives herself a little shake and moves forward. "Please, seat yourself." She goes to the table. "Will you have some wine? My mother is preparing a bite to eat."

"Thank you, but no." Juana settles herself into the settee Dolores had been using. She stares into the fire, her round face wrinkled in thought.

105

Pelegrina returns to the fire. Gertrudis settles herself beside her. "You have news?"

Juana glances at Pelegrina. "I don't know."

"You have heard rumors."

She nods uncertainly.

Gertrudis reaches for Pelegrina's hand.

Pelegrina looks at the newcomer. "I have heard nothing since late this afternoon, when a man came to say los insurrectos have captured my husband."

Juana closes her eyes. "Sí," she whispers. "And others. Lieutenant Hurtado and some of the soldiers. They have taken them to the camp."

Pelegrina shakes her head slightly. The names of the others clearly hold little meaning for her at this moment. She wets her dry lips with her tongue. "And his brothers?"

"They say Santiago went south and took Diego Sáenz with him."

Gertrudis swallows against the dry spot in her throat. So many men. "And Marcelino Abreú?"

"Possibly." Juana's round shoulders convulse in a shudder.

"Who shouldn't even be in Santa Fe, but safely at home in Tomé, instructing his students." Pelegrina moves restlessly in her seat. Her shoulders tighten into each other and her face pinches even more. "What will they do to them?"

Juana shakes her head and looks away. Gertrudis studies her. She really doesn't seem to know. Or doesn't want to think about what she's heard.

"And there's no one to send to find out," Gertrudis's mother says as she comes down the room from the kitchen. She's carrying a tray of food, which she takes to the table.

"Tules, if you will move your account books, we can eat properly. Then we can think more clearly about what has occurred."

Gertrudis's lips twitch. Even with destruction hanging over them, her mother will make sure those around her are fed.

And she's right to do so. Although none of the women eat much, the routine of the table, of breaking the bread and dipping it into the stew, helps restore a sense of normalcy. And the possibility for action.

"What's to be done?" Gertrudis asks as her mother carries the remnants to the kitchen.

Pelegrina presses her hands to her face. "I simply want to know what's happening."

"But there's no one to send," Juana says. "All the men are either with the rebels or fleeing from them. Or hiding."

Pelegrina shudders. "Not that hiding guarantees safety. Poor Señor Aponte."

"We'll have to go to the camp ourselves," Gertrudis says.

"No one is safe out there tonight," Juana protests.

Gertrudis's mother comes out of the kitchen, then turns left to one of the rooms that line the long wall opposite the fireplace. Gertrudis frowns. Surely Petra's stomach has settled by now. She turns back to her guests. "No one is likely to see us. Everyone's either inside their houses or at the camp."

"And how will we get close enough to see anything?" Juana asks. "There aren't many houses or other buildings between the west edge of town and the camp."

"There's the arroyo that crosses the road just before you get there," Pelegrina says slowly. "The cottonwoods on the top of its banks are fairly thick. We might shelter among them."

"It's too risky," Juana argues. "Our skirts will rustle and we'll be heard."

"Then we'll go dressed as men," Dolores says as she reenters the room. Her arms are full of clothing. She looks at Gertrudis. "Your brother left some items that he planned to sell to the presidio soldiers." She looks down. "We have pantalones y camisas y chaquetas, all in dark colors."

The three women at the table stare at her, then Pelegrina nods. "Anything is better than this waiting."

"But the children," Juana says.

Gertrudis pushes back from the table. "Petra can stay with them."

"She won't want to," Doña Dolores says.

"I know. But she's going to have to get used to thinking of a little one more than herself."

Juana glances at her inquiringly. Gertrudis turns away. She probably shouldn't have said anything, but Petra's condition won't be a secret much longer, anyway. "Come," she says. "Let's get dressed."

~ ~ ~ ~

The four women slip silently through Santa Fe's deserted streets. The only light is from the first-quarter moon. The ground has already dried from the brief rain earlier in the day, but the moisture has left the August air unusually chilly. The women's rebozos would have been warmer than the slouchy hats Dolores located among her son's trade goods, but the long narrow shawls are something only a woman would wear. They press the wide hat brims close around their faces until they can barely see.

They twist anxiously at each adobe-walled corner to check for watchers, then slip on through the empty byways. The sound of revelry in the camp west of town is loud in the still night.

The houses stop abruptly at the edge of town. The road ahead contains only an occasional building alongside patches of chile and squash. What moonlight there is fingers the walls and creates shadows among the plants, then disappears completely in the spot where the road dips to cross the arroyo. Campfire flickers just beyond the trees on the opposite bank.

The women pause and look at each other. "Are you certain you want to do this?" Juana Prada asks in a low voice. "The rumor is that they've killed the governor."

Gertrudis hears her mother's annoyed breath hiss between her teeth. The woman could have shared this bit of news earlier.

Not that the information would have made any difference to Pelegrina Abreú. "My husband and his brothers were with His Excellency when he fled last night," she says. "I need—" Her voice chokes, as if she can hardly bring herself to say what comes next. "I need to know." She pushes the hat brim farther toward her forehead. "Especially Ramón," she whispers.

The other women look at each other with shadowed eyes. Then Gertrudis moves forward and the rest follow.

They stop at the edge of the arroyo. Its bottom is still muddy from the afternoon rain. The women peer across and to the right, trying to see past the cottonwoods to the rebel camp and the tiny Rosario chapel at its further end.

"We need to cross to the other side," Gertrudis says.

"Someone will spot us," Juana mutters.

Doña Dolores shakes her head. "Not if we're quick about it. We're more likely to be seen if we remain here than if we're in among the cottonwoods."

Juana shudders. "Who else is in those trees?"

Gertrudis pushes her hat brim back and glares at her. "Then go home!"

Juana shivers, crosses her arms over her chest, and shakes her head. "Not by myself. Not tonight."

Gertrudis turns away. Her mother and Pelegrina are studying the opposite bank, plotting how best to reach it and where to shelter when they get there. "The big cottonwood in the center at the top," Dolores says. "The one with the dead log beside it."

Gertrudis nods.

Pelegrina peers to the right, up the arroyo's channel. "We need to cross there where it widens a little," she says. "The mud won't be so thick there."

Gertrudis nods. "Bueno." She glances at Juana, who's shivering now, her arms still tight around her chest. "Are you coming?"

Juana nods without looking at her.

"All right then." She turns to the others.

"Let's go," her mother says.

There's a burst of laughter from the rebel camp. The women's heads jerk toward it.

"Hurry!" Pelegrina hisses.

They edge halfway down the slope, then pick their way along the bank until Pelegrina tugs at Gertrudis's elbow and gestures toward the spot she has in mind. Gertrudis grimaces. The mud is more shallow here but it's still deep enough to suck at their shoes.

At least they don't have to worry about skirts blocking their view of the mud. The trousers make it easier for Gertrudis to see where's she's stepping and she's grateful for that, even though the unaccustomed fabric between her legs has begun to chafe her thighs.

Pelegrina is the first one across. Gertrudis follows her gingerly. She reaches the opposite bank and is halfway up it before she looks back. Juana is in the middle of the arroyo, her arms out as if balancing on a tightrope. Gertrudis's mother has reached safety, but is half-turned to give her a hand. Gertrudis turns away, toward Pelegrina, who's above her and moving toward the cottonwood and its downed log.

By the time Gertrudis reaches her, Pelegrina is flattened against the other side of the furrowed gray trunk, her back wedged into the space between two thick branches, and staring at the camp. Gertrudis positions herself behind another branch and peers forward.

Pelegrina doesn't turn her head. "It seems very quiet," she murmurs.

Gertrudis nods without looking at her. They're facing one end of what is essentially a long corridor lined with small cooking fires, tents, and piles of gear. It's an oddly peaceful scene. Men bend over the flames, preparing food. Others move quietly back and forth, alone or in small groups. They rearrange personal items, pat each other on the back, share drinks, and bend their heads to talk. The flat roof of the Rosario chapel is just visible beyond a cluster of tents at the far end of the space.

Doña Dolores and Juana reach the tree. They're breathing heavily. "That slope is steep," Juana complains.

Pelegrina's eyes flash at her. "Hush!"

The old lady edges past Juana and into the space next to Gertrudis. "What's happening?"

"Not much. Eating and drinking."

Then, beyond the chapel, a drum begins to sound. It's a steady beat, slow and deep. As the women listen, the speed increases, then the volume rises, comes nearer. A heartbeat, deep and all-encompassing. Gertrudis bites down on her breath, forcing it to stay even, not get sucked into the rhythm.

Someone in the camp shouts a command. The men by the fires straighten as others materialize from within and behind the tents. They face the approaching drum and stand waiting.

Then they surge toward it, blocking the women's view. Pelegrina takes a step away from the cover of the tree, craning her neck.

"No!" Gertrudis hisses. "Stay still!"

"I can't see!"

"It's too dangerous!"

"Hush!" Juana says. "They're coming back!"

She's right. Insurrectos surge into the long narrow space, at least three times as many as before. The size of the crowd pushes some of the men toward the arroyo. The women flatten themselves closer to the tree.

Then there's a shout from the other end of the camp. The drumming is louder now, closer. And there are guitars, echoing and expanding the heart-stopping beat. Gertrudis's fingers dig into the cottonwood's thick bark.

The space between the tents clears again as the rebels surge apart and pack together along its sides, behind the fires. A man dances down the resulting corridor. His feet kick sideways, then back toward each other, moving a ceremonial ball down the camp.

Then he kicks forward instead of to the side and the ball rolls into the light of the fire closest to the arroyo. Even as Gertrudis frowns in confusion, her stomach twists in horrified disbelief. He isn't kicking a ball. It's oval and has a hairy pelt attached to one end. Hair?

The dancer's feet reach, kick again. The oblong thing lifts off the ground, lurches to one side, and rolls to a stop in the open space between the tents and the trees. Governor Albino Pérez's dull eyes stare lifelessly at the hiding women. Bile bites Gertrudis's throat.

"¡Oh, Dios mío!" her mother hisses. There's a retching sound from the other side of the cottonwood. Juana.

Pelegrina is silent, her thin body leaning forward tight as a drawn rope. She turns a pale face toward Gertrudis. Not even the hat brim can block the shock in her eyes. "The governor," she chokes.

Gertrudis nods numbly, then her muscles tighten as she senses danger. Another rebel has come forward and is kicking at the head. If he looks up at the trees, he'll see the women peering out.

Then a hand grabs Gertrudis's elbow. Sharper and stronger than her mother's. A man's. She jerks and turns, ready to strike, but he's already released her. And it's not a rebel.

Albino Chacón, the only Santa Fe alcalde not at yesterday's battle, frowns at her from the shadows. He looks past her to Pelegrina and his brown eyes contract with pity. Then he turns back to Gertrudis. "You shouldn't be here, señora!" he hisses. "Please come away." He glances toward the fire-lit scene. "At least out of sight of the camp."

Gertrudis frowns. She doesn't want to leave but she knows the short thickset man is right. There's nothing they can do for the governor. And hovering here may give them more information, but it's dangerous. She nods reluctantly and she and the others follow him away from the trees toward the bottom of the arroyo.

Halfway down the slope, her mother speaks. "The governor—"

Chacón stops and turns. His usually pleasant face is grim in the moonlight. "They only brought the head to the camp. His Excellency's body lies in the road just north of Agua Fría, outside Salvador Martín's casa."

"But the head—"

"They cut it off and brought it to the camp. Kicked it all the way, from what I've been told."

Gertrudis bites back the bile in her throat. She turns toward Pelegrina, who's staring at the alcalde with eyes wide with fear.

He looks away, then seems to steady himself, and returns her gaze. His brows are heavy with regret. "Your husband wasn't with the governor when he fell," he says. "They captured him elsewhere."

She straightens. "He's at the camp?"

He half nods. "They brought him to the camp, but then—" He stops and looks down at his hands. "They killed him with

114

lances." He looks up at her, his eyes filled with pity. "I wish it were not so."

Pelegrina's hands go to her face and she crumples into Doña Dolores's arms.

Chacón turns to Gertrudis, his expression suddenly fierce. "You can't stay here!" He's a man devoted to his wife and three small children and doesn't frequent Gertrudis's gambling salon. She's always thought him rather weak, too friendly to have much substance or force, but tonight he's full of authority.

She scowls at him. "And what would you have us do? Governor Pérez is dead, as is Ramón Abreú and probably his brothers, as well."

He nods grimly. "Marcelino is. He and Ramón died together. I don't know about Santiago. No one has heard anything about him."

"And the others?" Juana Prada asks. "The men who were with them?"

He turns toward her. "I don't know. It is as God wills."

Doña Dolores, still supporting Pelegrina with one arm, crosses herself with the other hand, but Gertrudis turns on the alcalde in fury. "As God wills? This is your answer? Men have died and will keep dying, the rebels kick a man's severed head around their camp like a toy ball, and all you can say is 'It is as God wills'?"

He steps back involuntarily, but then a triumphant shout rises from the camp. He glances toward it, then turns to her mother, as the oldest of the four women. "You should return to your homes, Doña Dolores. It isn't safe here."

She has both arms around Pelegrina now, holding her compassionately, but the look she gives the alcalde is full of judgment. "The governor's body lies on the Camino Real for the birds to peck and the coyotes to eat," she says. "And those of the others?"

He spreads his hands, palms upward, and shakes his head. "I assume they are being held by the rebels."

"To cut off their heads as well?" Gertrudis demands.

Pelegrina groans and the alcalde gives Gertrudis a reproachful look. Her lips tighten. "Their bodies should be retrieved before they also are desecrated."

He spreads his hands again. "One man can do nothing against such a mob."

Her mother sniffs. "You were right, Gertrudis. Men are pretty much useless." She disengages from Pelegrina and moves around the alcalde, angling up the slope toward the camp. "Come, we'll go get them ourselves."

He leaps in front of her, booted feet slipping on the slope. "¡Por favor, Doña Dolores! Stop! Don't do this!"

She puts her hands on her hips and tilts her chin to look past her hat brim into his face. "You're the alcalde. You're the one who should do it."

He looks at his feet. "I have already tried. They told me the bodies of traitors cannot be buried in sacred ground and should be left for the vultures to eat."

Pelegrina puts her hands to her mouth. "Oh my darling!"

He turns toward her. "It may be that things will be calmer in a day or two. I will see then what I can do."

Gertrudis's mother glances at her. She nods back and turns to Chacón. "When you have retrieved the bodies, bring them to me. They will be safer at my house than anywhere else I can think of." She chuckles mirthlessly. "No one will expect me to get involved if there's no money to be made from it."

"And I will talk to Padre Ortiz about a proper burial," her mother says. "Bodies of traitors, indeed!"

And then the women return to the Barceló casa. Pelegrina weeps silently as they slip through the streets, but by the time they arrive, she's eerily silent. She enters the house like a tall, hatted shadow.

The children look up from the fireside, where Petra is telling a story. She stops in midsentence when she sees Gertrudis's face. Her hand creeps to her belly.

Luis scrambles up and runs to his mother. She kneels in front of him and he reaches for her. "¿Mamá?"

She takes his hands and opens her mouth but no words come out. She ducks her chin, swallows, and raises her head to gaze into his frightened face. "I have something to tell you, alma mía," she says, her voice quavering. She takes a deep breath and steadies it. "You must be very brave."

As he leans toward her, Gertrudis Barceló crosses to the fireplace, kneels, and pulls her foster daughters into her arms. The shadows from the flames hollow her eyes.

CHAPTER 7

August 11, 1837: A Clash of Perspectives
(Santiago Abreú and Diego Sáenz)

Ensign Diego Sáenz wakes shuddering with cold in the dim light of early dawn, then realizes it's not the chill that's pulled him back into consciousness. Rawhide straps bite his ankles and wrists. He's lying on his side, arms bound behind his back. His shoulders ache. There's also a smell. The sharp bitterness of an improperly cared for latrine. He turns his head as best he can, searching for the source. His eyes focus on a bare plaza enclosed by two-story adobe buildings. Where—?

Then he remembers.

The flight south across the golden Autumn grassland. The taste of escape on his lips, fear mixed with elation, eyes flicking over the landscape, then back to his jefe, current District Judge and former Nuevo México Governor Santiago Abreú. If anyone can get them out of this, he can.

And then the Santo Domingo warriors. Looming up out of the soil itself, terrible in their war finery. Moving in from every direction with that ground-eating run. The silence as the circle tightened. The scrape of his breath in his throat. The shrill cry of a hawk overhead.

Then the warriors move closer, lances raised. The horses screaming in fear. The white set of the judge's face, his sword slashing madly, though with no hope.

And finally rough hands, tearing the coat from his back, tossing him corpselike over the rump of his own mount. Dust and the stink of horse dung in his nostrils, then the barren plaza of the pueblo and its double-story buildings. The rawhide for him and the stocks for his jefe.

Diego turns his head toward the rough-beamed cepo del reo in the center of the square. The elegant and well-spoken District Judge Santiago Abreú, is clamped between its rough-hewn grey-weathered boards, feet and hands. The top piece is so thick that his chin barely reaches the upper edge. His pale face tilts awkwardly to the right above the holes that imprison his wrists.

Diego's stomach turns. This is his jefe, former governor of New Mexico and brother to the prefect of Río Arriba as well as the esteemed Tomé schoolmaster José Cleto Marcelino Abreú. But still he is imprisoned like a common criminal in the stocks of Santo Domingo, his posterior supported by a clumsy bit of old stump, its sides wet with feces and urine.

As Diego watches, Abreú's eyes open. He shifts slightly, but he can't move more than a few inches. His bare ankles are clamped tightly in the rough holes in the lower planks. The warriors have taken his boots. The pale skin looks almost obscenely naked.

Diego's gaze turns back to his boss's narrow face. A strand of golden-brown hair has fallen into his eyes. "Ensign," Abreú croaks.

"Sí, jefe."

"Forgive me." His voice is slightly stronger now. Less hoarse. "I should not have attempted to flee south."

"There was no other choice."

119

"Perhaps east. The mountains."

"I'm sure los insurrectos are there, also."

The judge closes his eyes. A shudder runs through his body. Then he grimaces. "I apologize for the smell."

Diego shrugs as much as he can against the ropes. "The Pueblo dogs have been busy."

He's rewarded with a tiny smile, a crinkle at the corner of the eyes. Somewhere behind them, a door opens and shuts with a thud. "I should have sent you home," his jefe says.

"I wouldn't have gone."

The judge tries to nod, but his neck won't bend that far. "You would have if I'd ordered you to."

Diego can't argue with this. He doesn't want it to be true, but he knows it is. He's always done whatever task his superiors set him. "How can I serve you, jefe?" he asks simply.

"You're a good man, Diego."

Even here, in the predicament they're in, the statement warms him. It's unusual for Santiago Abreú to praise his subordinates. He's a fair man, but he's more given to orders than compliments or confidences.

"I am at your service, sir," Diego answers. Behind them, more doors scrape open, then thud shut. Now there's a murmur of voices. He twists toward the sound.

Abreú tries to lift his head, but he can't move more than a few inches. "These damn stocks," he says. "I know there are those who'd say not being able to move my head simply reinforces my usual somewhat narrow perspective on things, but this is ridiculous."

The ensign grins, suddenly hopeful. The judge is getting his sardonic humor back. He turns a little further. "There are three men and two women approaching," he says. "The women carry water, I think."

"I'd prefer that they bring cleaning cloths."

"You would let them touch you?"

"I don't think I have a choice in the matter." He closes his eyes, then opens them again and squints as if the sun is in his eyes. Diego follows his gaze. The sky is beginning to brighten toward day. The judge can't turn his head away from it.

Dirt crunches under a mocassined foot. Diego turns to the newcomers. The men's faces are shadowed by the blankets over their heads. Diego shudders involuntarily again, but this time it's not from the cold.

One of the men says something in the Santo Domingo language and a woman steps toward Diego and tosses a blanket over his back. He hunches his shoulders a little, trying to move it closer to his chest, but she doesn't reach to assist him. She's wearing traditional Pueblo garb, a white wool dress that reaches to her knees and exposes her right shoulder and arm, but she seems oblivious to the chill. She stares expressionlessly at Diego for a long moment, then moves away.

"That would have been more useful last night," Santiago Abreú says.

Diego looks up. They've released the former governor from the stocks. He's standing beside the ugly wooden contraption, rubbing his wrists and rolling his head from side to side, stretching his neck. Another woman, also in traditional dress, hands him a gourd and he takes it and drinks thirstily. "Gracias," he says, handing it back to her. Then he gestures toward Diego. "And for my aide as well, por favor."

The woman turns to her container, dips more water into the gourd, and crosses to the ensign. He tries to push himself into a sitting position, but he's bound too tightly. The first woman approaches, grabs his shoulder, and yanks him to his feet. The blanket falls to the ground.

When the dipper is lifted to his lips, half the liquid pours down his chin and onto his dirty shirt. Neither woman reaches to wipe it away, though the one who grabbed him picks up the blanket and slings it over her shoulder.

Another man speaks and the woman with the water puts the gourd back into her container and moves behind Diego. The rawhide around his wrists tightens briefly, relaxes, then loosens further as she releases it.

He has a brief, glorious moment of stretching freedom, arms wide, then she moves in front of him, grabs his hands, wrenches them into position over his stomach, and rewinds and tightens the rawhide.

Diego glances at Santiago Abreú apologetically. For one instant there— But then he sees that the jefe has also been tied hand and foot. Two more women appear with water and cleaning materials and begin dousing the area around the stocks, cleansing it of his waste.

A girl of perhaps twelve comes out of a nearby house door with a small basket and hands the prisoners bits of bread and meat. Diego winces as he maneuvers the food to his mouth with his bound hands. Everything seems stiff this morning.

"Gracias," Abreú says politely when she gives him a second piece of bread.

"There is only one reason we feed you," the largest of the three men growls. "It will enable you to endure your punishment longer."

Abreú's fair skin flushes, but his voice is icy. "Any punishment you inflict on me and my aide will be revisited upon you ten-fold."

The youngest man laughs, his face lighting with glee. "There is no one left to protect you, Excellency!"

The judge's scowl deepens. "You have forgotten what happened after your last insurrection. How we returned and conquered your people more thoroughly than before."

"That was many generations ago," the first man says. "And your own ancestors were not here, so you don't understand the scope of that insurrection, how thoroughly we cleansed those like you from the land. And how many españoles died when they tried to reclaim it. A land that was never theirs in the first place."

Abreú's mouth opens to respond, but the oldest of the three men says, "Enough!" He turns and waves a hand toward a distant corner. A cluster of adolescent boys materializes from the shadows. They advance across the plaza in a phalanx of brown-muscled torsos and faces like rock. Diego's bowels twist. He wishes he hadn't taken the woman's food.

The boys move past him to Santiago Abreú and unbind him. He reacts quickly, twisting like grease in their hands. He's halfway across the plaza before they catch up to him. The first to reach him has a knife tucked into his waistband. In one motion, Abreú snatches it and swings. A thin trail of blood appears on the boy's chest. Abreú moves in but the

123

boy sidesteps, circling warily left. The judge turns, following him.

There's a sudden shout overhead. The boy and the man don't look up, but Diego does. Sunlight touches the flat tops of the buildings, the sky a luminous pale blue beyond. People stand on the roofs, black against the light. Have they been there all along?

The judge has glimpsed them, too. As he and the boy move slowly left, then right, each watching for an opening, he lifts his voice. "This one is a mere child!" he bellows. "Give me a grown warrior to fight and we'll settle this once and for all!" The rising sun touches his hair and glints it into a halo of brown gold. "Send me a warrior!" he cries. "If I die, I die, but I will die on my feet like a man!"

"Ah, but then you will die too easily and with honor." The oldest of the three men makes a motion to the boy, who steps back.

Abreú turns toward the elder with a scowl. "I would not die easily."

The old man moves to the center of the plaza, pitching his voice loud enough for the people above to hear. "But there would be honor in such a hard-fought death. What is it your people say? Even though we are made of the same clay, there's a difference between a chamber pot and a pitcher?" His eyes glint in amusement, then harden. "You do not deserve to die in a way that bestows honor."

He makes a small, commanding gesture. Three young men step from the walls nearest Abreú and swiftly disarm him, then bundle him back to the stocks. They clamp his hands and feet into place, step back, and give him small smiles of satisfaction. "It is good to see a man of your kind in that mechanism," the tallest one says. "It gives me great pleasure."

"May I have the pleasure of ripping off your balls!" Abreú snarls, his head twisted sideways again.

The man laughs, says something in his language to the others, and they all chuckle grimly.

"What is it you want from me?"

The old man steps forward again, into Abreú's line of sight. "You will see soon enough." He lifts his gaze toward the housetops and waves a hand. The dark forms melt away. Then he turns back to the cepo del reo. "We have given you food and now we too must fortify ourselves for what lies ahead. While we do so, you would be wise to reflect on the crimes you and your people have committed against the pueblo you call Santo Domingo, so you may understand why we do what we do."

Abreú stares at the old man blankly. The elder turns and moves away. Abreú tries to follow him with his eyes, but the top board blocks his sight.

Diego, still standing, can see every inch of the old man's implacable back. He forces the trembling from his voice. "He's going inside."

The judge's eyes close, then open. "Are you still upright?"

"Sí."

"Sit, if you can."

Diego blinks at his jefe in surprise. He cannot recall a time he has sat in the presence of his commander, unless they were both on a horse.

"That's a command, ensign."

125

He lets his knees bend then, and sinks reluctantly, awkwardly, to the ground. The rawhide strips cut into his wrists and ankles. The sun, now over the tops of the buildings, glares pitilessly into the dusty plaza. Diego closes his eyes and turns his head, trying to find relief.

He suddenly has an intense need to urinate. He begins to count backward from one thousand, trying to distract himself. It's a trick he learned on campaign against the Navajo. The pressure in his bladder fades but is replaced by an overwhelming desire for sleep. In spite of his best efforts, his head nods and he dozes off.

~ ~ ~ ~

He startles awake to a wet sound splatting against the cepo del reo. Two small boys stand in front of it, a small basket of overripe tomatoes at their feet. Pulp stains the gray wood a hand's breadth below and left of Abreú's face.

"You missed," the judge says sardonically. "My three-year-old nephew can throw better than that."

"I wasn't trying to hit you," the larger of the two boys says. "I was trying to scare you."

"It'll take more than that to frighten me."

The smaller boy reaches for another piece of spoiled fruit and flings it at the boards. It hits the former governor's forehead. The boys give each other gap-toothed grins and scoop more fruit from the basket. Half a dozen children run toward them with grass and mud in their hands and join the fun. By the time they're out of supplies, Abreú's face is spattered and sticky with tomato pulp and grass seed, and Diego has also been hit.

But the children aren't finished. When their hands are empty, they turn on Diego and begin using their feet, darting in, then out, aiming for his ribcage. He doubles forward, curling into a ball, and they go after his back and head. He closes his eyes. Small but surprisingly strong fingers yank his hair. His bladder is really aching now. Pain slices his bowels. He curls more tightly, elbows to his sides, trying to hold it in.

"¡Chamacos!" a man's voice calls. "Let your fathers have some of the fun!"

Diego opens his eyes and lifts his head. The children have backed away into a semicircle around him and the judge. They grin unashamedly at the newcomer. "We were playing warrior, grandfather," one of them says.

The man is white-haired and tiny. His eyes twinkle at the children, then his face sobers. "Warriors do not attack prisoners who have been bound and await justice."

Abreú's face twists with contempt. The tomato pulp, mud, and grass seed have turned his expression into a gruesome mask, even though he can't see the old man directly. "If you were true warriors, you would accept a duel to the death."

The man moves into the judge's line of vision. "The time for fighting is over. Now is the time for justice."

"In that case you will release me immediately! I am the man appointed judge over you. None of you have any authority for what you have done!"

The old man's lips curve into a smile, but his eyes are stone cold. "Ah, yes, His Excellency Santiago Abreú," he says. "The man appointed by those of la Ciudad de México to be our governor and then later made judge over us by

127

those same legislators. People who believe themselves anointed by the Divine Spirit to decide who will rule a land they have never seen."

"Land they possess and therefore rule!"

"Land they know nothing of." The old man turns away. "But we speak of things best discussed before all the people." He waves a hand at the children. "Go, chamacos. Clean yourselves and prepare for the council. You will learn this day how justice is done in the town of the Kewa, the place the Spanish call Santo Domingo."

The children drift from the plaza. The white-haired man follows them.

The sun is almost directly overhead now. It pours into the plaza, heating it to oven temperatures. Diego's cramps worsen. The pressure is unstoppable. It's only a matter of how he can best keep the urine from soiling his entire body.

He shifts, pushing himself into a kneeling position, then works his knees as far apart as his bound ankles will allow and looks up at the sky, trying to ignore his body's betrayal. The liquid pours out. Most of it seeps into his clothes. What does reach the ground pools at his knees. He groans and tries to inch backward and away from it.

Abreú, who can't see him but can tell what is happening from the sounds Diego is trying to suppress, chuckles. "Our bodies work against us continually, don't they?" he asks.

Before the ensign can answer, a drum starts up at the edge of the plaza. He turns his head. People pour from the buildings and gather along the sides of the square.

The three men who accompanied the women with the water appear again. They aren't wearing blankets now. Their bare brown chests gleam in the sunlight. They stand waiting until the man who shooed off the children joins them. He wears a massive silver-and-turquoise necklace and carries his cane of office, a polished wood staff with a silver tip on the end. When he reaches the other men, they step back, giving him precedence.

He moves toward the cepo del reo, stops two arms' length in front of it, and stares at Abreú's face. Without turning his head, he raises his voice and says something in his own language.

A young woman approaches with a pottery bowl full of water. He speaks to her and she nods and moves toward the stocks. Two paces away, she moves to one side so she's in Abreú's line of vision and studies him thoughtfully.

Then a smile lights her eyes. She lifts the bowl and flings its contents at the judge's head, drenching him and the board. The mud from the children's game has dried on his face and the water darkens the resulting mask but doesn't remove it. Low laughter ripples through the watching crowd.

The old man chuckles. Then his face flattens and he moves to take the young woman's place. He stares at Abreú for a long moment, then turns to the onlookers and lifts a hand. The plaza goes silent.

His voice is low but carrying. "It is the custom of the Kewa people to speak of the crimes of those whom we punish so they may have an opportunity to explain themselves." His gaze touches Diego, then returns to the stocks. "You, Santiago Abreú, former governor of Nuevo México and the man those in la Ciudad de México appointed judge of this district, have much to account for."

"I will say nothing to you! You have no right to restrain me or demand explanations!"

"But we have done so."

"You will pay for this!"

Diego feels a surge of pure pride and love for his jefe. The man is magnificent, even with mud and grass seed plastered on his face, and his hands and feet gripped by the stocks.

The old man seems unimpressed. He moves on as if Abreú hasn't responded. "For generations, we of the Kewa have been punished mightily for much smaller infractions than yours. Infractions against laws not of our making. For the sin of existence. You have participated in those punishments." His eyes flick to Abreú's hands and feet. "You are now encased in the mechanism you yourself once ordered to hold men revered by my people." His gaze moves around the plaza. "People you believe to be of less value than your horse."

Abreú's brows contract. "I have never said such a thing. The law does not allow it."

"But you feel it in your heart."

The former governor scowls. "Do not tell me what I feel."

The old man nods. "It is a true statement that the eyes we see, but the heart we know not. But it is also true that a man's actions show us what is inside him. What is it your priests say? By their fruits you will know them?" He shifts slightly, as if getting ready to make a speech, and raises his voice. The very ravens curving through the air overhead can hear him now. "No man can tell all that another feels. Because this is so, I will help you understand what I and my people have felt under the long and heavy hand of you and your kind."

Abreú closes his eyes as if he knows what he's about to hear and is weary beyond words.

"Open your eyes, Excellency!" The old man springs forward, his burning gaze inches from the judge's face. "Hear me!"

Abreú's eyes open, then flick sideways and up. He blinks once, adjusting to the sun, then stares stubbornly at the sky.

The Pueblo leader steps back. He turns to his people and points at the former governor's face. "This!" he bellows. "This contempt! This conviction that only he has the right to speak! To feel! This arrogance is what we condemn!"

Abreú's eyes drop to the old man. His brow contracts in what appears to be genuine confusion. "But I was put in authority over you by the Congress of los Estados Unidos Mexicanos," he says. "They placed me in that position. It was not of my doing."

The other man's face twists in disgust. "The Congress of the Estados Unidos Mexicanos!" he spits. "What is that to us? Have its members walked this land, hunted these mountains, pursued the buffalo across the plains to the east?"

He turns away from the stocks, speaking now more to the onlookers than the prisoner. "We live on this land in harmony with all things, seeking to exist in peace among ourselves and with others. We take from the earth only what we need. With prayer and right living, we acknowledge what she provides. We have done this since the beginning."

He gestures toward the prisoner. "And then this race of men came. They told us their ruler across the wide seas had the authority to seize what no man has the right to own. Even though we knew they were wrong, we made room for them. In exchange for our hospitality, they stole our women and our corn and drove us with whips to dig gold and precious stones from the sacred mountain."

He turns, facing east and raises both hands. "They forced us to pry into the soil of Mount Chalchihuitl, over whose peaks the sun lifts each morning. In the past, she has willingly given us turquoise, the stone of safety and life." His fingers touch the necklace on his chest, then his arms drop to his sides. "But the españoles wanted more, ever more. They forced us to tear into Chalchihuitl's soil with their tools, to dig ever deeper, always searching, never satisfied with what they were given."

He turns back to the cepo del reo and stares at the former governor, his voice flat. "So we threw you out. We and the other pueblos banded together and sent you back where you came from."

"And then we returned," Abreú says. "You couldn't defeat us for long."

"We had been infected," the old man says. "We fought against the poison, but it had invaded us. We desired the goods of the Spanish, the men who wormed their way into our women's hearts, the children they begat upon them."

A murmur of protest whispers across the plaza. He lifts his hand and slowly turns to take in each corner. "Yes, I know. The desires of the flesh and the love of one's children are not to be resisted. As it was then, so it remains. I do not blame. I simply state what occurred. For good or ill, it was done. When the Spanish returned, we did not fight them hard enough. Them and their laws and their bigotries."

He jerks his chin toward Abreú. "This man is the result of that return and those laws. A rico who places himself over us because someone else said he could, not because we of the

Kewa acknowledged his wisdom and authority to judge us. A man—" His eyes form narrow slits and his voice shakes with anger. "A man who believes the authority bestowed on him by men far to the south allows him to give a stranger the right to destroy the very thing that sustains us and all the peoples they call indios!"

Abreú's brow contracts. "What are you talking about, old man?"

"Still no respect!" This isn't the pueblo elder, but the youngest of the three who first approached. The one who spoke so harshly earlier in the day. "He speaks of the stone of protection, what you Spanish call turquesa, and of Mount Chalchihuitl. The mountain you handed over to El Sonoreño Ortiz, a person with no honor." He steps closer to the stocks and leans in, his spittle hitting Abreú's face. "You have given our mother to be raped!"

Then he straightens and looks deferentially toward the old man. The Pueblo leader nods as if in answer to an unspoken question and moves away to stand with the others.

The young man turns back to the cepo del reo and takes an obsidian-blade knife from his waistband. He paces in front of the stocks, showing the weapon's black notches and sharp point to the crowd. Then he positions himself sideways in front of the boards.

Diego cranes his neck, trying to see.

The man's knife arm sweeps up, then down past Abreú's head, toward his hands. The judge screams. Something falls to the ground at the warrior's feet. He laughs contemptuously, bends, and picks it up. Then he turns, waving what looks like a very short, pale stick, and moves toward the crowd, showing off his prize.

Diego peers at Abreú's face. His skin is almost white under the mud-and-seed mask. He's twisting his neck, trying to look down, but the wood plank won't allow him enough movement. Diego's gaze drops. His stomach twists. Blood covers the judge's right hand. His index finger is missing.

Then the angry young man is back, blocking Diego's view, leaning toward the judge. "Admit your wrongs!" he roars.

Abreú's voice is steady in spite of the pain he must be feeling. "That mountain had never been claimed by Santo Domingo or any other pueblo."

"It was not ours to claim! It belongs to all!"

"You all still have access."

"With your permission! And after Ortiz and his miners have stripped it of its power!" The knife flashes upward again. "You refuse to listen! Shall I take your ear as well?"

"Take the issue to the courts," Abreú says. "That is the way of civilized men."

"And who sits as judge in that court?" The warrior turns to the crowd and flings an arm toward the stocks. "Behold the judge!" Then he faces Abreú again, a glint in his eyes. "It was your right hand which signed those papers, was it not?"

Abreú doesn't reply. Diego peers forward. The former governor's face is pale as ice.

The man with the knife turns his head and barks a command. A young boy moves into the plaza. He carries a strip of narrow white cloth in one hand and a finger-thick stick the length of his forearm in the other.

A woman follows him. The boy hands her the cloth. She moves around the cepo del reo and wraps the strip of cotton once, then twice more, around Abreú's upper arm. She pulls it tight, crosses the ends, and nods to the boy. He places the stick in the center of the cross. She ties it into place, grips both ends, and twists, forcing the binding into Abreú's skin. The boy reaches for the ends of the cloth and secures them, tightening further.

The judge groans through clenched teeth. His forehead is damp with sweat.

The man with the knife laughs mirthlessly. "This is only the beginning of your pain, you who think you have the right to judge us, to give away what can't be possessed."

The woman steps away and leads the boy back to the watching crowd. The obsidian blade rises into the air. "And now the judgment!" the warrior cries. "A knife of stone from the earth which feeds us! Our mother has given us the weapon by which to enact her revenge!"

His arm whips forward. The knife flashes downward once, twice, then again, and suddenly Abreú is screaming—a high, thin shriek of disbelief as much as pain.

The warrior steps back, his head lifted and proud, blood dripping from the blade. "Do not fear," he says. "The binding will keep you from bleeding too quickly." He turns to Diego and raises the object in his other hand. Diego blinks, not wanting to believe his eyes. It's all one piece—three fingers, a thumb, a blood-smeared palm, a dripping wrist. His stomach twists. He bends forward, trying not to retch.

The warrior laughs triumphantly. "Your jefe is a man after all, is he not? His blood is the same color as ours!"

Diego's stomach is suddenly still, gripped by fury at the sacrilege. He straightens and swipes his tongue over his cracked lips. "What is your name?" he demands.

The man throws his head back and laughs. "That is your answer?"

Abreú's eyes open in his white face. Diego's question seems to have given him fresh courage. "You will pay personally for this crime," he says through gritted teeth. "You may cut my body to pieces but you will pay."

A slow smile spreads across the warrior's face. "You speak as a man with authority." He half turns toward the elder with the silver-tipped cane. "He speaks as a man with authority!"

Amusement glints in the eyes of the Pueblo leader. He steps forward, walks slowly to the stocks, stops in front of it, then turns to the watching crowd and raises his hand in a signal that he will speak. "The people of this pueblo choose their leaders and give them authority to make decisions on their behalf," he says in a carrying voice. "Is this man with the severed hand one you wish to be in authority over you? Have you chosen him?"

The watchers gaze back at him. Then one man takes a single step forward. "I have not chosen him."

On the far side of the square, someone else raises their voice. "I have not chosen him."

And now another, to Diego's left. "He is not of my choosing."

And another. A woman this time. "Nor of mine."

Diego braces himself, waiting for the shouting to begin, the drums that will pound the crowd into a single deadly unit. But there is only silence. It fills the space between the high-walled buildings more powerfully than a thousand voices. He shivers in spite of the heat.

"It is not your right to choose." Abreú's voice is weak, but it still carries.

Diego turns his head. Admiration surges through him. There's true dignity in a man who can insist on the law in these circumstances. When he's already lost a hand and is in danger of losing much more.

The man with the cane of authority gazes at the former governor expressionlessly. "Even now, you speak without understanding, in the voice of your people and its arrogance." He sounds almost sad. "You refuse to open your ears." He turns, returns to his place, and makes a small gesture to the man with the black knife.

"He is a government official!" Diego protests.

The young man ignores him. He gazes at the stocks for a long moment, then turns toward the crowd.

Another boy comes forward with more white cotton and a slightly thicker stick. A woman follows. They move behind the cepo del reo. The woman bends over Abreú's right leg and wraps the cloth around his thigh, a hand's-breadth above the knee.

Diego's stomach twists. There's an uncontrollable burning in his throat, then his mouth. Vomit spews out, splattering his face and shirt. He bends his head toward his shoulder, trying to wipe the worst from his chin.

Then Abreú screams.

The warrior steps back from the cepo, holding up a bloody foot, and turns slowly so all can see.

Diego can't breathe. A gray haze edges his vision. His throat closes. There's a stretch of silence, then the crunch of knife hitting bone. And more screaming. A male voice—the man with the knife?—says something Diego can't make out, then there's a shout. Abreú screams again, a high shriek of pain, then blackness closes around Diego's head.

~ ~ ~ ~

When Diego comes to, the plaza seems to contain only the long purple shadows of late afternoon. He lies on his side, still bound, his cheek flattened in a smear of vomit. The smell of it roils his empty stomach. He makes a great effort and rolls away from the mess. A hand grabs his shoulder and forces him into a sitting position.

The angry warrior crouches beside him, his knife now back in his waistband. "Do you finally understand what becomes of those who presume to judge without authority?" he demands. He grabs Diego by the hair and forces his gaze toward the cepo del reo. "Do you see?"

The ensign stares at the heavy gray beams, now spattered with dry blood. On the ground beside the stocks lies the torso of a man, his face turned away. The dying light skims over his gold-brown hair and drops to a bare foot on the earth beside it. A severed hand lies next to the foot. A hand with a missing digit.

Diego's stomach heaves, but nothing comes out. The warrior's fingers jerk his hair, twisting his head and forcing his gaze elsewhere.

Halfway across the plaza, two short logs rest in the dirt. They're bent oddly, as if they have knees. He blinks, then understands. They aren't logs, they're legs. He takes a ragged breath, trying to stay afloat.

And with the breath comes fury. He jerks his hair from the warrior's grasp and lets out a bellow of rage. "You fool!

He was a district judge! A former governor! You will be punished for this!" He glares at the man, who smirks back at him. "Tell me your name!" Diego howls. "Tell me your name!"

The smirk vanishes into incredulity. "You want my name?" Then the warrior's face fills with pure glittering hatred, a malice born of years of barely suppressed anger. He straightens and yanks the obsidian blade from his waist.

Diego opens his mouth to protest, but he has no time. The knife plunges into his chest, once, twice, then again.

As the ensign's breath flees his body, the angry warrior cries, "¡Me llamo Consecuencias!"

CHAPTER 8

August 12–September 10, 1837:

A Different Kind of Leader

(José Angel Gonzales)

José Angel Gonzales, newly made rebel governor of Nuevo México, places his hands flat on the big oak desk in front of him, flexes his fingers against the wood, and wishes it was round instead of flat. A buffalo lance. Or the braided leather reins of a horse, saddle creaking beneath him. He rises impatiently from the throne-like chair behind the desk and paces to the door, then back again.

The room is filled with the trappings of power: delicate tables, ornate candle holders, carved boxes, brass clocks. So unlike his mother's parents' home at Taos Pueblo. He stops and stares into a gilt-edged mirror. Long black hair neatly braided and pulled forward over his shoulders, high thin Comanche nose. Or is it Pawnee? Or Spanish?

He grimaces and turns away. Genízaro. That's what los españoles call him. He doesn't know if it's true. Technically, a genízaro is someone from the non-Pueblo tribes who's been rescued and baptized into the Spanish religion, or a descendant of someone who has. But the origins of his father's father remain a mystery. All he knows is that the man was a coyote, the child of either an anglo or Spanish man and an Indian or Spanish woman. His chin lifts. Whatever the mixture in his blood, on his mother's side he is a son of Taos Pueblo. And now he is ruler over them all.

He paces again to the open door. The space beyond is empty. The adobe palacio echoes with silence. Most of his rebel forces have returned to their homes and he is left in Santa Fe to govern a people who don't seek him out.

He turns back into the room with a sick feeling in his stomach. He may hold the position of governor, but he hasn't been trained in the art of politics. He doesn't know how to proceed. He looks again into a mirror and stares at himself, trying to see himself as others do.

His height, broad shoulders, and ox-like neck are those of a cibolero, a buffalo hunter, not a governor. And he's good at that. His skill has earned the respect of his neighbors and compañeros. However, the ability to bring down a buffalo means nothing to the ricos, the alcaldes, the priests. He growls in disgust at his own weakness and turns toward the door.

A short, rather thickset man is standing there, watching him. He has wavy almost-black hair and pale skin and is clutching an elegant beaver-felt hat in both hands. He bobs his head at Gonzales and wets his lips with his tongue. "Your Excellency—"

"Governor!" Gonzales snaps. "I do not answer to such high-flown titles."

"I apologize, Excel—" The man stops, looking confused. Then his shoulders straighten and he begins again. "If I'm not disturbing you—"

Gonzales waves him into the room and returns to the desk. He has a sudden urge to stand behind it, use it as a kind of bulwark. This Spaniard has a rico look about him, for all his nervousness, and will be watching for any sign of weakness. "What is it?" His tone is not as brusque as he'd like it to be.

The man positions himself in front of the desk. "I have a petition." He looks down at his hat.

"Yes?"

He lifts his head. "Forgive me. I should begin by telling you my name and position."

Gonzales nods, watching him.

The other man shifts his feet, steadying himself. "Me llamo José Albino Chacón. I am the third alcalde of Santa Fe, elected alongside—"

"I know who the other two are. We captured them at La Mesilla."

Chacón bobs his head. "They have now been returned to their families and are grateful. I convey their thanks to you."

Gonzales nods, trying to look gracious but feeling irritated instead. Of course the men were returned to their homes. Is this the part he must play now? Being thanked for doing what is right and just? But there's more to this visit than polite expressions of gratitude, especially since such thanks should have been conveyed by the men themselves, not Chacón. "And your petition?" he asks abruptly.

The alcalde takes a deep breath. "His Excellency Governor Pérez—"

"Is dead." Gonzales braces himself, ready to defend the actions of his men.

Chacón nods. "Sí. And his body lies unburied on the road just north of the village of Aqua Fría."

"As an example to all who oppress those beneath them."

"It is— Unseemly."

Gonzales scowls. This Spanish whelp is telling him what's unseemly? After the abuses his kind have heaped upon the vecinos of this land? "Pérez was unseemly!" he snaps. "Every bit of him!"

Chacón nods and looks away. "Forgive me, Excel— Governor. What I meant to say is that the corpse is unclothed." He glances at Gonzales, then returns his eyes to the floor. "Or so I am told. The body lies outside Salvador Martín's house."

"The father of Tomás Martín, the presidio corporal who was captured at La Mesilla?"

The third alcalde of Santa Fe nods without looking up.

Gonzales's lips thin. Does the man think his decisions as governor will be biased by the loyalties of Martín's son? A man can't control his adult children. But perhaps the ricos don't understand this simple truth. His lips curl in contempt as he gestures for Chacón to continue.

"Don Salvador wishes to remove the corpse so his women folk may leave their home without being exposed to such a sight."

"Then he should move it."

The alcalde looks him full in the face, his expression almost stern. "He wishes only to live in peace. He has no desire to offend you or your men."

The governor's lips twist again. "And since his son is a presidio soldier and Martín himself sheltered Pérez for a few moments before his death, he's reluctant to draw attention to himself."

The alcalde's brows rise in surprise, though he's doing his best not to look alarmed. Gonzales grins in satisfaction. Does the man think he knows nothing? Then he sobers. After all, it

143

took courage to approach him with this petition. "But you are willing to risk drawing attention to yourself?"

Albino Chacón's chin rises. "It is my duty as alcalde to see to the removal and burial of any corpse left lying on a public roadway. I seek your permission to do so."

His permission. Gonzales studies the other man's face. Does Chacón realize just how little control he actually has? The insurrectos have placed him as governor in the palacio. They can just as easily remove him. Chacón is undoubtedly a loyalist, for all his hat-holding. If he uses the burial of Pérez's headless body to rally opposition to the rebellion, there will be no holding back the more rabid insurrectos still camped west of town. They're already taking provisions from the populace without paying for them.

Not that they have any funds to pay with. But that's an issue for another time. The alcalde is watching Gonzales' face and seems to read at least some of what he's thinking. "I propose to take the corpse away under cover of darkness," Chacón says. "A woman of Santa Fe has offered to prepare it for burial."

Gonzales's eyebrows rise in surprise. "A woman? She is a brave one."

A small smile lightens Chacón's face. "Gertrudis Barceló is not an ordinary woman."

"Ah. This is she who is called Doña Tules? The woman with the gambling salon?"

The alcalde nods. He looks down at his hat again, pointedly acknowledging the rebel governor's authority, awaiting his decision.

Gonzales stares at the surface of his desk. He runs his hand over the warm, slightly pitted wood, considering, then lifts his head. "You may remove the body of the traitor Pérez to the house of Señora Gertrudis Barceló and see that it is conveyed from there to be buried." He raises a hand. "However, you must do both these things at night and take care that no one sees you."

A flash of irritation crosses Chacón's face, then he draws himself up. "I thank you, Governor and bid you good day." He bows stiffly, turns, and goes out.

Gonzales sinks into the chair behind the desk and gazes at the empty doorway. Satisfaction twitches his lips. Even the ricos obey him. And he feels confident he did the right thing.

Now if that confidence will only get him through the assembly he's called. On the last Sunday of the month, after mass at Santa Fe's parish church, the ricos from up and down the river will be here to discuss what to tell Mexico City about recent events and also what to do about Nuevo México's fragile financial condition.

He moves uncomfortably in the chair. That is, most of the wealthy and influential will be here. The priest at Tomé has sent word he's too ill to attend. He's a man with much influence along the lower river. His absence doesn't bode well.

But even the governor can't force the man to come to Santa Fe. José Angel doesn't really want to be here himself.

He closes his eyes and wonders what Ramona and the children are doing. His lips curve upward. What a delight she is. After his first and then his second wife died, he hadn't been able to bear living in Don Fernando de Taos anymore. Ramona Bernal of Santa Cruz de la Cañada, that plump, tender, and hardy woman, has been a delightful surprise. Not only was she willing to add his children to her own, but at thirty-seven she isn't weary of life. Or the marriage bed.

145

His smile deepens as he remembers certain passages in that bed. Then he sighs. Life would be so much easier if he were home. But he who risks nothing has nothing, and sometimes it is necessary for a man to risk much for his compañeros. He braces his hands on the arms of the chair and lifts himself into action.

~ ~ ~ ~

Over the next few weeks, José Angel wishes more than once that he's back in Santa Cruz with his family. The petitions, the anxious voices, and the demand for decisions are unending. And then the 27th of August arrives. The day of the assembly.

They meet in the long narrow building on the east side of the plaza that is home to the Santa Fe city council, a space with a row of small windows just under the vigas and one door at the end opposite the table where the governor and council members sit. Benches for the ricos who aren't on the Council face them, though some audience members—including Antonio Abad Montoya and his brother—stand along the wall.

The new Secretary of State, Donaciano Vigil, sits beside the governor and reads the agenda items out one by one. The first order of business is to approve the rebel actions to this point, including naming Gonzales as governor.

The red-headed Santa Fe priest Juan Felipe Ortiz coughs nervously when this comes up, but his fellow council member Pedro José Perea gives him a sharp look and they continue. Everyone present votes in favor, although Judge Esteban Pino frowns as he does so.

Then the assembly moves on to the process of approving the distribution of Pérez's possessions and addressing the demands of his creditors. Here they hit a snag. Vigil's staff has made a list of the items Pérez owned and their present location, but it doesn't seem to be complete. In addition, some things, such as the man's camp bed and a dressing table, have disappeared. These particular items apparently left town with his housekeeper.

To further complicate the process, Pérez didn't own all the items on the list. For example, the gilt-edged mirrors still hanging in the governor's office were borrowed from Francisco Sarracino, who hasn't been heard from since shortly after the battle at La Mesilla. Gonzales suppresses a groan and shifts impatiently in his chair.

In addition, the list of Pérez's creditors keeps getting longer. As the meeting extends into early evening, more men drift in, murmur the pertinent information to a clerk at the back of the room, then settle onto the benches to watch the proceedings.

As a servant brings candles, Gonzales tries to focus on Judge Esteban Pino, who's providing painfully extensive details about the legal process required for identifying the creditors of a deceased person and cataloging the demands on their estate. The governor's eyelids drift down and he forces them open, straightens his shoulders, and tries to look attentive.

Then a brown-bearded American merchant with a worried expression enters the room. Pino continues his explanation, but everyone else watches the man lean toward the clerk and murmur a question. The clerk looks up and shakes his head.

147

The americano frowns, nods, and straightens but, instead of joining the other debtors, moves toward the front of the room.

Donaciano Vigil rises from Gonzales's side and meets the newcomer halfway. They confer quietly, then the secretary returns to the table and stands just behind the governor's right shoulder. José Angel turns and looks up at him.

"There are also American demands," Vigil says into his ear. "Not personal debts, but notes on the Treasury. Too many to go into today."

Gonzales suppresses a groan. So now they'll need to deal with government debts as well. It's becoming overwhelming. Then he realizes that this is an excellent excuse to adjourn for the day. He turns back to the table and holds up a hand. Judge Pino stops in midsentence and looks at him expectantly.

The governor blinks in surprise, feeling the power. He tries to keep the satisfaction of it from coloring his voice. "I've just been told that there are additional debts that must be taken into account." He glances at the merchant, who's still standing halfway up the room. "These are not personal debts, but demands against the Treasury by the americano traders. A complete list must be compiled before we can do anything more."

"Americans!" Judge Pino spits. "How will we know what they tell us is true?"

Padre Ortiz leans forward, his red head bobbing as he registers his agreement.

The governor ignores them. He looks down the room. Antonio Abad grins at him and he suppresses an answering smile. "Today's meeting is over," he says. "We will meet again tomorrow morning."

The ricos at the table look at each other in surprise, but Gonzales simply rises and moves toward the back of the room. He nods to the American merchant as he passes and meets Montoya by the door.

The other man grins at him companionably. "Are you enjoying yourself?" he asks.

Gonzales allows himself a small smile. "I'd rather be hunting buffalo."

He repeats the phrase to himself late the next morning, at the end of a tediously long session of sorting out the claims. The debts to the merchants are substantial and, even after the clearly fraudulent personal demands are removed from the list, there's not enough money to cover everything. There will have to be an auction of Pérez's goods.

This event occurs at the palacio, where Vigil and the others go through the furniture and other things and assess their value. The bull-headed Padre Antonio José Martínez of Don Fernando de Taos inserts himself into almost every decision, raising objections at every turn, setting aside items he insists belong to the families of Pérez's dead officials.

But finally it's done. What little can be sold is auctioned off and the money distributed. The Treasury has been almost emptied to meet at least some of the demands of the American creditors. The traders aren't happy, but there's nothing more to be done.

Only Sarracino's mirrors remain, still hanging in the governor's office. Until there's clear information about the man's fate, that's where they'll stay.

Now the assembly's real work begins. They spend the next day arguing about how to reassure Mexico City that, unlike the Texans two years ago, Nuevo México isn't interested in independence. They simply want redress for their grievances.

Governor Gonzales is bemused and then annoyed at the length of time it takes to decide the obvious and to put together a committee to put it in writing. This is followed by the tedium of choosing the members of said committee. Eventually, Padre Martínez, Alcalde Esquibel, and Manuel Armijo, of all people, are named to it.

But the meeting still isn't over. The assembled group wishes to identify the specific points to be included in the committee's statement. Esquibel pushes for explicit language about Pérez, with detailed examples of his arrogance and immoral behavior. This prompts a long harangue from Judge Pino about the importance of obeying the law, particularly the 1836 Constitution. Antonio Abad Montoya responds to Pino's remarks with elegiac praise for the 1824 constitution, universal suffrage, local elections, and so forth. "We reject the constitution of 1836!" he ends with a flourish.

Manuel Armijo and Padre Martínez don't look happy, but they nod agreement. The committee's report will include language that rejects the federal control imposed by the 1836 constitution and beg for more involvement in choosing Nuevo México's governors.

In the meantime, there's the issue of how much authority the governor the rebels have named can legally wield, since he hasn't yet been confirmed by Mexico City. Armijo proposes a resolution that will give Gonzales the power to act as circumstances require while respecting federal law.

The cibolero forces himself to lean back in his chair as he tries to keep the confusion from his face. Exactly what does that mean? And who will decide what particular circumstances require? Gonzales alone? Will Judge Pino want to weigh in? And Manuel Armijo? After all, he was governor eight years ago. It seems odd that he's not seeking for a larger role in the administration. The man makes Gonzales uneasy.

But that's not all he has to be uneasy about. The assembly wraps up late Tuesday. Early Wednesday morning, a deputation arrives at the palacio with the scar-faced El Quemado Vigil at its head. These are men who fought at La Mesilla and they're unhappy. There were too many ricos involved in the assembly and no final decision about taxes.

The men eye Gonzales as if he's now a rico himself. He suppresses a quease of discomfort and answers them reassuringly. El Quemado seems convinced of his good intentions, but the others shake their heads as they step from the palacio portal and head back to what's left of the rebel camp at the edge of town.

Gonzales suppresses a sigh as he watches them go. Governing is no easy task. He almost feels sympathy for Albino Pérez, that bastard.

But then both insurrectos and ricos head home over the next few days. Santa Fe seems to expand and settle in the late-August quiet.

This town is a beautiful place. The cottonwoods at the corner of the plaza deepen toward gold and the flag in its center lifts gently in the breeze, its green, white, and red stripes bright against the blue sky. He wonders if Ramona would be willing to move here. A land at peace with itself, some semblance of fairness for all, and his esposa beside him. What riches.

~ ~ ~ ~

But a week later, the governor's daydreams are smashed. It's the first Sunday of September and he's just returned from mass. As Gonzales steps onto the palacio portal, Padre Antonio José Martínez springs from a bench along the wall. "Excellency!" he exclaims.

"I don't answer to that term," the governor says automatically.

"I beg your pardon," the priest says. "It has been a difficult journey. We have ridden all night." Another man steps forward. He's more slender than Antonio José, but there's something about the jaw that says they're related.

Gonzales glances at him, then turns to the priest. "You have come from Don Fernando?"

Martínez's thin hair drops onto his forehead as he nods. His face is lined with fatigue. "Your men there are threatening to kill my brother and me!" He looks at the man beside him, whose eyes are fixed on Gonzales. "They followed us down the river! It's a miracle we escaped!"

The governor turns toward the palacio door and gestures them to follow. As they enter, a servant girl appears, carrying a bundle of clothes. "Could you bring us some food?" he says to her. "And wine?"

She pauses, nods, then disappears. He settles his guests in his office and is formally introduced to the padre's brother, Taos Subprefect José Santiago Martínez. Then the food arrives. Gonzales pulls up a small table and his visitors eat like men who've travelled all night. Afterward, a little calmer now, the priest explains that a parishioner came to him early Saturday morning with word that the rebels were gathering to attack him and his brother. Apparently, the Martínezes haven't been vocal enough in their disapproval of the Pérez administration.

"What do they want me to do?" Martínez sputters. "Turn every sermon into a diatribe against the man and his perceived sins? The mass is for looking into one's own heart, not that of others!"

The governor looks at the subprefect, who puts down his tortía and pulls a folded paper from his waistcoat pocket. "They've also issued this." He starts to hand it to Gonzales, then extends it to his brother. "Here, you read it."

The padre looks at the document as if it will scorch his fingers. "I know what it says." He turns to Gonzales. "It's another proclamation, one that makes Esquibel's August pronouncement look like a love letter." He stabs a piece of meat with his fork as if he'd like to stab something else, something alive. "Los insurrectos are threatening to move south to Alburquerque and beyond and steal everything in their path on the way. Everything owned by a rico, that is." He pauses, his food in the air. "They say they want to redistribute New Mexico's resources and they'll kill anyone who speaks against them."

The subprefect leans forward and peers anxiously into Gonzales' face. "There were men behind us all the way from Don Fernando," he says. "I'm sure of it." His shoulders tighten. "And the rebels there aren't the only ones who are restless. We went through Santa Cruz at midnight and even at that hour there were campfires everywhere. The place is crawling with men who should be home harvesting their crops."

His brother the padre looks at Gonzales. "Your men."

The governor stirs uneasily. At least some of those men are angry about the result of the assembly. Who knows if they're still truly his? "It's not that simple anymore," he says. He nods toward the proclamation. "What else does it say?"

"Not much of substance." The padre pokes a finger at it, moving it toward Gonzales as if he can hardly bear to touch it.

The rebel leader pretends not to see it. He may be able to sign his name, but reading doesn't come easily to him. He's not about to try it in front of the highly-educated padre. Gonzales stares at Sarracino's mirrors. He's suddenly filled with a great weariness. "Let us rest on the matter."

Antonio José looks disgusted but Santiago Martínez seems relieved. "A good night's rest would be welcome," he murmurs.

The governor is still pondering how to proceed and the complexities of governing when the padre returns the next morning with more news. His brother José María has arrived in the capital with a message. The citizens of Don Fernando de Taos are begging Antonio José to return and help them restore order. They promise he won't be harmed if he does so.

The padre is taking no chances. He wants Gonzales to go with him.

The rebel governor stares at him, taking it in. Martínez is educated, a rico from an old Spanish family which owns a broad swath of the Taos Valley. As the priest at both Don

Fernando and Taos Pueblo, he also has spiritual authority. And the personality to assert it. In all the time José Angel lived in the Taos area, he never saw Martínez look even slightly worried about anything.

But now he's afraid and has come to him, the genízaro, for help. Gonzales feels an undeniable glow of satisfaction. Then he wonders if he should leave the capital. If he's not here, will angry insurrectos try to attack it? Or ricos attempt to regain control?

But this is Padre Martínez asking him.

Padre Martínez. Asking him.

He nods to the priest. "Yes, I'll go with you."

The other man almost seems to collapse in relief. "Gracias." Then he hesitates. "I'd like to go today, if that's possible. My brothers are anxious to return to their families."

Donaciano Vigil appears in the doorway. Gonzales motions him in. Taking a whole troop of presidio soldiers wouldn't be wise. The Don Fernando insurrectos would take it amiss. Besides, the troops are needed here. Vigil will be a good substitute. He represents the ricos and the military and is also a government official, a symbol of Gonzales' power.

Something stirs uneasily in the governor's chest. Wielding power still makes him uncomfortable. How will his compañeros react to an assertion of authority on his part? Then he steels himself. The rebels need to understand that he's responsible to everyone in Nuevo México, not just them.

~ ~ ~ ~

155

They leave that afternoon and ride hard, arriving late the next day. The mood in Don Fernando isn't quite as friendly as the note had implied. Rebels cluster in the middle of the dusty plaza and others patrol the massive wooden gates at its four corners. The church stands just outside and to the west of the square. More men are stationed around it.

The insurrecto who stands directly in front of the church door has his arms folded and his feet braced for trouble. It's Juan Antonio Vigil, the one called El Coyote. His thin face is dark with suppressed anger as he looks the priest in the eyes.

"My son," the padre says, both hands out in a kind of half benediction.

"You may have sons, but I'm not one of them," Vigil says flatly.

Martínez's hands drop to his sides. Donaciano Vigil moves forward. El Coyote jerks his chin at him. "Cousin," he says. It's more of a warning than a greeting. The sergeant looks at the padre, who glances at the governor.

Gonzales steps forward. "Buenos días, compañero," he says politely.

The rebel's face softens. "Buenos días, General. Are you well? How is Santa Fe treating you?"

Gonzales smiles. "As well as can be expected." He shrugs. "Politicians."

"Like this one." He glares at Padre Martínez. "This man of Don Fernando de Taos who is really of Santa Fe." He turns his head and spits on the ground. "And la Ciudad de México." He looks back at the priest, his face sardonic. "Have you received any new orders lately?"

Martínez stiffens. "I answer only to God."

Gonzales looks at him in alarm. This tone won't soften hearts.

Martínez seems to catch his concern. His face changes, moving from anger to caution, then something resembling humility. "And the voices of my parishioners when they come to me with their concerns," he adds.

El Coyote snorts, his expression a mixture of amusement and contempt. He jerks his head toward the padre's walled house, which stands behind the church. "We'll be coming this evening to express what you call our concerns. You'd better be prepared to respond to them."

The padre's shoulders jerk back. He glares at the insurrecto, then turns and marches toward his house. Gonzales stifles a sigh, then turns to the two Vigils, who are carefully avoiding each other's eyes. "So," he says to El Coyote. "All is not well?"

The rebel points his chin toward the departing priest. "That one doesn't know how to keep his mouth shut. Or maybe he thinks he doesn't have to because he's a rico. It's been a month since we rose and he's still preaching that we must submit to authority no matter how tyrannical it is. I'm surprised he's not also telling us to give to Caesar what is Caesar's and to God what is God's." He turns his head and spits again. "Of course, the only thing the church really wants us to give it is our money, crops, and flocks."

"Martínez has never been one to ask more of the poor than they can afford," the governor says mildly.

"But he makes the decision about what fees should be paid and by whom. We never know for certain what he's going to decide. It's all in his power, not ours. And he refuses to allow our dead to be buried inside the church."

"That's been forbidden for decades," Donaciano Vigil says. "He'll be answerable to his church superiors if he does that."

The rebel glares at him. "He should be answering to us, not to them! The people are in charge here, not the church!" He moves impatiently. "And he hates us, the coyotes and the genízaros. If a person isn't born pure Spanish, he thinks they're less than dirt."

"Wasn't he born in Abiquiu?" The sergeant turns to the governor. "Wasn't it settled by rescued Indians?"

"Rescued!" El Coyote spits. "Rescued or enslaved? He was born there, but his blood is purely español. Just ask him!" He scowls at Gonzales. "And you consort with him! Have you forgotten where you come from? Are you turning Spanish on us? Don't you remember who your parents were? Or do you need to be reminded?"

Anger thickens the governor's chest. His hands curl into fists. "That's enough!"

El Coyote's face changes. He steps back. "It was only a joke."

Gonzales stares at him. He's surprised both at the ferocity of his own emotion and the deep satisfaction in seeing the other man cower. Six months ago he would have laughed off the veiled threat and been embarrassed at his own reaction. Now he turns abruptly away, toward the padre's house.

He's still mulling over his confused feelings that evening when there's a knock on the outer gate. A small group of Don Fernando insurrectos files into the sala, which is lit only by the flames in the corner fireplace and the candles in the three-pronged holder on the table. The newcomers stand at the edge of the light, their faces unreadable.

El Coyote isn't one of them, but the Montoya brothers' relative Pablo is. And he's the man in charge. He isn't a big man. In fact he's downright short and wiry. But his shoulders are proud, his eyes are shrewd in his weather-beaten face, and his chin is lifted higher than Padre Martínez's as he stares around the room. He nods politely to Gonzales, then focuses on the priest.

"You will announce your agreement with the principles of the rebellion," the rebel says flatly. "And you will no longer require baptism or other fees for church functions." He pauses, studying Martínez's averted face. "Also, when a family wishes it, you will bury their dead inside the church."

The priest's long head jerks at this, but his mouth remains closed.

Pablo's eyes narrow. "Most importantly, you will cease preaching against the insurrection. If you do not, there will be consequences." He looks around the room, at the bookcase with its leather-bound volumes, the decanter of wine beside the candelabrum on the dainty American-made side table. When his gaze returns to Martínez, it sparks with suppressed triumph. "You have three days to appear before us and make a formal declaration. If we find your statement acceptable, you will be allowed to continue to reside in our community."

The padre's long jaw tightens and his fists clench. For a brief moment, Gonzales thinks he'll strike out, but his voice is low and almost humble as he says, "I will appear before you."

"And acknowledge our conditions? We won't tolerate a sermon."

Martínez's lips twist, but he merely nods and says, "In two days."

Pablo studies him for a long moment, then swings abruptly toward the door. The others follow him out. When the room is empty, the padre turns to Gonzales. "What have we come to?" he asks bleakly.

José Angel looks away. Now he's part of the "we" of the governing classes. He's not sure if he should be flattered or worried. He only knows it fills him with disquiet.

Martínez clasps his hands behind his back and begins pacing the room. "I don't understand why they're so angry with me," he says. "I've always been careful not to overburden my parishioners with demands. As it is, most don't pay the baptism or marriage fees. Yet I and my household must eat. And the church building must be maintained in proper order." He turns toward Gonzales. "And this demand to bury the dead inside the church! That is strictly forbidden and they know it!"

"They believe it protects them in the hereafter," Donaciano Vigil says from the corner.

The governor turns in surprise. He'd forgotten the sergeant was in the room.

Vigil glances at him, then the padre. "My grandmother always said that the closer the dead were to the altar, the more intercession they'd receive from the Virgin."

"The more likely their rotting body is to send poisonous fumes into the nostrils of the priest," Martínez sniffs. "Even if I agree to set aside all fees, I can't do anything about the rule forbidding in-church burials and I wouldn't want to if I could. It's a filthy custom."

Vigil shrugs and drops his eyes. Gonzales watches Martínez pace.

Two days later, the padre speaks to the rebels. Somehow, he avoids promises of burial inside the church. A thin-lipped Pablo Montoya accepts his stilted statement of support and reform, and the governor finally feels free to leave for the capital.

~ ~ ~ ~

He and Sargento Vigil take their time. Gonzales is in no hurry to return to the governor's palace. Its rooms are larger than home, but they contain no wife, no laughing children. They ride the barren hills above the stone-strewn banks of the río del Norte, camp that night among the rocks, and drop the next day toward the river and its bright foliage. The cottonwoods are gloriously golden and somehow comforting.

The presidio sergeant seems to appreciate them, too. He's an easy travel companion. He speaks if talk is wished for and is silent if it is not. And Gonzales is sick of talk. As his mount moves south, his mind returns to El Coyote Vigil in front of the Don Fernando de Taos church. His thin, contemptuous face. And his words, accusing Gonzales of forgetting where he came from, turning Spanish.

A growl fills José Angel's throat. How dare he speak in such a way?

Donaciano Vigil gives him an inquiring look, but the governor turns his head. No, he hasn't forgotten the precepts of his parents or the arrogances of a man like Padre Martínez toward his parishioners. He brought the priest back to Taos to face the rebels and promise better behavior in future, didn't he? Did that mean nothing?

And yet, a part of him knows El Coyote's words sting because there's truth in them. "Turning Spanish" is another way of saying he's gotten above himself, has begun to act differently.

It's true. He has. With the governorship has come conversations with educated men such as Donaciano Vigil, meetings with powerful ricos like Pedro Perea and Judge Pino. Even Padre Martínez comes to him for help.

And he's become used to being obeyed. Didn't he just now turn away from the sergeant with the full expectation that the man will accept his snub? A few months ago, he wouldn't have done such a thing.

Gonzales grimaces. He has to admit it. Being responded to in this way makes him feel good. Then he frowns. And why shouldn't it? He's a man, too!

And yet— How long will it last? Vigil is a good man, but he will obey whoever is in authority. Manuel Armijo waits in the wings. Given the right combination of circumstances, he'll pounce, ready and eager to take over. After all, he's not only a rico, he has experience governing. And incentive to do so. He knows how to make the position worth his while.

José Angel's mount stumbles, bringing him back to the present. He pats the warm flank and speaks soothingly, then flicks the reins and breaks into a trot. One of Ramona's favorite sayings is "el pez que busca anzuelo, busca su duelo"—the fish that goes for the hook looks for his funeral. She's right. If you look for trouble, you're sure to find it. Pondering what may be is of no use. In the meantime, it's a glorious fall day and he has a pleasant companion.

He slows and turns to Donaciano Vigil. "I understand you were born in Santa Fe," he says. "What was it like there when you were a child?"

They speak only of pleasant things as the road leaves the hills and dips toward the river, then moves past the fields of Los Luceros and the pueblo of San Juan. Eventually, the dirt track bends southeast to Santa Cruz.

It crosses the plaza here and heads straight to Santa Fe, but instead of following it, Gonzales turns off toward home.

The sergeant doesn't look startled at this apparent change in plans or say anything about the duties that await them both in the capital. A smile tugs at Gonzales's lips. There are advantages to being governor. He doesn't have to explain himself.

Then he shifts in his saddle. Is he indeed becoming more Spanish than Indian?

However, there's no time to answer this question, because here is Ramona peering from the gate, a yard full of excited children behind her. She's in his arms as soon as his feet hit the ground. "I heard you were in Don Fernando," she says. "I hoped you would find time to come to me." She smiles into his eyes, then turns to Vigil, who doffs his hat. "Forgive me," she says. "I was so happy to see mi esposo that I forgot myself." She curtseys sweetly. "I am María Ramona Bernal."

The big man introduces himself gravely, then looks from her to Gonzales. "You will wish to speak privately." He tilts his head toward the children, who have broken into a noisy game of tag. "If you don't mind, I will treat myself to a visit with los chamacos. It has been almost a week since I've seen my own." Without waiting for permission, he moves toward them.

Gonzales smiles into Ramona's eyes as she catches his hand in hers and tugs him toward the house door. How he has missed her.

But even her luscious curves and sweet ways can't distract him for long. He must return to his duties. He and Vigil leave the next day and head south again, through the browning hills. In the west, the river bosque is alive with golden cottonwoods. Yet even the glories of Fall can't distract José Angel from the memory of El Coyote's words. Has he truly forgotten where he came from?

Certainly not the poverty, the laughter, the love. But the sense of being lower than others? Yes, that has left him.

As far as he can tell, this is a good thing. He wishes every man, woman, and child of Nuevo México to feel equal to those around them. Neither high nor low. Simply people.

He shakes his head. He knows that's impossible. The human soul requires both someone to look down on and someone else to look up to. It's the way of the world.

Gonzales frowns. If El Coyote thinks he's forgotten who his parents were, what do the ricos think, especially those of the lower river? If they believe him to be getting above himself, they'll be searching even now for a way to put him back in his place.

His spine quivers at the thought. If they decide that such a one as he shouldn't be governor— But he will not dwell on such ideas. To do so is to look for trouble where there may be nothing but shadows.

He's still doing his best to maintain this perspective the next day when he and Donaciano Vigil ride through the last of the hills just north of Santa Fe. It's easy enough to do at this moment. It's Monday, the eleventh of September in the year 1837. The air is sweet and cool, the junipers beside the road are blue-green in the sun, and the cottonwoods in the hollows are turning ever more golden. A light breeze scatters the heart-shaped leaves that have already fallen across the road and the animals' hooves crunch them pleasantly underfoot.

He is José Angel Gonzales, governor of the land in which he was born. Nuevo México's Secretary of State rides at his right hand. Even the bits of straw in the adobe walls of the old guardhouse on the north edge of town glow in the sunlight. He breathes it all in with a small, contented smile.

Then he and Vigil turn into the plaza.

There are soldiers stationed along the portal in front of the governor's quarters, one before each post. Two more stand beside each door. Their stance is very like that of El Coyote before the Don Fernando de Taos church.

One of the men turns his head, sees the travelers, and opens the nearest door just enough to speak into the interior. He steps back and the door swings wide. Santa Fe's first and second alcaldes emerge. Albino Chacón follows them, his eyes on the ground.

There's something about the implacable set of the two alcaldes' faces that stiffens Gonzales's spine. He and Vigil rein in side by side, facing the portal. The two Santa Fe officials step to the edge and stand watching.

Gonzales waits, his eyes on the first alcalde. It is not the governor's place to speak first.

"Don José Angel," the man says. There is no respect in his voice. And he hasn't addressed him as governor.

So it has come. Gonzales glances at Vigil, who's watching the men on the portal with narrowed eyes.

165

The alcalde keeps his focus on Gonzales. "There is word from the south," he says, then stops as if waiting for the governor to speak. When he doesn't, the other man's shoulders shift slightly, then he says, "A meeting has been held at Tomé," and stops.

Gonzales suppresses his impatience and tries to speak calmly. "And the purpose of this meeting?"

"The said assembly was convened at the request of the padre of Tomé."

The priest who refused to attend the assembly two weeks ago. Gonzales opens his mouth to prod the alcalde further, then closes it. He won't give him the satisfaction.

There's a long pause. The first and second alcalde look at each other. Behind them, Albino Chacón moves to one side and shoots Gonzales a half-apologetic, half-defensive look, as if asking forgiveness for something he hasn't done.

"Before I proceed further on that topic," the first alcalde says, "I must inform you that the leadership of the presidio has changed."

Gonzales raises his eyebrows but doesn't speak.

The other man hesitates. Then his chin lifts. "Just as the rebels of the north decided who would govern them, so the presidio soldiers have also chosen their leader. The garrison has been reorganized under the command of Captain José Caballero, who is out of town at the moment. He requested me to notify you of said restructuring." He glances at Donaciano Vigil, then turns back to Gonzales. "However, informing you of this change is not the primary reason I am here to meet you this morning."

A stillness comes over the governor. "Speak what you have come to say."

The man settles himself onto his heels as if preparing to launch into a memorized speech. "I am authorized to inform you that on Friday last, a meeting was convened in Tomé at the request of Padre —"

Gonzales makes an impatient gesture. He's already said that.

The man gives him an irritated look and goes on. "The subject meeting was for the purpose of addressing the continued threats to the safety of the people of Nuevo México." He clears his throat and reaches for his breast pocket. "I have here the results of that discussion." He pulls out a piece of paper and makes a show of unfolding it, then holds it out at arm's length, level with his chest.

"In the post of Tomé," he reads. He pauses and glances past Gonzales. His voice takes on a deeper tone, as if he wants it to carry. "In the post of Tomé," he begins again.

The governor turns slightly and sees that a small group of men has gathered around the base of the plaza flagpole.

The alcalde continues. "On said eighth day of the current year, 1837, the inhabitants of said post and of Santa María de Belén having assembled with their respective alcaldes, the parochial curate of the first, the lieutenant of the active militia and the honored citizen Manuel Armijo—"

The governor grimaces. Armijo. Of course. This missive sounds like something he would write. Gonzales closes his eyes, listening for the key points buried beneath the flowing words.

"To sustain our tranquility or die in defense of the laws—" the other man intones. Then, "no authority is recognized other than the prefect of Alburquerque." And a bit later, "under the command of Citizen Manuel Armijo–"

Gonzales raises an eyebrow. Citizen, not former governor. Are they unsure about the wisdom of giving Armijo military power? Or do they hope using this term will placate the insurrectos?

More men have gathered near the flag. They stare intently toward the palacio. The alcalde's voice rises. "—The commandant shall take whatever measures may appear to him to be convenient, and if he put forth his hand for anything, it shall be with the condition of reimbursement, which will be made religiously."

Gonzales' lips twitch. Now it's commandant, not citizen or governor. And he'll pay for what he takes, which means his men are more righteous than the penniless rebels, who can't afford to do so. Gonzales's jaw tightens. It is always the way. The rich win because they are rich.

Finally, the alcalde is finished. He lowers the document and looks into Gonzales's face. "The people of Santa Fe agree with this plan laid out at Tomé," he says. "They have gone to Captain Caballero and demanded to be allowed to participate in returning the capital to the proper authorities."

Demanded to be allowed? If the stone in his stomach wasn't so heavy, Gonzales could almost laugh. He barely listens as the alcalde focuses again on the crowd at the flag-pole and raises his voice to repeat in simpler words that Manuel Armijo is in the process of organizing a force to re-take Santa Fe and subdue the men who put Gonzales in power.

Then he drops his voice and speaks directly to the governor. "As I have just said, the people in Santa Fe are eager to restore legitimate order. In addition, three-quarters of the residents of Alburquerque and farther south also support us.

You have no chance of succeeding in your quest to topple the legitimate government. You would do well to come quietly."

Gonzales looks at him thoughtfully. Quest to topple? He and his compañeros have already succeeded in doing so. The only question is whether they—and Gonzales—can hold it. His mind flashes to El Coyote's words to him, Pablo Montoya's fierce anger. Do they still trust him? Consider him their leader? Would they respond to his call to defend the capital against Armijo and his men?

Even if they did, what are the feelings of the people of Santa Fe? If the alcalde is telling the truth, they'll resist the rebels this time. He glances at Donaciano Vigil, who sits beside him with an expressionless face. Where would his loyalties be in such a fight?

Gonzales's eyes flick back to the portal, past the two alcaldes to Albino Chacón, who's studying the ground again. This is the man who will suffer the most from a battle for the capital. He and people like Gertrudis Barceló.

The governor's gaze drops. His hands rest lightly on the saddle's pommel, the long leather reins loose between his fingers. He can turn in an instant and career out of town, north to Ramona and the insurrectos of Santa Cruz, Don Fernando, and elsewhere. If the opinions of El Coyote and Pablo Montoya truly reflect the population, their neighbors will rise when called on. All they need is a demonstration that their governor is still more Indian than Spanish.

But holding that position has already changed the way Gonzales thinks. It wouldn't be dignified to flee. And it could be counterproductive in the long run. For a moment, he's a cibolero again, studying the herd of buffalo before him, considering which way it will turn.

"You would do well to come quietly," the alcalde says again, more insistently this time.

Gonzales purses his lips. "Where is it you plan to take me?"

The other man jerks his head toward the door behind him. "There is room for prisoners as well as the governor here in the palacio. The document containing your oath to uphold the agreement at Tomé waits inside for your signature."

Gonzales's jaw tightens. Uphold an agreement he didn't help create? It's such a rico way of doing things. He turns toward the men who watch from the flagpole. They stare back at him, waiting to see what will happen. His eyes shift to the soldiers in front of the portal. Their grip shifts on their weapons and their feet adjust, ready for action. He's trapped. If he tries to flee now, a lance will find his back.

Then his face relaxes. Only ricos would be foolish enough to believe a man swore such an oath willingly. And a coerced oath does not bind the one forced to speak it.

He swings from the saddle, brushes past the alcaldes, and strides into the palacio one more time.

CHAPTER 9

Mid–Late September 1837: A Gift For Words
(Manuel Armijo)

Manuel Armijo positions himself in front of one of the big gilt-edged mirrors in the Nuevo México governor's room and adjusts the plume on his bicorne hat. He's not only Interim Governor, he's Commandant. Head of the presidio troops as well as New Mexico's militia. He needs to look the part, especially since the rebels have once again moved south out of Santa Cruz de la Cañada.

He scowls at the mirror. Damned insurrectos. If they would just stay quiet for another month or so, he'd have more than enough soldiers to deal with them. The Chihuahua commander will send the necessary troops and it will all be over. But no, the idiot rebels had to stir themselves up again before he has the necessary men and equipment to meet them.

Armijo's eyes narrow at the image in the mirror. The hat isn't perfectly straight. As he adjusts it, Donaciano Vigil appears in the open doorway. Armijo frowns officiously.

"Excuse me, Your Excellency," the newly reappointed secretary of state says. He proffers a carefully sealed letter. "A response has come from Judge Pino."

"Ah." Armijo starts toward him, then changes his mind and goes to the large oak desk at the far end of the room. He positions himself behind it and rest his hands lightly on the newly polished surface. "You have not opened it?"

"No, Excellency." Vigil moves up the room and places the letter on the desk.

Armijo stares at it. He sent Pino a request early yesterday, begging him to take command of the loyalist troops. After all, the judge is a man experienced in negotiation, one who's known for fighting corruption wherever he finds it, speaking his mind regardless of the potential consequences. The rebels will trust him almost in spite of themselves. And, if the situation does come to bloodshed, it'll be on his hands, not Armijo's.

But will Pino do what the interim governor has asked? He's at his place in Galisteo, which is about seven leagues southeast. A rider on a fast horse could have brought his answer long since, if it was positive.

However, Vigil is watching. A leader must look decisive, no matter how anxious he feels. Armijo picks up the missive and carefully slits it open, then sinks into the big chair behind him. The extra pounds he's added these last few years make standing for any length of time uncomfortable. He glances up at Vigil. "The air here in Santa Fe is insalubrious to my old leg injury," he says.

Vigil nods, his face noncommittal. "Is there anything else?"

Armijo waves a hand toward a chair by the fireplace. "You might as well remain while I examine this piece of correspondence. It will undoubtedly demand further action." He looks down at Pino's message. There's the obligatory greeting, then— He scans to the end. A growl rises in his throat despite his best effort to suppress it.

Vigil looks up. "Bad news, Excellency?" he asks sympathetically.

"He says he is indisposed, that he wasn't trained as a military man, and that he knows nothing of battle tactics." Armijo tosses the letter onto the desk. Idiot. Coward. The judge doesn't want the paisanos turning against him when their friends and family members die. That's his real reason for refusing.

But Armijo can't say any of these things. He must restrain himself. Think. "It was my hope that his gift for words and his reputation for honesty would make what he calls 'battle tactics' unnecessary," he says, trying to keep the petulance from his voice.

"But you have those attributes as well, if not more so than the judge."

Armijo's eyes narrow. Is that sarcasm? It's always difficult to tell with Donaciano Vigil. However, the broad face is as bland as ever and there's no amusement or anything else in those dark eyes. No apparent reference to the complications of Armijo's administration in the late 1820s: the American trappers and their complaints about his integrity.

"Judge Pino's presence during discussions with the insurgents would have been beneficial," the commandant responds mildly. He leans back and suddenly realizes he's still wearing his hat. He takes it off and turns it in his hands, studying the curving white plume.

"Just before the letter came, I received another report on the rebel movements," Vigil says. "There are about three thousand of them camped in the hills five leagues north of here, near the ruins of Cuyumungue." He hesitates, then adds, "Our scout spotted Pueblo warriors among them, despite the fact that you told them to stay home. There seem to be about three hundred."

173

Armijo scowls. He places the hat on the desk. "All from Santo Domingo, no doubt."

"He couldn't get close enough to tell." The secretary shifts slightly in his seat. "However, he did meet someone who confirmed that Pablo Montoya is leading the overall force."

"The rebels are expanding their range of influence," Armijo observes. "Montoya is one of those genízaros from Abiquiu."

The secretary's face is carefully neutral again. "That may be. He seems to have moved to Taos."

"Unfortunately, many of his men are related to citizens here in the capital as well as down river," Armijo continues in a more thoughtful tone. "Our Nuevo México family ties are so widespread that it is inappropriate to institute open conflict with the rebels as we would los indios bárbaros, the Navajo or Comanche." He spreads his hands, palms up. "We must seek to conciliate, not conquer. Indeed, although our words may be supported by weapons, we must resort to arms only in the event of the most dramatic of catastrophes. As a last desperate measure."

Vigil's lips twitch slightly at the rhetoric, then his face smooths out again. "It is as you say," he says. "I pray there is no need for more bloodshed."

Armijo pushes himself from his chair and begins pacing the length of the room. "The first volley in our bloodless campaign must be a communication to Pablo Montoya. One he can have read aloud to his forces." He passes a mirror and his eyes narrow at his reflection. He runs his fingers through his black hair. There's still plenty of it, even if he is almost fifty.

"A proclamation?" Vigil asks.

"No, I don't believe so. For the time being, I shall send a mere letter. However—" He reaches the door and turns back toward the desk, his eyes on the vigas as he thinks it through. "It is imperative that we dispatch several copies of said letter, each by a different messenger and all of them unsealed." His eyes crinkle in amusement as he drops them to Vigil. "I desire most heartily that this important correspondence make it through the rebel lines to its intended destination."

The secretary chuckles.

Armijo reaches the desk and settles into his chair. "It is exceedingly evident that many innocent persons have been beguiled into participating in this rebellion. I would not wish them to be injured or killed as a result of the untruths they've been told. The knowledge of my deep concern for the well-being of my countrymen may well induce them to turn away from their misapprehensions." He smiles beguilingly. "After all, more flies gather for a drop of honey than for a hundred drops of bile." Then his face hardens. "Let the negotiations begin."

~ ~ ~ ~

And so they do. Pablo Montoya appears more than willing to remain camped among the rocks and sand hills near the old pueblo north of the capital to receive Armijo's letters. He can't seem to resist responding to subsequent messages, as Armijo skillfully addresses the rebels' concerns without suggesting concrete solutions to any of them, and takes every opportunity to remind Montoya of the superiority of the loyalists' training, funding, and arms.

175

Although there's no evidence that the number of rebels has been reduced by Armijo's disinformation campaign, he's still satisfied with it. He's taken the initiative and controls the discussion.

After two days of jockeying, he also points out that José Angel Gonzales is technically still the rebels' supreme commander. Pablo Montoya should be explaining himself to him, not Armijo. After all, placing the insurrecto camp so close to the capital puts Gonzales's life at risk. If they attack, he will die.

In response to this observation, Montoya sends a missive for Gonzales. Armijo smiles complacently when he shows it to the prisoner. "They place your life at great risk," he says.

The rebel governor turns away and stares at the room's pitted adobe wall. Armijo reaches out and pats his shoulder. "Do not fear," he says. "We will arrange it between us."

He turns to leave, his lips twitching with satisfaction, the words of his next message to the camp already forming in his head. Now that Gonzales understands the danger in which his compañeros have placed him, it's time to invite Pablo Montoya and his friends to the palacio. Time to meet face-to-face and inspire a little anxiety in them, as well as their jefe.

But they aren't easily inspired. Montoya enters the commandant's office first. He's followed by Alcalde Esquibel, Antonio Abad and Desiderio Montoya, the scar-faced El Quemado Vigil who injured Manuel Aponte so badly at La Mesilla, and others Armijo doesn't recognize.

He awaits them in the chair behind his desk. He's had all the other seats removed. The room is stark without Francisco Sarracino's mirrors, which he retrieved yesterday. The newcomers cluster in the rectangular space, politely take off their

176

hats, and stand watching him. Armijo's lips twitch with satisfaction.

"I summoned you here this morning—" he begins.

"We were invited." Antonio Abad Montoya is behind the others, but he's tall enough to see Armijo. He scowls at the governor. "We came of our own free will, as free men who have a right to say what we think."

Armijo gives him an overly patient look, as one would a child. "We are meeting together this morning to determine how we may best accomplish a peaceful coexistence for the people of Nuevo México—" The men in his audience glance at each other and adjust their stance as if preparing themselves for a long speech.

Then the door behind them opens. Captain José Caballero enters the room. His hair may be streaked with gray, but his height and erect stance give him an authority that stiffens the rebels' spines. Or maybe it's just the uniform. The left corner of his cape is tossed back over his shoulder and his right hand rests on his sword. He removes his hat with the left, makes a sweeping bow to Armijo, then steps smartly across the room and stations himself along the whitewashed wall. The other officers of the presidio follow him in, including Donaciano Vigil in his sargento uniform. They spread themselves around the edges of the room, hands behind their backs, gazing steadily forward.

Armijo lets his gaze drift from Caballero to the cluster of rebels, who've pulled closer together in the center of the room. Antonio Abad looks mutinous, but the others are more stunned than angry.

"I believe you are all acquainted with the presidio officers," Armijo says. He stands from the chair and tucks a hand into his waistcoat, Napoleon style.

"We met some of them at La Mesilla," Antonio Abad answers. Pablo chuckles at this and the shoulders of the rebels seem to relax and yet grow more defiant at the same time. After all, they won that fight.

"Under different leadership," Armijo says dryly.

"If I may, Excellency?" Captain Caballero asks.

Armijo nods. Caballero turns toward the rebels, but his eyes focus on Pablo. "Please rest assured that I and my men have no desire to meet you again on the field of battle. We wish only for a peaceful resolution to this crisis."

"That's because we'd beat you again." It isn't Antonio Abad's voice. Perhaps Esquibel's? Armijo's lips tighten. His fingers impatiently drum the desk. Then he forces his expression back into its habitual smoothness, spreads his hands, palms up, and moves his gaze slowly across the group of rebels, making eye contact with each of them.

"Mis amigos," he says. "I wish above all things to avoid bloodshed. Everyone in this room springs from the same soil. We are all the descendants of men and women who ventured north together into the wilds and struggled valiantly side by side to establish themselves in a strange land and to create a way of life in which we can coexist in peace."

He makes a welcoming gesture, as if pulling the rebels towards himself. "Come, let us reason together and facilitate a solution to the issues that have created this dissension among us." His gaze settles on Pablo. "In the recent correspondence with which you honored me, you expressed yourself most eloquently, my friend."

Antonio Abad glares at him over the heads of the others. Armijo has gone too far. Everyone here knows Pablo has no skill with words.

The interim governor forges smoothly on, his eyes still fixed on the rebel leader. "You have expressed a deep concern about the potential new taxes."

"Potential?" Esquibel snaps from the middle of the group. "They're as certain as death!"

Armijo allows himself a small, mischievous smile. "Nothing is certain in this life, mi amigo. Not if the correct individual is guiding events." He pauses, glances around the room, then continues blandly. "But if that individual is to be successful in arranging circumstances in a way which is beneficial to all, they must be accorded the respect they deserve as a duly appointed representative of the National Congress and President."

Esquibel pushes himself forward. "No more appointments!" He jabs a finger into the air. "We must return to the free election of our representatives!"

The other men nod. "Our alcaldes must be elected by their vecinos," someone adds.

"That's right." Desiderio Montoya moves forward. He runs one hand through his long curly black hair and slaps his hat against his leg with the other. "No more appointments! Only elections!" These are clearly slogans that have been repeated more than once in the rebel camp. The young man's eyes shine with enthusiasm as the others nod their agreement.

Armijo looks away. His fingers twitch against the side of his leg. The governorship has always been an appointed office, as have Nuevo México's judges. "I apprehend your

179

concern," he says smoothly. He lets his eyes roam over the rebels' faces. Perhaps because of their excitement, they've let down their guard and moved slightly away from each other and toward his desk.

"Undoubtedly, there ought to be a mechanism which allows each community to voice its opinion as part of the mechanism for identifying the appropriate alcalde or prefect and so forth," he says.

The rebels nod warily. Armijo spreads his hands. "You see? Our differences are easily dealt with. It's only a matter of coming to me peaceably." He smiles benevolently. "After all, we are all family here."

He's rewarded with a few tentative smiles. He stands, moves from behind the desk and positions himself at one end. "And now that we are in concurrence, we must discuss how best to maintain the strength of our agreement on all sides."

Antonio Abad eyes him suspiciously. "What exactly is it that we've agreed to?"

Armijo spreads his hands again. "Why, that you, mis vecinos of the North, will disperse to your homes and crops while I do my utmost to elevate your concerns to the highest officials in our most gracious government." He looks at Pablo, who's watching him with narrowed eyes. "This is, after all, the outcome for which you expressed such an ardent desire," he says. "A resolution to the dissension between us."

The rebel leader frowns. "Taxes!" he says. "Taxes and representation!"

"And the end of church fees," El Quemado adds.

They're so single-minded. Armijo suppresses a flash of irritation and forces himself to chuckle as he focuses on the man's scarred face. "As all of us know, the government has no jurisdiction over religious fees. That is a matter you must address with the priests."

Pablo's face tightens. "We've done that."

Armijo manages to throw real concern into his expression and voice. "And have you reached a resolution that satisfies your concerns?" When the other man nods reluctantly, he says, "Ah, excellent! Most excellent!" He looks around the room. "Then all that remains is to identify those who will act as security for the good behavior of your compañeros."

The rebel leader frowns. "Security?"

This time, Armijo allows a little impatience into his voice. "Your letters expressed a desire for the release of José Angel Gonzales. As you know, he is being held here in the palacio as surety against the unlikely event that foolish and uninformed men will seek once again to shed the blood of their countrymen."

He glances around the room. He has their full attention now. "In a gesture of magnanimity, I have not pursued official charges against José Angel, although there are most certainly grounds for doing so. The man led a traitorous rebellion against our beloved country, one which resulted in the deaths of many illustrious officials."

Antonio Abad stirs irritably. Armijo holds up a warning hand. "Whatever you or I may feel about the righteousness of Gonzales's actions, in the halls of power in Mexico City, he is considered a perverse and indefatigable traitor. I have every cause to continue to hold him."

"He has repented of his deeds," Pablo says.

Armijo's eyes narrow. And how would he know that? Have los insurrectos been communicating outside official channels? But he decides not to pursue the matter. "I concur with your belief that he is no longer a threat to the security of the nation," he says smoothly. "It is also evident to me that those of you who fought at La Mesilla did so for what you believed at the time to be the good of Nuevo México. However, it is manifest to me that you now understand the error of your ways and repent of the bloodshed which occurred as a result. Certainly, your presence here today demonstrates your chagrin at your participation in that fateful event."

He glances around the room. They seem softened by this statement. Less wary. Or perhaps simply confused. It's time to come to the point. "Be that as it may," he continues, "the central government of our fair land requires some among you to stand bond for the continued beneficent behavior of your compañeros."

"Bond?" Antonio Abad spits. "So you want money?"

"No, no, you misunderstand me." Armijo's fingers flick against his trousers. He tucks his hand back inside his waistcoat. "It is simple enough. It is paramount to retain the most prominent of your men in custody as an assurance that there will be no further disruption of Nuevo México's peace." He pauses, letting the idea settle. "Men such as José Angel Gonzales, who I have been informed you would like to have released, and your leader Pablo Montoya, of course."

A kind of tremor runs through the little group in the center of the room. Pablo stares at Armijo, while his companions glance uneasily at each other.

Armijo's palm itches. He's so close. He plunges on. "It goes without saying that the authority to determine who will be restrained and who will go home lies solely in my hands. If I choose to allow it, other men may take the place of the two I have named." He lets this sink in before he continues. "However, given the stature of the men I have mentioned and their value in the eyes of the officials in la Ciudad de México, it would be appropriate for both Pablo and José Angel to be replaced by more than one man. Two each would suffice."

There is silence in the center of the room. None of them look at each other. Armijo's lips twitch with satisfaction.

"Of course, not just any two men will do," he continues. "The men chosen must be people of consequence. Men known by Mexico City as having been active in early August. Men willing to accept their role as spokesmen for the concerns of their neighbors as we of Nuevo México move forward together toward a peaceful coexistence."

The rebels look at each other uneasily. Even the implied promise that those who stay behind will speak for the insurgency isn't a selling point. Prison in Santa Fe is not a laughing matter, especially when there's no telling how long the confinement might go on.

"The men who volunteer for such a responsibility will be protecting your leaders," Armijo continues. "They will be heroes among their vecinos because they have protected José Angel Gonzales and Pablo Montoya, who will undoubtedly be safer well away from the capital. Many citizens here are unhappy about incidents which occurred during the rebel occupation, the death of beloved officials, the taking of goods without payment, and so forth, and hold them responsible." His gaze locks onto Desiderio Montoya's. "It would be a kind and loyal action to take their place."

Desiderio turns to his brother. "We together can replace Don Pablo."

Antonio Abad frowns.

"For the cause," Desiderio says.

Antonio Abad's frown deepens, but he nods his agreement.

"And for José Angel Gonzales?" Armijo asks blandly. "For the man who acted so nobly and gave himself up so willingly after the Plan of Tomé?"

Alcalde Esquibel lifts a hand. "I will stand for Don José Angel."

Armijo smiles at him benevolently. "You are an excellent and honorable man, mi amigo. I have always said so." Inside his waistcoat, his fingers twitch against his chest. Another. He needs another. He forces his eyes to move blandly from one rebel to another. "Unfortunately, our illustrious government officials in la Ciudad de México will ask me why there is only one man to replace the commander of La Mesilla. It will be difficult to explain that no valued man of arms willingly volunteered to stand in for the cibolero Gonzales."

El Quemado Vigil steps forward, the burn scars vivid against his brown skin. "I will do it."

Armijo's fingers stop twitching. He suppresses his relieved exhalation and turns toward Captain Caballero. "If you will kindly see these men to their rooms and release José Gonzales from his, then our conference may come to an end."

Caballero's lips twitch as he salutes. Armijo's not sure if he's impressed or annoyed. But the captain moves quickly enough away from the wall and toward Esquibel. Someone else is already at El Quemado's elbow and the Montoya brothers are moving toward Sergeant Vigil, whose habitual mask has slipped for a moment. He looks as if he'd like to hit somebody, and not a rebel.

Armijo turns away. He doesn't really care if his men approve of what he's done. He removes his hand from his waistcoat and begins circulating through the remaining insurrectos, clapping this one on the shoulder, shaking another one's hand, asking after a third's mother.

He has accomplished his task, and with only a gift for words. The relief is almost unbearable. He must reward himself tonight with that special bottle of brandy from El Paso. And perhaps a visit to an americano merchant tomorrow to replace Sarracino's mirrors.

CHAPTER 10

October 1837: Doubtful Safety

(The Perea Family)

Francisco's mother is furious. He can glimpse her ahead and to the right, when he leans sideways to peer around his Uncle Leandro's shoulders. She's seated on cushions in the back of a cumbersome two-wheeled carreta, cradling baby José Ynes. The hooves of the brown-spotted ox pulling the cart have raised a cloud of dust. Her head and shoulders are swathed against it in her blackest rebozo, so Francisco can't see her face, but he still knows she's angry. Her back is straight as an arrow, despite the lurching cart.

She didn't want to leave Bernalillo for Santa Fe. It's too far to drag a six-month-old infant and she doesn't believe the Perea hacienda beside the river is in any danger from los insurrectos of Río Arriba. There's little likelihood they'll venture so far south, almost to Alburquerque. Furthermore, if Francisco's father and uncle and grandfather would stay home where they belong, there'd be no danger from Navajos or anyone else.

Her brother Mariano Chávez is in Santa Fe, of course. He's Manuel Armijo's second in command, in recognition of his past position as interim governor and as a result of his impulsive nomination of Armijo as commandant, or governor, or whatever the man's calling himself these days. She still doesn't understand why Mariano dragged his family to the capital with him. He could have just as easily left them south of Alburquerque at Los Padillas or even with her at Bernalillo. Surely it's safe enough.

In her opinion, the safety of Santa Fe, on the other hand, is doubtful. Especially now, when it's full of soldiers and the chaos they carry with them. Besides, the rebels are more likely to attack there than anywhere else. If her husband and his brother and father had any sense, they and everyone connected with them would stay at home where they belong. But no one listens to her, of course. She's a mere woman.

That's how she wound down last night. Thinking about it now, seven-and-a-half-year-old Francisco grins and digs his chin into Tío Leandro's shoulder to keep from laughing out loud. His mother is one of the most powerful people he knows. That's why she's so furious. The Perea men won this particular argument and she's not used to losing. Francisco leans forward again, stifling his laughter.

His uncle jerks away from Francisco's chin. "Stop doing that. You have a sharp face."

"Lo siento," Francisco says, more or less apologetically. Leandro may be only fourteen, but he's still his tío. And he's been to the capital before. At least twice. "What is Santa Fe like, uncle?" Francisco asks.

"It's just a town of peones and politicians."

"I suppose Mamá will insist that we rent a house and live in a civilized manner."

"Given the number of families also following the militia north, she may not be able to find anything, and then we'll be forced to stay with Mariano and María Lavinia."

Francisco groans dramatically.

"What's the matter? Don't you like your cousin José Francisco?"

187

"I wish we didn't have the same name, but I don't mind him. He's only four. But when they stopped in Bernalillo on their way north, Mamá's bossy little sister was with them."

"You mean Longina? She isn't so bad."

"She's eleven, which means she's older than me and thinks she can tell me what to do. And when she and my sisters get together, life is a misery." His voice rises. "All she and Rufina and Petra do is order me around! And because she's my tía, she's the worst of them all! As if she's a queen!"

On the dusty road ahead, his mother's black-clad form turns toward Francisco's voice. He ducks behind his uncle's back.

Leandro chuckles and waves cheerfully at his sister-in-law. After a long minute, he says, "You can look now. She's turned away. Though I think she's still indignada, so I advise obedience and caution whenever possible."

Francisco shudders dramatically and Leandro chuckles again. "You'll like Santa Fe," he says. "There's always something going on in the plaza." His tone turns thoughtful. "And there should be people there with wool fleeces to sell. And buy."

"What else?"

Leandro chuckles. "There's money to be made. That's all I need to know. But I'm sure you have other questions."

José Francisco grins and proceeds to ask another one. He doesn't stop until they halt to camp for the night on the rocky, cactus-strewn plain at the foot of La Bajada. His tío heads off to help with the animals and Francisco tries to make himself useful around the fire.

His mother is still irritable. After the evening meal, she seats herself on a large rock at the edge of the firelight, tucks José Ynes under her rebozo to nurse, and frowns at her husband. "We shouldn't be stopping here. It's too close to the pueblos. We may have circled around Santo Domingo, but we're still within an easy ride of that nest of treachery. We could all be murdered in our beds."

Francisco's father crosses his arms and gazes at her impassively. She scowls and twitches the edge of the rebozo farther over the baby's head. "Not that we have beds to sleep on."

Her father-in-law stumps into the firelight, Francisco's younger brother Joaquín trailing behind. She frowns at the five-year-old, then Francisco. "Go get your blankets and bring them back here."

The boys' shoulders slump. They don't want to sleep by the fire like the girls. They want to bed down at the edge of camp near the animals and the wagons of household goods, beside Tío Leandro and the other men travelling with them.

However, they both know better than to complain when their mother's in this mood. They spread their sleeping rolls on the other side of the fire from the girls and put their heads together, whispering in the dark and watching orange sparks fly upward.

"What will Santa Fe be like?" Joaquín asks, and Francisco repeats what Leandro has told him—people everywhere, a plaza filled with animals and freight wagons, a gambling game called monte, and a wheel people use for betting.

"And it's crowded," he finishes. "We might have to stay with Tío Mariano and Tía Lavinia."

189

"Oh no!" Joaquín covers his face dramatically. "Anything but Longina, Rufina, and Petra in one house for more than two days!"

"José Francisco will be there," his brother points out. "So it will be three against three."

Joaquín grimaces. "He's only four. He won't be much help!"

"Will you stop talking?" Rufina grumbles from across the fire.

The five-year-old covers his ears. "It's starting already!"

~ ~ ~ ~

Both boys recover their good humor over the next two days. The closer they get to Santa Fe, the more there is to see. Small groups of soldiers camp between the walled compounds that hug the road. In the fields, people gather the last of the pumpkins, and goats and sheep browse among what remains of the cornstalks. The youngsters responsible for the animals wave at the passersby and the Perea children wave back.

Francisco feels a burst of pride at his family's little caravan. His gray-haired but still stalwart grandfather, Pedro José de los Dolores Perea, rico of Bernalillo and member of Nuevo México's ruling council, rides at the head of his wagons, family, and retainers. He nods gravely to the various people they meet on the road, but he doesn't stop to chat. Francisco's father, Juan Dolores, rides beside him.

The brown-walled adobe houses begin to appear more frequently. Then the road turns east and the walls become connected, blocking it in. There are sounds ahead, of oxen lowing, donkeys braying. And people. A low murmur and occasional shouts. Is it a matanza? Francisco peers around his tío's shoulder, trying to see past his mother's carreta and his grandfather's and father's horses.

"It's the Santa Fe plaza," Leandro says over his shoulder. A shiver of excitement tightens Francisco's chest.

Then his grandfather and father reach what seems to be a wide spot in the road. Don Pedro raises an arm. The Perea wagons and animals grind to a halt. Francisco clutches his uncle's shirt and leans farther out. Beyond his abuelo's horse is the back end of a big wagon. And a donkey. A whole cluster of them, from the sound of it. Leandro clicks his heels against his mount's side and they edge closer.

This puts them beside the carreta. There's a lump under Francisco's mother's rebozo where the baby is sleeping. She clutches it as she twists irritably toward the front of the cart. "I can't see a thing," she grumbles.

Leandro's horse is taller than the ox hitched to the cart, but Francisco's view is still pinched by the buildings on either side of the outlet and blocked by his grandfather and father. He leans farther out, teetering dangerously. "There are wagons," he tells his mother. "Carretas like ours and also large covered ones with four wheels that look like boats."

Leandro nods. "Those are the ones the americano traders use to bring goods from the East."

"I'm surprised any of the americanos are still here," Francisco's mother says. "If they had any sense, they'd be back in Missouri by now. Francisco, stop twisting around like that. You're going to fall off if you're not careful." As she speaks, the carreta lurches sideways. Her grip tightens on Ynes. "Good heavens! What was that?"

191

A pig grunts as it passes, then another one bumps the cart. It's a fat mamá puerco, followed by two stoats. One of them stops to poop. Francisco's mother wrinkles her nose in disgust. Francisco buries his chin in his uncle's back and tries not to laugh.

"Filthy beasts," his mother mutters. She shakes her head. "I knew this was a bad idea."

Up ahead, Don Pedro gives a shout and waves his hand, motioning the little caravan forward. The ox begins to move, the carreta lurches into action, and the Perea family inches into the Santa Fe plaza.

They angle toward the far northeast corner and a cluster of three rangy mountain cottonwoods. Francisco twists his head from side to side, trying to take in everything at once. There are more americano covered wagons, simple ones like those carrying his family's household goods, and carretas the size of his mother's, though these contain everything from firewood to baby goats to piles of shaggy wool fleeces.

And there are people. More than Francisco's ever seen in one place. Teamsters, americano merchants in smooth suits, Pueblo men in blankets and wrapped leggings, Nuevo México ladies in fine dresses. Children run this way and that. Soldiers go to and fro, with and without weapons, and wind their way between the mules, burros, oxen, and pigs. Some people have set up camp right in the plaza. Off to his right, an old woman with a black rebozo on her shoulders stirs a pot that smells of red chile and pork.

The boy's stomach grumbles. Then he tilts his head. She doesn't look like the type of person who would sleep outside. Doesn't she have a house and courtyard of her own? Is she a refugee, too, but without a place to stay?

Hope touches his chest. There are so many people here. Maybe others who are also related to his tío Mariano have arrived before the Pereas. Maybe the house is already full and there isn't room for more. Or there's only room for the adults and the girls. His eyes brighten. If that happens, he and Joaquín and the other Francisco will be forced to sleep out of doors. Or at least with the animals.

They pass a tall pole with the national flag flapping at its top. Leandro pokes Francisco with an elbow and points left, toward a long adobe building with a bunch of doors shaded by a long covered porch. People come in and out of the doors on the left, the ones close together. "Those are the rooms where the presidio soldiers and their families live," Leandro says over his shoulder. "On the other side is the palacio, where His Excellency Governor Manuel Armijo lives. The guard house is there too and behind it the calabozo where prisoners are kept."

Francisco nods. The cluster of trees they've been heading for is at the far end of the building. More Pueblan women sit beneath them with baskets of corn, bread, and other food for sale. Francisco's stomach growls again. Tío Leandro's horse moves to the right and he has a moment of hope that they'll go ahead of the others and get something to eat.

But Leandro is only trying to get closer to the carreta and Francisco's mother. She's twisting this way and that. Her frown is anxious now, instead of angry. She looks up at her brother-in-law. "Where did Juan Dolores go?" she asks. Her eyes light on Francisco. "And where are your brother and sisters?"

193

Francisco is about to protest that he's not responsible for his siblings when his father's tall horse appears at the end of the street that heads east from just beyond the cottonwoods.

"Papá is right there," he says, pointing.

She twists, but she can't turn far enough to see. "I hate this cart," she grumbles.

But then his father trots toward them and looks down at her. "The casa is halfway down that street ahead," he says. "Mariano has found two houses, side by side, with an adjoining courtyard."

She allows herself a small smile. "You mean Lavinia has found them and Mariano has paid the rent, of which we will contribute our share."

His eyes twinkle. "My sister is a very efficient woman. There will be plenty of room for us all." He grins at Francisco. "Even for the boys."

Francisco wrinkles his nose and his father chuckles and turns back to the carreta. "If your carriage will follow me, milady."

She narrows her eyes at him, but her lips twitch in amusement, not annoyance. Francisco's heart lifts and he jiggles in anticipation. "This will be fun," he says to Leandro's back as they begin moving again.

However, before the midday meal is over, he's not so sure about that. His blue-eyed cousin José Francisco Chávez is almost half Francisco's age, but he's latched onto Joaquín and himself and he doesn't intend to let go. When the Chávezes passed through Bernalillo on the way north, the four-year-old had been tired from the journey and not very talkative or active. He's apparently recovered completely,

194

because he's full of energy and ideas and they all seem child-ish to the almost-eight Francisco.

After the meal, the two younger boys run into the shared adobe-walled courtyard and immediately begin a game of "who's the noisiest chicken?" Francisco slumps onto a bench along the wall and glumly watches them run in circles around the beehive-shaped adobe cook oven as they squawk and flap their arms at each other.

Then his gloom is interrupted by a girl's voice asking, "What are you doing?"

He knows who it is before he looks up. His scowl deep-ens. Tía María Dolores Longina Chávez, otherwise known as La Mandona, the bossy girl, stands at the end of the bench. As usual, her hands are on her hips, her hair is in careful brown ringlets, and her dark eyes are bright with disapprov-al.

He gestures towards his brother and cousin. "I'm watch-ing them."

"They don't need to be watched. They're inside the court-yard."

"One of them might fall."

"We need more wood for the kitchen fire."

"Get it yourself."

"Josefa said to tell you to bring it."

One of the things he hates most about Longina is that she calls his mother by her first name. Yes, they're sisters, but it still sounds disrespectful. "Get it yourself," he says again.

"Well!" she huffs. Then she whirls and heads for the house. He goes back to watching his brother and cousin. They have sticks in their hands now and are pretending to be fighting cocks, though they're jabbing the air more than they are each other.

His mother appears in the doorway, the baby in her arms. "José Francisco Perea!" she snaps.

His spine straightens. He can't help it. It always does when she uses that tone. Especially when it's accompanied by his full name. Longina peers around her, smirking, and he sticks his tongue out at her.

"That will be enough!" his mother says. "I sent Longina out to tell you to bring in wood because I didn't have the time and energy to come tell you myself! And yet here I am!"

He drops his eyes.

"Do I need to tell you myself?"

"No, Mamá."

"The next time she tells you I said to do something, you will do it! Do you hear me?"

"Yes, Mamá."

She whirls and is gone. La Mandona stays behind, one hand on her hip, smirking triumphantly.

Francisco scowls, gets up, and heads to the woodpile. He carries an armload inside and is immediately given other chores. He helps reposition the long table in the sala, then shifts boxes and blankets from one room to another. He breathes a sigh of relief when he's sent outside again to stack the firewood that's been delivered while he was in the house. He doesn't like stacking wood but he'd rather do that than be indoors.

~ ~ ~ ~

Two mornings later, he and Joaquín are taking care of yet another firewood delivery when the military officers arrive. Don Pedro must have known they were coming, because he opens the gate for them himself. The tall young man in the blue coat and flat-brimmed black hat stays near the entrance, but the other two move with the boys' grandfather toward the bench and stand next to it, talking in low voices.

Francisco and his brother stop what they're doing and stare openly. Their abuelo looks up and catches them looking, but instead of frowning at their rude behavior, he beckons them closer. "Come chamacos," he says.

He turns to his visitors. The short stout man has taken off his helmet and tucked it under one arm. Its long black horsehair tail streams behind him, almost touching the ground. The man shifts it slightly and gives the children a friendly smile.

The other man is tall and has gray-streaked hair. He stands so straight, you would know he was a soldier even if he wasn't in uniform. He glances at the boys and looks away as they approach. Their grandfather puts his hands on their shoulders. "These are my grandsons, José Francisco and Joaquín Perea, los hijos of my son Juan Dolores," he says.

The men nod to the children, the short one with a smile, the other with a cool stare. "Children, this is Captain Pedro José Muñoz of the Vera Cruz dragoons and Captain José Caballero of the Santa Fe presidio. These are the men who are keeping us safe from los insurrectos."

Captain Muñoz chuckles and turns toward the man by the gate. "Please do not pass that sentiment on to Commandant Armijo, Don Donaciano," he says with a grin.

The other man's eyes twinkle at him, "Never fear. My motto is always 'hear, see, and be silent'." Then he catches Captain Caballero's stony eye and his gaze drops.

Captain Caballero turns to the boys' grandfather. "We have much to discuss, Don Pedro."

"Of course, of course!" He gestures toward the house. "Please, come in!"

Francisco and Joaquín turn back to their work as the men head to the door, the younger one trailing behind. At the threshold, Captain Caballero stops and turns. "Sargento Vigil, you will remain in the courtyard."

Captain Muñoz and Don Pedro look at him in surprise and the sergeant opens his mouth as if to argue, then drops his gaze and nods. "Yes, sir." When the door closes, he moves to a bench, drops onto it, takes off his hat, places it beside him, runs a hand through his wavy black hair, and looks at the ground.

The boys watch him out of the corner of their eyes. They stack a few more pieces of wood, then drift over to the bench and stand in front of him. "Why doesn't he like you?" Joaquín asks tentatively.

Don Donaciano looks up. "I have too many friends and relatives." A smile tugs the corners of his mouth and his shoulders lift in a tiny shrug. "He thinks I'm going to tell los insurrectos in Santa Cruz de la Cañada that Commandant Armijo still isn't certain how many soldiers are coming from Chihuahua or when they'll arrive."

"There are soldiers coming?"

"Yes, but we don't know how many or when they'll get here. If the rebels decided to attack now, they might well succeed in retaking the city."

"But we have the militia, too," Francisco says. "They're all here in Santa Fe instead of at home where they belong." Donaciano Vigil's eyebrows quirk upward and the boy grins. "That's what my mother says."

"She may be right. It's hard to say. Captain Caballero worries that I'll pass word to my connections in La Cañada and los insurrectos will descend on us again." He glances at the house door. "He trusts your abuelo, of course. He's a member of Nuevo México's Council."

The boys stare at him, puzzled by the irony in his voice. He smiles at them apologetically "Don Pedro is a good man. He's as unlikely to help the rebels as I am. But he wasn't captured at La Mesilla and then maneuvered into working for the rebel governor."

The house door opens. In one fluid motion, the sergeant grabs his hat, places it on his head, and stands. The boys cross to the woodpile and go back to work as their grandfather sees the visitors out.

But when he turns from the half-shut gate, Don Pedro doesn't head inside. Instead, he stands watching the boys for a long minute, then crosses to them. They stop what they're doing and look up.

"You are good chamacos," he says gruffly. "I think you deserve a reward for all you've accomplished today and also for how well you've adjusted to life here in Santa Fe."

They haven't actually seen much of Santa Fe. As if he knows what Francisco's thinking, Don Pedro says, "You haven't had an opportunity to explore yet, have you?" He glances up at the sky, then reaches into his vest pocket and keeps his fingers there as he looks at the children. "If you will promise to use good judgment and not go beyond the streets immediately around the plaza, I will tell your mother you are running errands for me and will return by sundown." He pulls out two small silver coins. "This will be enough to buy you each a tortía and bowl of stew on the plaza."

The boys take the coins, their faces splitting with joy. "Now, be good and come back before sundown," their abuelo says, but they're already halfway out the gate before he's finished his sentence.

~ ~ ~ ~

It takes Francisco and Joaquín longer than it should to reach the plaza. The house yards behind half-open gates are so interesting. And then there are the people in the street itself. The men in broad face-shading hats and smaller americano ones. The women wrapped in long rebozos, and the girls in bright skirts and cool-looking blouses.

A carreta filled with chickens in wicker baskets trundles by, its ungreased axles squealing. A boy leads a burro piled with firewood. A pig roots in the dirt, looking for something to eat. A mother cat disappears into an alley with a kitten in her mouth.

Joaquín wants to follow, but Francisco tugs on his elbow. "We're almost to the plaza," he says. "Listen!"

Joaquín's head turns. Indistinct voices, the bawl of an ox, a man's voice rising above the rest. A donkey brays and another one answers it. The boys scamper toward the square, then halt at the corner, near the cluster of trees. The plaza is crowded, but there's no one sitting under the cottonwoods or along the palacio portal, or anyone stirring a pot of stew. Francisco frowns in disappointment. He's hungry.

But then they venture further in, to the first posts that support the portal roof. Joaquín tugs at Francisco's elbow and points to the left, toward an open door.

Sergeant Donaciano Vigil steps into the square. He stands, fist on his hips, studying his surroundings, then turns and moves toward the boys. He sees them and lifts a hand in greeting, but keeps going, angling toward the palacio's big gate. However, he doesn't go inside. Instead he moves down the portal toward the intersecting street beyond.

"I wonder where he's going," Joaquín says.

Francisco shrugs. "I know a way to find out." They grin at each other. There's no one here to tell them they can't follow. No one watching, in spite of the crowd.

They hurry after the sergeant, but by the time the boys reach the end of the building, he's disappeared.

There are more doors on their right, with more people coming in and out under the porch that shades them. The boys don't notice. On the left hand side of the street, a gate stands invitingly half open. Music spills out. Guitars and a violin. Francisco and Joaquín move toward the sound.

Under a portal that spans the far side of the courtyard, two men sit on three-legged stools and strum guitars. A silver-haired man stands behind them, playing a violin. The instruments blend in a tune designed for dancing.

Which is what the girl in the middle of the courtyard is doing. She turns slowly, her eyes closed in concentration. Her hands lift over her head and clap in time to the music. Or is the song responding to her hands? Sunlight sparks her curly brown waist-length hair with gold. The boys move forward, tugged by an invisible thread.

The older of the two guitar players sees them and smiles, then looks back at the girl. The beat increases and she speeds up, twirling in place. Her knee-length full skirt flares around her bare legs and feet.

"¡Olé!" the younger guitar player cries. He twitches his head to flip his black hair out of his eyes, then begins slapping the front of his instrument with his palms, like a drum. The other guitar speeds up and the rhythm increases in both intensity and volume. The dancer twirls faster in response. Joaquín laughs aloud.

She stumbles, losing the beat, and tilts to one side as if she's going to fall. Francisco darts toward her, but she catches herself, and turns toward him.

Francisco's voice catches his throat, then he swallows and says, "Perdóneme." He glances as his brother. "That is, pardon us."

She giggles and covers her mouth with her hand. The younger guitar player trills his fingers across the strings, then thumps the wood one last time, making a loud, triumphant sound, and the music breaks off. The three children laugh, Francisco in relief and sheer joy.

The man with the violin smiles at the boys. "Welcome," he says. Then he glances at the girl. "It is well?"

She smiles and nods and moves toward Francisco and his brother. "You are most welcome," she says shyly. "My name is María Refugio Sisneros and this is the house of my adoptive mother María Gertrudis Barceló." She waves a small brown hand toward the musicians. "These are her friends. Please join us."

Francisco steps forward but Joaquín hangs back. "Grandfather said to stay on the streets near the plaza," he says.

"What is that?" The violin player cups a hand to his ear. "Your grandfather? And what is his name?"

"Our abuelo is Señor Pedro José de los Dolores Perea," Francisco says proudly.

"Ah, Don Pedro, the council member." The man studies the boys. "You must be his son Juan Dolores's children. I heard that you had arrived."

"And with a new brother," the older guitar player says.

María Refugio looks at the boys with new interest. "You have a baby brother?"

Francisco nods.

"I like babies," she says. "We're going to have one here early next year."

The men exchange a glance. "Perhaps our visitors would like something to drink," the violin player says.

"Forgive me." It's a general apology, but with a special smile for Francisco, whose heart flutters in response. His eyes trail her to the door into the house. A shadow seems to cross the sun, then lift when she reappears a few minutes later, followed by a maid with a tray of drinks and bizcochitos.

Then another woman steps from the house. She's wearing what Francisco thinks must be an americana dress. It has sleeves that puff at the top of her arm, a tiny waist, and wide skirts. Her red-tinted black hair is twisted in long curls around her face, with the rest of it in a complicated braided knot at the back.

The men rise when they see her. "Doña Tules," they murmur respectfully.

She smiles and nods at them, then turns to the girl, who takes her by the hand and leads her to Francisco and Joaquín. "Mamá, these are the boys I spoke of," María Refugio says.

Francisco gives the lady a small bow. "We are José Francisco and Joaquín Perea," he says. "The sons of Juan Dolores Perea and Josefa Mercedes Chávez, and the grandsons of Pedro José de los Dolores Perea."

The woman's eyes sparkle as she smiles at the boys. "It is a true pleasure to meet you. I hope you will convey my greetings to your parents and your grandfather."

"They have a new baby brother," Refugio says.

The woman's smile deepens as she looks at the girl. "Perhaps we can arrange for you to visit them and meet him."

The girl looks at the boys. Francisco nods speechlessly. Joaquín stretches onto his toes. "We can go now!" he says.

Doña Tules laughs. "Perhaps not today. I must first pay a call on your mother."

Francisco nods again, still speechless. Her eyes twinkle at him. Then she waves toward the tray the maid has placed on a small table on the portal. "But please, refresh yourselves." She turns to the musicians. "And you also, of course. I must return to my monte table or the players will lose their enthusiasm for the game."

The violin player chuckles and the younger guitar player sweeps his hair from his eyes and laughs. "¡La diligencia es madre de la buena ventura!" he says. He slaps the guitar's wooden body, making it boom.

Doña Tules laughs. "Yes, I have found that to be a true saying. In fact, I believe that diligence is the *only* mother of good fortune." She turns toward the door, then looks back at the boys. "I am most pleased to make your acquaintance." She smiles at the girl. "You did well, niña."

Refugio beams at her, then turns to the men and boys and waves her hand at the tray. "Please, refresh yourselves!"

Francisco and Joaquín each take a cookie and a tumbler of fruit-flavored water and settle onto a bench. The men talk politely for a while, then withdraw into the house. The music begins again, this time inside.

However, Refugio doesn't leave. She sits on a low stool and asks the boys questions. Where do they live? Do they like Santa Fe? How many siblings and cousins do they have? She's so kind and so interested and so sparkling. Francisco could sit here forever.

They talk and talk. Then suddenly, Joaquín pokes Francisco in the side. "Grandfather said to return before sundown."

Francisco looks away from the girl to the sky above the courtyard. It's changed from bright blue to a pale orangey-pink. Shadows have begun to edge the portal. He makes a little face of disappointment and rises to his feet. "We need to go home."

Refugio nods, stands, and puts out her hand to him. "You will come again?"

He can feel his face getting hot. There's a strange lump in his throat. He nods and she smiles at him, then gives her hand to his brother. "And you also, Joaquín?"

The five-year-old grins at her. "If you have cookies again."

Her voice peals with laughter. "Oh, we always have cookies of one kind or another!"

Francisco smiles and pokes his brother in the ribs. "Let's go then," he pretend-grumbles.

Joaquín is still chortling as they leave the gate. Then he stops in his tracks. Francisco, behind him but looking back at Refugio, almost falls over him. "Watch out!" he says.

Then he sees the reason for his brother's abrupt halt.

Longina stands halfway up the street toward the plaza, her hands on her hips. Rufina and María Petra are on either side, staring at the boys with open mouths. "You just wait until I tell your mother where you've been!" Longina says triumphantly. "She'll never let you out of the house again!" She whirls and runs back toward the square, the other girls behind her.

"¡Mandona!" Francisco spits.

Joaquín bites his lower lip. "We were supposed to stay in the plaza," he says in a small voice.

Francisco's chin juts out. "Abuelo said to stay in the streets near the plaza and that's where we were." He glances at the Barceló gate. He hopes Refugio hasn't heard any of this. She's so different from Longina. So sweet and kind. Surely nothing bad can happen because he talked to her.

But it can. At the evening meal, his mother is pale with anger at the news of the boys' escapade, as she calls it. Fortunately, most of her fury is directed at their father. "That is the kind of person who lives in this city!" she hisses at him across the table. "This woman who owns a gambling den, a drinking establishment! Whose daughter is pregnant by some americano who's fled back to Missouri!"

"¿Refugio?" Francisco asks blankly. "A baby?"

His mother waves a hand at him. "Her sister. That is, her foster sister. The Gutierrez girl." Then she frowns. "Did you see her?"

"We met María Refugio Sisneros and Doña Tules."

"The woman's name is María Gertrudis Barceló. Only her fellow gamblers call her Tules!"

"And those of us who have known her since she arrived in Santa Fe over ten years ago," his grandfather says, reaching for another tortía. "Or before that, when she and her family moved to Tomé from Sonora."

Her lips tighten against each other. It's not polite to contradict one's father-in-law. However, she can still let her feelings be known. Her eyes snap at Francisco's father. "Our sons are too young to be visiting such a house!"

"We didn't go inside," Francisco says. He pushes his food aside. He's lost his appetite.

"She said she wanted to come—" Joaquín glances at Francisco. "Give her money? Pay—"

Francisco looks at his mother. "Pay you a call."

His mother scowls at him, then turns abruptly to the maid, who's bringing in the meat. "If María Gertrudis Barceló, otherwise known as Doña Tules, comes to visit, I am not at home!"

"Now Josefa," Francisco's father says. She glares at him, but he continues anyway, though his voice gentles. "If you go on like this, you will only make enemies here, not friends."

Her face is stony. "The only friends I need are my family." She pushes back from the table. "Excuse me. The baby is calling."

At the other end of the table, Rufina and Petra toy with their food and exchange glances. Francisco glowers at them. Though it's not really their fault. It's that stupid Mandona's.

~ ~ ~ ~

207

Francisco's still fuming when Captain Caballero visits again the following week. This is someone his mother approves of. She welcomes the presidio commander with smiles and conversation and cake, tells the maid to make hot chocolate, and sends next door for her husband and father-in-law, who've been visiting with Tío Mariano all morning.

Francisco and Joaquín are in the far corner of the sala helping Tío Leandro clean the dirt and seed burrs out of the long-haired churro fleeces he's bought since they arrived.

Francisco's father gives them a small nod when he and their grandfather come in, but Don Pedro sees only the presidio Captain. "There is news?" he asks as soon as the greetings are over and the men have settled into high-backed chairs at the long table.

The man nods his gray-streaked head. "From Las Truchas."

"The village east of Santa Cruz and Chimayó on the mountain road to Don Fernando de Taos?"

"Sí. It seems the rebels are mobilizing to come south again. I must decide how to respond."

Francisco's mother looks up from the banco, where she's retired with her knitting. Her eyes spark with anger but she doesn't speak. Francisco's father glances at her, then turns back to their visitor with a slight frown. "You must decide? Isn't that Armijo's responsibility?"

The captain shifts in his chair, as if he's suddenly uncomfortable. "The commandant is in Alburquerque, where it's warmer. His leg wound was acting up and he went home." He turns to Francisco's grandfather. "Don Pedro, I've come to ask your opinion, as a member of the Council. It's—" He glances toward the banco and lowers his voice. "It's a delicate situation."

Josefa glares at them, her lips a thin, angry line. She looks at the children in the corner and her mouth twitches in annoyance. Francisco's hands stall in the strands of fiber, waiting to be sent from the room, but her eyes drop to her work.

Leandro tugs on the other side of the fleece to get the boy's attention, then shakes his head slightly and jerks his chin toward the wool. Francisco grins and goes back to work, ears open, mouth shut.

Captain Caballero leans toward Francisco's grandfather. "Before he left, Armijo gave me orders to execute the rebel prisoners if there's further unrest."

Tío Leandro's breath whistles between his teeth. Francisco glances at him. His uncle's own hands are still now, his head tilted toward the table.

"All four of them?" Don Pedro asks.

"Those were his instructions."

"Do you know for certain that the rebels are rising? Could it be a false alarm?"

"Nothing is certain." The captain's weight shifts again. "I fear the consequences of killing the prisoners, especially the alcalde. Such a spark could cause a small fire to become a conflagration."

"The death of four well-loved men would be more than a spark," Francisco's father says drily.

"Perhaps I should send someone to investigate," Caballero says. "Someone leading enough presidio men to convince los insurrectos we mean business, yet not so many as to antagonize them."

There's a long silence. Francisco can't see the men's faces, but he thinks he sees his grandfather nod. Captain Caballero rises from his chair and the others follow him. As he moves toward the door, he nods to Francisco's mother. "Thank you for the refreshments, Doña Josefa," he says politely. He turns to Francisco's abuelo. "And to you, Don Pedro, for your advice."

The old man chuckles. "I offered more questions than advice."

"But you helped me to clarify my thinking and identify a plan of action."

"More importantly, you can be confident Armijo will have someone else to blame if he doesn't like what you've done," Francisco's father says drily.

Don Pedro gives him a warning look, then turns to the captain. "Please let us know what your men discover." He glances toward Francisco's mother, who's sitting in the banco, her knitting in her lap, the expression on her face more sick than angry. He turns back to the presidio commander. "So we may take appropriate action."

Francisco's chest tightens, though he's not sure if it's from excitement or dread. As the men go into the courtyard, his mother rises and leaves the room.

She's very quiet the rest of the day and all of the next. Until the evening meal, when she turns to Francisco's father. "Has there been word yet from Captain Caballero's men?" she asks.

He and Don Pedro exchange glances. "There is no need for concern," Francisco's grandfather says a little grumpily.

Her hands drop to the table and flatten there. She looks from her husband to her father-in-law and back again. "What has happened?"

Francisco's father glances at the children.

Her lips tighten. "This affects them, as well. Tell me."

"Before Caballero could arrange for men to go out to reconnoiter, he received a letter from the new alcalde at Santa Cruz, the one who replaced Esquibel. The insurgents are dividing their forces and plan to march toward Santa Fe from different directions."

She goes very still. The skin around her lips is white. In the corner, baby Ynes begins to fuss. His mother glances at Rufina and she slips away from the table to him.

"Which means that Caballero's men are needed here," Francisco's mother says grimly. "Because he can't protect us from all directions at once." A shiver runs down Francisco's spine.

"Yes," his father says. He opens his mouth to continue, then seems to think better of it.

Rufina brings her the baby. She takes him blindly and clutches him to her chest. "What now?"

The men exchange another look. Her back stiffens. "Tell me!"

"The governor's instructions—"

"To execute the prisoners?" She looks from one man to the other. "But if that happens, the rebels will be even angrier than they already are! Surely Armijo understands that!"

"Nothing has been decided," Don Pedro says reassuringly. "The captain is waiting for further information from the north."

Now it's her turn to open her mouth and close it again without speaking. She looks down at the now-quiet baby, reaches for a tortía, and sits staring at it. The others finish the meal in silence, then the men disappear into Tío Mariano's side of the compound. Francisco's mother goes to her room.

~ ~ ~ ~

But she's present the next day when Captains Caballero and Muñoz arrive. The presidio commander hasn't heard anything more from the north. However, he has received instructions from Armijo. The prisoners are to be executed. The men's faces are anxious as they drop into the armchairs in front of the fire and lean toward each other.

Tío Leandro is on the banco, whittling a weaving shuttle. Francisco's mother hovers near the long table on the other side of the room. Don Pedro turns toward her. "Could you send someone for Mariano? I believe he will wish to hear what the officers have to say."

Then he spots Francisco and Joaquín by the door, playing with a top. He frowns at them, though not unkindly. "Vamos, chamacos, por favor," he says. "This conversation is not for your ears."

They rise reluctantly and go into the courtyard. The toy won't work here. The ground isn't hard and smooth like the floor inside. Francisco moves restlessly. The bright October air seems too cheerful for the news the men are discussing. He stacks a few pieces of firewood, then wanders over to the bench to pet a chicken Joaquín has caught. It pecks at his fingers, looking for food. Francisco chuckles, picks up some sand, and offers it instead. The hen pokes at his palm.

212

The house door opens and Longina comes out. "Don't you have anything useful to do?" she demands.

"Abuelo sent us outside," Francisco says. He tries to sound indifferent but he can't quite keep the bitterness from his voice. "The conversation was too important for us to hear."

She smirks and smooths her skirt. "That's because you're so young." She flips her hair over her shoulders. "It is a woman's place to prepare refreshments and take them to the men. We hear things."

Joaquín releases the hen, who flutters to the ground. "What things?"

She tilts her head to one side. "If you want to know, you'll have to say please."

"Please."

"Say, 'please my beloved aunt.'"

Francisco rolls his eyes. But Joaquín is less stubborn than he is. "Por favor querida tía," he says. He folds his hands together imploringly. "Please."

She smiles complacently and looks at Francisco. "Now you say it."

He glowers at her. She shrugs and turns toward the door. He mutters something under his breath. She turns back. "¿Qué?"

"I said, 'please my beloved aunt.'"

She gives him a slit-eyed disbelieving look, then her face changes to eagerness. She clearly wants to tell them what she's heard. She moves toward the bench and seats herself, a boy on each side. "The governor sent a letter to Captain Caballero, telling him to kill the rebel prisoners."

Francisco frowns. "We heard that part."

213

She tosses her head. Her brown curls bounce in the sun. "But you didn't hear the part about how he doesn't want to and that Don Pedro and Mariano and your father don't want him to, either." She frowns. "I don't understand it. Los insurrectos are murderers and thieves. They should be punished." Then she shrugs. "But Don Pedro and the others have decided the captain and his subordinate officers should send a letter to Governor Armijo, refusing to obey."

The boys stare at her. "But the governor is in charge," Joaquín says. "They have to do what he says. He'll be angry if they don't. He could come back with more militia and make them do it."

She shrugs and looks pleased with herself. "Maybe we'll have two revolutions."

Francisco frowns, trying to understand. Joaquín stares at their aunt, his eyes wide with fear. The house door opens and Tío Leandro comes out. Longina is looking down at her hands, touching her fingers together one at a time, and doesn't notice. As he moves into the yard, she says complacently, "And the rebels will murder half of Santa Fe and then be killed themselves!"

Leandro frowns. "What's that you say?"

She turns toward him. "Captain Caballero and the others are going to defy the governor and let the rebel prisoners live," she says. "Then los insurrectos will take over Santa Fe and murder and pillage, but Commandant Armijo will come back and defeat them once and for all." She nods at him. "That's what I think."

Leandro is in front of the bench in three steps. He glares down at her. "You bloodthirsty girl, what kind of nonsense is this? Look at Joaquín! You've made him cry!"

Joaquín wipes his face with his sleeve. "I'm not crying."

Longina's lips curl contemptuously. "That's because he's still a child."

"You're the child!" Leandro's hands clench and unclench at his sides. "You hear a small part of a conversation and think you know everything that was said! You take a bit of information and leap to conclusions that are untenable and monstrous!"

Her mouth opens, then closes stubbornly, her eyes mutinous.

"At your young age you already gossip and fear monger!" His lips curl in disgust. "What is it they say? 'By the evenings we get to know about the days?' As a woman, you'll be insufferable!"

She jerks as if he's slapped her, then jumps up and rushes past him and into the house.

Leandro turns to the boys. "Let me explain. Because he is both commandant and interim governor, Manuel Armijo has the authority to order that the four prisoners be executed. However, Captain Caballero and others like your father and uncle and grandfather are worried that doing so will incite the rebels to invade Santa Fe, not discourage them. So they've worked out a plan. The Montoyas and the others will be killed only if the rebels try to enter the city, but not before."

"Oh," Joaquín says. He scrubs at his face again. "I wasn't crying."

His tío grins sympathetically. "I know."

"But what about los insurrectos?" Francisco asks. "Will they still come south?"

215

Leandro shrugs. "Captain Caballero doesn't think so. But there's no point in killing their leaders before they've actually done anything. That would just make things worse."

"But Governor Armijo said to do it."

He nods. "Sí. The presidio officers are sending him a letter explaining what they will do and why."

"They're brave men to contradict orders like that."

"Yes, they are. Now we must wait and see what happens."

Francisco nods. He looks at Joaquín, who's watching the hen peck at the ground by the woodpile and scrubbing surreptitiously at his cheeks.

"I'm going to take a few of those fleeces we cleaned to some of the americano merchants, to find out how much they'll offer me for them," Leandro says. "Do you two want to come with me?" Joaquín turns toward him eagerly and Francisco nods. It would be good to get away from the house.

When Leandro has concluded his business, he buys the boys a cone of piloncillo to share. It's half-eaten by the time they return to the house and their hands are sticky with sugary brown goodness when they enter the courtyard.

Longina sees them licking their fingers but, surprisingly, turns away without remonstrating.

She's remarkably silent in the following days. On Sunday, she doesn't react when Francisco lags behind the rest of the family after Mass to say a shy "hello" to María Refugio Sisneros. And she makes no comment when news comes that Armijo has accepted Caballero's plan of action, the rebel threat has dissolved, and the men in the presidio jail will definitely not be executed. Francisco thinks she's disappointed that nothing exciting has happened. At least she's not bossing him or Joaquín around.

Because of this, he's feeling kinder toward her when he finds her in the courtyard late one morning, poking a stick into a sputtering fire in the dome-shaped adobe oven. Longina's face and skirt are streaked with ash and her hair tumbles around her forehead as if she's forgotten to comb it. "Stupid thing!" she grumbles.

Francisco moves closer. He peers over her shoulder.

"It's not burning right," she says sulkily.

"I think you've put too much wood in at once."

She scowls at him. "Then you do it! Boys are so much better and nicer than girls, anyway!"

He steps back. "I didn't say that."

"Leandro did!" She flounces away.

Francisco bends over the oven's arched opening, peers inside, then carefully reaches in and maneuvers two logs from the top of the stack. Something at the back shifts, then the flames begin popping enthusiastically. He turns away and discovers Longina on the bench, her arms folded over her chest and her chin almost touching them.

Francisco moves cautiously toward her. "What is it?"

She shakes her head without looking up. "He hates me." She sniffs and scrubs at her face with her closed fist. "He thinks I'm a stupid little girl without a brain in her head."

"But you are a little girl."

She lifts her head. "I'm not. I'll be twelve next year."

He frowns in confusion.

"Your mother was married when she was fourteen. And our mother was only a year older than that when she married Papá."

He pulls back. "Married?"

"Don't look at me like that!" She scrubs at her face again and pushes herself from the bench. Then she looks down at her skirt and brushes at it with the side of her hand, trying to get the ash off. "I'll be old enough to wed in the next year or so." Then she sniffles. "But he doesn't care. He hates me."

"Maybe he wouldn't hate you so much if you would stop being such a gossip and fear monger."

Her head jerks up and her hands move to her hips. Then they drop. Her shoulders hunch inward as she moves to the door and goes inside.

Franscisco watches her go. Poor tía. Then his lips curve into a tiny smile. He can't help it. If La Mandona is worried about Tío Leandro's opinion of her, she might lose some of her bossiness. That would be nice.

His mother comes out of the house door with Joaquín close behind. Her head and shoulders are wrapped in a rebozo and she's carrying a shopping basket. "I have news for the two of you," she says briskly. "Now that things have settled down and we've decided to stay for the winter, it's time to take advantage of all Santa Fe has to offer." She looks Francisco up and down. "You both need new clothes. And Lavinia's found a school for your cousin. I've asked your father to locate one for the two of you, as well."

The boys' shoulders slump as they look at each other. Their mother laughs. "Through the temple of toil one enters the temple of fame," she says, turning toward the gate. "Come. First we will shop for solid americano shoes." The boys roll their eyes at each other but they obediently follow her into the street.

CHAPTER 11

November–December 1837: Rebellious Souls
(Padre Antonio José Martínez)

"Ten years, José Santiago," Padre Martínez says. He waves a hand at the papers scattered across his desk—certificates acknowledging his value to the churches and communities he's served, commendations from the vicar general himself—and scowls.

Then he looks up at his brother, who's in the chair opposite, his hands flat on its wooden armrests. "Ten years I've been pastor in this parish," Antonio José continues. "I've ministered to the poor, taught their children to read and write, and listened to their endless confessions. I've exhorted them to godly behavior and admonished their sins. I've been a true father to them."

He looks down at his desk, picks up a piece of paper, and waves it in the air. "And this is how they repay me! More demands and threats! And orders! Orders, of all things!" He's practically spitting now. He slaps the missive onto the wood. "From these— These peasants!" He leans forward and peers down at the awkward scrawl at the bottom of the sheet, which is barely visible in the firelight. "It's hardly literate. Juan Antonio Vigil never could spell."

"Antonio Vigil the coyote?" Santiago asks. "The one with the genízaro mother and who knows what americano father?"

"Of course, Antonio Vigil the coyote. It's always him. Or Pablo Montoya. Demanding written assurances that no padre in Nuevo México will ever again ask for an offering or tithe of any kind." His voice deepens in disgust. "I and my fellow priests are to live on the scraps of whatever our parishioners care to feed us. We aren't to even ask, much less demand, that they do their duty. I thought we settled this back in September!"

"I suppose they want you to reaffirm your promises now that Armijo has retaken Santa Fe. To confirm that you're still willing to do what the rebels want even though the loyalists are back in control."

His brother's jaw tightens. "They'll be sorry they've taken this attitude when the troops get here from Chihuahua."

Santiago's gaze sharpens. "Is it certain?"

Antonio José nods. "I had a letter from Santa Fe yesterday. Armijo has received word that the troops are on their way, though when they'll arrive is difficult to predict."

"Not soon enough. In the meantime, El Coyote will continue to foment trouble. And he seems to speak to people's hearts. He's very eloquent."

"I'll give him eloquence." The priest stares past his brother, into space. "I do believe it's time for me to remind my flock just where they're positioned in the greater scheme of creation," he says slowly. "El Coyote Vigil forgets that two can play the game of speaking to people's hearts. And I have authority he's never dreamed of." His lips curve in satisfaction. "The man isn't as clever as he thinks."

Santiago's brows contract. "Please be careful, hermano. Remember that whatever you say will be taken as coming from me and the rest of the family as much as from you. I have children, you know."

Antonio José comes out of his trance. His eyes light with genuine warmth. "And another on the way. How is Luz holding up?"

"This child is a kicker. She's worried it's going to be another boy."

The padre laughs. "With three already, another could be a bit of a burden. I'll say an extra prayer that the baby will settle." He pushes himself to his feet. "And be a nice docile female."

Santiago nods toward the letter on the desk. "What will you do about that? Should I intervene in my role as subprefect?"

"Do you truly want to remind these rebellious souls who appointed you to that position? They already chased us out of town once."

Santiago grimaces. "I suppose not. However, I do have the authority to confine some of the more troublesome ones for a few days, if that would be helpful."

Antonio José shakes his head. "Jails seem to create insurrections these days, instead of discouraging them." He moves around the desk and puts a hand on his brother's shoulder. "This coming Sunday, I'll give them a sermon they won't forget and appeal directly to their sense of duty to God as well as those he's placed over them."

Santiago chuckles wryly. "I'm not sure El Coyote Vigil believes God has placed anyone over him. Not without his express permission."

"It's not him I'll be preaching to."

~ ~ ~ ~

El Coyote is nowhere in sight the following Sunday, but he's present on Tuesday. It's December 12, the feast day of the Virgin of Guadalupe, for whom the church was named. The Virgin's image is carried reverently around the plaza and back to the church, then honored in the subsequent mass. Afterward, Padre Martínez turns to his flock and spreads his hands beseechingly.

"I stand before you today as a representative of our Holy Mother," he says. The congregation stirs. Perhaps they're tired from the procession and then standing through the service. Impatient for this afternoon's dancing and feast. "This is a holy day," he goes on. "A day of thanksgiving to Our Lady of Guadalupe for all She has given us and for Her care for us." His voice lifts, carrying into the far corners. "We owe Her gratitude and devotion and obedience."

Their feet shift on the hard-packed dirt floor, settling in. The padre and his congregation have known each other since he was a small boy. He's been their pastor for ten years and they've grown familiar with his sermonic rhythms. He's just hitting his stride. Feasting and dancing will have to wait.

He turns slightly and raises his hand toward the painting of Our Lady on the wall beside the altar. "As the Blessed Virgin spoke to Juan Diego on a hilltop outside la Ciudad de México over three hundred years ago, so She speaks to you here today."

He turns back to face his parishioners. "She says unto you, 'Yo soy tu Madre. Nunca te preocupes. Que vives bajo de mi amparo.'" He pauses a moment, letting it sink in.

"That is correct. She says, 'I am your Mother. Never worry. Your lives are under My protection."

The crowd stirs slightly, perhaps wondering where he's going with this. It's not an exact repeat of what he said on Sunday. Or is it? El Coyote Vigil watches him with narrowed eyes. Santiago, beside his pregnant wife, smiles slightly. Juan Aragón, the Don Fernando de Taos magistrate, folds his hands over his ample belly and nods as if to say, "Keep going."

Padre Martínez begins pacing back and forth in front of the altar, pitching his voice to the back of the room. "Our Lady La Guadalupana is your mother," he says. "She will protect you. She will wrap you in Her arms and comfort you when there is no comfort left. As She gave the Indian convert Juan Diego a sign with Her face on his mantle and more signs with roses in December, so She will give you signs of Her favor."

Then he whirls to face them, eyes flashing. He jabs his finger into the air. "But you must deserve Her favor! You must repent of your hardheartedness and your presumption! You must come humbly to Her with a pure heart and clean hands! Do not grasp for what is not yours! Do not elevate yourselves above your station! Seek to live simply and humbly, to be worthy of the love of the Virgin of Guadalupe!"

Old ladies wrapped in black rebozos nod back at him. A young matron weeps quietly as she tucks her children closer to her skirts. El Coyote Vigil stares defiantly until even his eyes drop before the priest's stern gaze.

Satisfaction surges through Padre Martínez's chest. He lowers his voice, gentling his tone. "Come, let us pray together." He turns, kneels before the altar, and lifts his voice so it can be heard behind him all the way to the doors. "Dios te salve, María," he begins. "Hail Mary, full of grace—"

There's a small hesitation, then they join in, saying it with him. When the prayer is finished, he begins again. Then again. After three iterations, the voices are stronger and more unified. Again he repeats the words. The sound behind him begins to soften into the smooth flow of acquiescence and proper prayerfulness.

When he feels the time is right, the priest rises and faces his people. His eyes sweep over the silent, bowed heads. Even El Coyote looks subdued.

"Go in peace," Padre Martínez says solemnly, careful to keep the glee from his voice. "Depart in good order, knowing your only true safety is in La Guadalupana and in respect for the command Her Son has given us." He pauses, waiting for them to wonder which command he's referring to, then intones, "Entonces denle al César lo que es del César y a Dios lo que es de Dios."

They stir, gazing back at him, and he nods. "That's right. To Caesar what is Caesar's, to God what is God's. Obedience to authority, not rebellion." He glances at El Coyote, whose jaw has tightened, though his eyes are still on the floor.

The padre raises his hands for the final blessing. He speaks the words, then waves toward the door. "Now vamos!" he says jovially. "Celebrate! Eat! Dance! It is the feast day of our Lady of Guadalupe!"

They smile back at him, all except Vigil, who's already turning toward the exit. The congregation pours out, the children's voices erupting gleefully as they hit the clear December day.

Martínez watches them until the building is empty, then smiles with satisfaction, turns, and genuflects one final time before the altar.

~ ~ ~ ~

But the battle for the soul of Don Fernando de Taos is merely engaged, not won. Two days later, the padre has a visit from El Coyote Vigil, Pablo Montoya, and José Angel Gonzales.

It's late afternoon and the sun is already setting when they pound on the gate. The padre goes out to them and stands considering them and the empty street. Across the way, the sunlight is rich on the back of the golden-brown walls of the church.

His eyes drop to El Coyote's face. There's only animosity there. Pablo Montoya stands behind him and to one side, his sharp eyes focused on the hat in his hands. Gonzales is beside him, studying the ground.

So it's only El Coyote he truly has to deal with this time. Martínez steps back, motioning them across the courtyard and into the house. Inside, he turns to the housekeeper. "Refreshments, María, por favor," he says genially. He turns to the men. "Chocolate, perhaps? Or wine?"

"We won't be here long enough for refreshments," El Coyote says flatly.

"At least let me offer you a seat." Martínez ushers them toward the big wooden chairs by the fire, then stands waiting. Gonzales and Montoya settle first, still looking self-conscious. El Coyote scowls, then sits on the front edge of the chair farthest from the flames.

Martínez's lips quirk with amusement as he settles himself, forearms flat on the broad arms of his chair like a judge of old. "And how can I help you gentlemen today?" he asks blandly.

Gonzales and Montoya look at El Coyote, who leans forward. "You will stop preaching dissension."

"Dissension?"

The housekeeper arrives with their drinks, a deep red wine from Bernalillo. Normally, the host would wait until the others are served, but the padre doubts his visitors will take anything if he doesn't. "What do you mean?" he asks as he reaches for the tray.

He lifts a goblet, watches the others take theirs, waits for the woman to place the decanter on the little table on the other side of the room, then sips carefully, proving the wine is safe. "If you would explain yourself," he says courteously.

El Coyote leans down, puts his goblet on the floor beside his feet, then straightens and scowls at the priest. "That sermon on the feast day. You told us to abase ourselves."

Martínez sips his wine, then says calmly, "I quoted the Gospels."

"For your own ends!" He's coiled tight as a mountain lion ready to pounce.

The padre looks into his goblet, then raises his eyes and holds the rebel's gaze. "You believe I am your enemy. This is not the case." He looks at the other men, who are cautiously sipping their drinks. "If you will spare me the time, I will explain myself." They look at him noncommittally. He turns to El Coyote, who jerks his head in impatient agreement.

Martínez rises, crosses the room to the small table, and places his goblet beside the decanter. Then he returns to his

226

seat, leans back, puts his elbows on the armrests, touches his forefingers together, and looks into El Coyote's narrow face. The other man's mouth twists in irritation, but he doesn't speak.

"I wish, as I believe you do, for a country in which every man has a voice," the priest says. "This latest set of laws from Mexico City is not much to my liking, especially the new restrictions regarding who can vote. And I am deeply concerned about the impact of a return of the sales tax. Losing the exemption that has been in place so long will be a hardship for all of us."

"Some of us more than others," José Angel Gonzales says.

Martínez nods. "Truly spoken." He frowns slightly, trying to find the most appropriate words. "However, the Holy Scripture tells us that destroying life is a great sin."

El Coyote Vigil scowls, but the priest continues. "Especially when that life is that of the men God has placed in authority over us."

The other man's scowl deepens. His feet scuff the floor as if he wants only to escape. Or stand and fight. Martínez focuses on Montoya and Gonzales and drops his hands into his lap. "It is a matter of strategy," he says. "Just as a parent is more likely to respond favorably to a child's well-spoken and respectful request, so those over us—"

"We are not children!" El Coyote surges out of his chair, hitting the wine goblet with his foot and sending it sideways onto the hard-packed floor. The red liquid spreads toward the padre's feet.

He glances down. He should call the housekeeper to clean it up, but he's unwilling to break the flow of the conversation. He focuses instead on the other man's angry face. "It seems to me that you rebels have acted very much like children," he says quietly.

El Coyote's fists clench, though he stays beside the chair. "Who are you to judge how we act? To give us advice?"

Martínez draws himself up. "I am your pastor!"

"Put in place by other men just like yourself! ¡Ricos!"

"I have used my wealth wisely, both to educate myself for the service of my community and also to feed those made destitute by the irresponsible actions of you and your fellow insurrectos."

He glances toward the others, who are watching warily, then refocuses on El Coyote. He can't keep the impatience from his voice any longer. "There were no men left in the Taos valley this fall to tend to the harvest. They had all gone south to do battle against those who—" He stops. There's nothing to be gained by belaboring the evil and futility of rebellion against appointed authority.

"They had all gone south," he repeats, more calmly this time. "The harvest remained in the fields. The women and children and old men brought in what little they could, but that was all consumed within a few weeks. By mid-November, many suffered from lack of food. In the face of their affliction, I and my family opened our storehouses and gave freely to anyone who requested assistance." He lifts his chin. "We have continued to provide what we can, regardless of their family's affiliation. We ask only if they are in need."

"As if you have a right to ask such a question!" El Coyote spits.

"It is our grain. We have every right to determine that it's being used wisely."

"You mean you make our women grovel before you to prove their humility and gratitude for the assistance you bestow on them so graciously." He makes "graciously" sound like an insult. He swings a fist, as if he'd like to use it on the priest, but Martínez crosses his arms and gazes at him impassively.

The rebel turns away and begins pacing the width of the room. Into the darkness, then back to the fire, then into the shadows again. "This is the problem," he says. "This is what must change." He faces the priest. "The power of people like you over those who are poorer or less well connected. The right of officials in la Ciudad de México to appoint strangers to settle our quarrels. The right of outsiders to decide who among us can vote and who can't."

"And the right of the rich to decide when or how much the poor will eat," José Angel Gonzales says. "Or how much they pay for their sustenance." His eyes are dark with pain as they meet the padre's. "The people have so little. The new sales tax will place an unbearable burden on them."

"The Council has sent a petition to Mexico City asking that Nuevo México again be exempted from the sales tax."

"You hope it was sent!" El Coyote snorts. "Governor Pérez had every intention of collecting those taxes!"

Pablo Montoya chuckles grimly. "At least we solved that problem."

"Not permanently." The padre glances at El Coyote, who's still pacing, then turns to the others. "All the insurrection has accomplished is to anger the federal government and unleash the power of the military upon us."

El Coyote swings back toward the fire. "So Armijo says. However, if and when his imaginary troops arrive from Chihuahua, we'll be ready for them."

"They'll arrive." Martínez turns to Gonzales. "Even now, there could be time to fend off what is coming. You understand strategy. When to pull back, when to charge. Soft words now may be all that's needed to turn away chastisement—"

"Soft words!" Pablo Montoya snorts. "We can't eat soft words!"

"I and my family have provided grain—"

"There is still hunger," Gonzales says quietly. His face is shadowed with concern. "Here and in Chimayó and elsewhere."

The priest spreads his hands, palms up in a hopeless gesture. "We have given all we can."

El Coyote swings toward him. "You have not even begun to give!" He waves a hand at the comfortable room, its wooden chairs, the little table with the wine decanter catching the light. The bookcase in the corner, crowded with leather bindings. "You think you live simply. You have never fought to scrape together the priest-fees necessary to be born and to die, or taken the food from your children's mouths because it was required to pay the grain tithes. You and every priest in the land should be hanged for what you do to us!"

Martínez draws himself up. "You exaggerate. And you threaten the lives of the men of the church. You could be thrown in jail for such talk."

El Coyote stops in midstride, his face stony. "We'll put you in jail instead. And we'll do more than that, if you don't meet our demands."

The priest looks at the other two men. They stare back at him, their expressions almost as hard as El Coyote's. For the first time since they arrived, he feels a tremor of concern. "What do you want?" he asks quietly.

"The church has funds," Pablo Montoya says.

"The poor fund has already been depleted. What's left is set aside for candles, for paying my pittance, for—"

"You don't know what a pittance is!" El Coyote snaps.

The padre studies his face, then the others'. Their eyes are hard as the black rock of La Mesilla.

El Coyote holds out a hand, palm up. "The funds," he says. Then he grins wolfishly. "Or the jail in Santa Cruz, where your brother has no jurisdiction." His head tilts and his eyes narrow. "Or we can take you both there. The road through the mountains is closed due to the snow. We'd have to take the route above the river." Mischief tilts his lips. "That section can be quite icy this time of year."

"The rocks there can be dangerous," Pablo Montoya agrees, his eyes on Martínez' face. Gonzales says nothing. His gaze is more watchful than angry now, but it's still not friendly.

Martinez throws up his hands. "All right," he says. "I'll hand over the church funds and you can distribute them as you see fit." He turns toward his desk. "However, I hope you will use good judgment in how you share this out." He bends over a drawer and pulls out a small bag of coins. "Remember, I have already agreed not to request contributions for my services. You are milking the cow dry."

"As you have milked us these many years," El Coyote snarls.

And then they are gone, without a formal goodby. The priest sinks into his chair and stares at the fire as the spilled red wine continues to soak into the floor.

The housekeeper is scrubbing at the stain the next afternoon when a disheveled Santiago arrives. In spite of El Coyote's implied promise that they'll leave him alone, the insurrectos have grabbed the subprefect, held him overnight, and extracted an oath of loyalty to the insurgency. He's wild-eyed and shaking.

"I thought they were going to kill me," he says as he enters the house. Antonio José leads him to a chair by the fire, pours him a goblet of wine, then sinks into the seat opposite.

Santiago drinks deeply, draws a long, settling breath, then looks at Antonio José. "You must stop."

The priest's jaw tightens.

"¡Maldición!" His brother leans forward, his eyes snapping. "I could have been killed! And they told me about your little interview with El Coyote and the others. You were fortunate all they wanted was money." He drinks again, then sets the goblet on the chair's broad arm. "You must moderate your language."

The padre stares at his brother. Santiago has always been the compliant one, the sibling who'll do whatever he's told, the one who believes Antonio José can do no wrong. He's never spoken to him this way before. And he's clearly not going to be talked out of his opinion this time.

And maybe he shouldn't be. He has children and a pregnant wife.

"Very well," the priest says unwillingly. "I will do as you say."

Relief washes Santiago's face. "Thank you, mi hermano." He pushes himself to his feet. "I must hurry home. Luz will be beside herself with fear."

Antonio José follows him to the door, his mind already playing with words for his next sermon. He must soften his stance. Find a way to caution their restless hearts without risking his brother's life. Or his own. Moderate his words.

He manages to do so until Christmas Eve and the traditional midnight mass. As he lifts the cup, speaks the traditional words, he ponders what he will say. How can one speak of el Niño Jesús without mentioning our duty to him? Why He came? Our sinfulness? Our need to be as children before His Father and those He's placed over us?

When he turns to speak to the congregation, he tries to keep his voice mild, his words gentle. But they are his flock. He has a duty to call them to repentance, to admonish them to live as they ought.

Their faces gaze quietly back at him in the light of the flickering candles and when he has finished, they go silently back to their homes. He breathes a prayer of thanksgiving. Perhaps he's turned the tide. Perhaps they'll truly repent and there will no longer be fertile ground for rebel teaching here in the valley of Taos.

~ ~ ~ ~

But several nights later, as he and Santiago sit before the fire discussing candidates for herding the family flocks in the coming year, there's a pounding at the courtyard entrance.

Antonio José jerks to his feet, his heart hammering in his chest, but when he swings the wooden gate open, he discovers friends, not foes.

It's the Don Fernando magistrate Juan Aragón, surrounded by grim torch-bearing men carrying weapons—old, new, Spanish, americano.

"Padre," Aragón says, without preamble. "We come to protect you."

The priest frowns. "What is it?"

The magistrate cocks his head toward the street that separates the church from the plaza. "Hear that?"

Voices. A kind of low growl. The throb of a drum. Santiago comes out of the house door and stands on the threshold, staring toward it. "El Coyote," he says. It isn't a question.

Juan Aragón nods. "And Pablo Montoya."

"And José Angel Gonzales," someone else says. The reverence in the voice shivers the priest's spine. He steps aside and the magistrate and his followers enter the courtyard.

As the gate swings shut behind them, there's a shout at the far end of the lane, then a louder voice. "Hullo the house!" it bellows. "We want the padre!"

The gate bar drops into place. Another voice—nearer now—calls, "¡Padre! Padre come out to us!"

The magistrate's face is pale in the torchlight. "They were overheard in the taberna," he says. "Plotting more sedition."

"Thank God for wine," someone says sardonically.

Aragón's eyes twinkle in spite of the tension. "And for the intelligent young women who serve it." He turns back to the priest, his face somber. "You spoke too clearly the other night, mi amigo. They have decided you are a threat to the rebel cause and must be silenced."

The priest nods, acknowledging the words as he looks toward the wall and the lane beyond it. The crowd is louder now, but they're not shouting. They're chanting instead—a steady "¡Padre! ¡Padre! ¡Padre!" over and over again.

A shiver runs down his spine. Then he steels himself. "They won't stop until I speak to them."

Santiago moves toward him. "It's too dangerous."

"Let us guard you." Aragón turns to a cluster of men carrying americano rifles. "Two on each side of Don Antonio José," he says crisply. They move forward.

The priest closes his eyes. So it has come to this. He must speak to his flock guarded by men with guns. Sadness engulfs him. And then another emotion, a combination of anger and righteousness. His eyes snap open. How dare his people forget their duty and his authority over them?

He moves toward the wall facing the lane and reaches for a nearby bench. He positions it against the adobe, climbs up, and looks out.

The street is bright under a cold black sky lit more by the stars than the sliver of moon. Torches flare. Someone has built a bonfire near the back of the church.

In the courtyard, benches scrape the wall as Aragón's men shove them into place and climb into position. Padre Martínez drops his gaze to the lane immediately in front of the gate. It's filled with rebels, with more crowding in from either end. When they spot him and the men Aragón has brought, the chanting slows, then ceases.

He clears his throat. "My children!" he calls.

El Coyote Vigil pushes his way to the front of the crowd. "We are not your children!" he bellows. "We are adults!"

"You are all my children in God." The padre projects his voice as if he were in church, sending his words past the crowd into the intersecting streets. "I see you as the Holy Father, the Virgin Mary, and the infant Jesus see you. As you are their children, you are mine."

Vigil scowls. His gaze moves to the men stationed along the wall. "You have protection," he observes sardonically. His eyes return to Martinez. "We may be your children but you don't trust us."

Antonio José has a sudden urge to shout an imprecation at the man. To damn him to all eternity. He clenches his fists, fighting for calm.

Then Juan Aragón climbs up beside him and raises his hands for attention. The crowd's gaze shifts. "You have assembled here tonight to wreak harm on a citizen of Don Fernando de Taos," the magistrate says in his most formal courtroom voice. "Fortunately, that harm has been prevented and nothing has occurred which places you in danger of the law."

"Danger!" someone jeers from the back of the crowd. "As if you can touch us!"

Further down the wall, a man lifts his rifle and points it at the crowd. There's a small, restless movement below, then sudden quiet.

"Danger." Aragón's voice is flat, his expression hard. "The men inside this courtyard are here to protect a peaceable citizen who has every right to express his opinion as long as it does not incite violence." The implication is clear. At either end of the lane, men begin to slip away into the darkness.

"Who said anything about violence?" El Coyote's voice is still aggressive, but it's lost its sardonic edge. José Angel Gonzales appears at his elbow and speaks into his ear.

Vigil tilts his head, listening, then refocuses on the wall. "We have come to remind the padre that the people of his parish look to him to provide an example of appropriate behavior. An illustration of discretion."

Martínez's jaw tightens. Is that yet another threat?

Aragón glances at him, then leans forward and raises his hands for attention. "Let us all agree to speak discreetly and with great precision." He slowly turns his head, staring into the crowd as if making a note of each face. "You are mis vecinos. We see each other often. To act in anger now is to endanger our very existence as a community, to rend it apart. Let us not be foolish. Instead, let us retire to our homes in peace and reflect on the consequences we have avoided this night."

They stare at him blankly, absorbing his words. Then, after a long moment, the torches begin to drift toward the end of the lane and drop out of sight as their bearers round the corner, heading toward their own streets and houses. Someone throws water onto the fire behind the church. The smell of wet ashes drifts into the air.

El Coyote Vigil remains where he is, hands on his hips, and studies the priest and the magistrate, who still gaze out from the wall. Starlight glints on the weapons of the men beside them. The padre shifts his weight, preparing to speak again, but then Vigil takes a step back, turns, and disappears into the shadows.

The tallest of the guards turns toward the priest. "We'll take a look outside to make sure they've truly gone."

Antonio José nods wordlessly. He and Aragón climb down from the bench, meet Santiago as he joins them from farther down the wall, and return to the house.

The housekeeper and her daughter are there with wine and chocolate. The padre thanks them with a nod and lifts a goblet to the magistrate in a toast. "To discretion," he says with a small smile. He takes a deep breath without allowing his chest to move, the kind he's trained himself to take so that no one can see. "This should settle them. They know now that we'll stand and fight."

On the other end of the room, Santiago shakes his head as he paces the floor.

CHAPTER 12

January 1838: What Was Necessary
(Captain Pedro Muñoz)

Captain Muñoz tries to keep the elation from his face as he enters the commandant's office, but he can't keep it from his voice. "The Vera Cruz cavalry is riding in from Agua Fría at this very moment," he says.

For one second, the relief on Manuel Armijo's face is palpable. Then he reverts to his usual urbanity. "Excellent," he says, as if he has other things on his mind.

Muñoz feels a stab of annoyance. Then Armijo turns to Donaciano Vigil, who's standing in front of the desk. "And now is the propitious moment to send forth the proclamation of which we spoke."

Muñoz suppresses a grin. The language Armijo uses at times like this is always amusing.

"It is well past time to remind los insurrectos El Coyote Vigil and José Angel Gonzales that the fish which goes for the hook looks for his funeral," Armijo continues. He drums his fingers on the desk top. "They seem to have forgotten why Esquibel and the others remain incarcerated here in the capital."

Vigil nods. Armijo looks at Muñoz. "Am I to understand that Lieutenant Colonel Justiniani brings my official appointments, both as governor and principal commandant?"

"Sí, Excellency. He sent word requesting an audience to-morrow to congratulate you in person. At your convenience, of course."

Armijo's back straightens even more. He looks into the distance as if mentally considering the next day's itinerary. Then he nods. "Kindly extend to him my invitation for luncheon. And please plan to join us yourself." He turns to Vigil. "Now that my appointment as governor has arrived, we must convene the Council to reaffirm their request to ex-empt Nuevo México from the taxes in question. It will have more significance with my official signature attached."

"Yes, Excellency." Vigil turns, nods to Muñoz, and leaves the room.

The captain says a few more polite words to Armijo, then bows himself out. He doesn't allow his face to relax its dip-lomatically bland expression until he's on the palacio portal, putting on his hat. He's torn between amusement and annoy-ance. Originally, he'd felt a certain affection for Manuel Armijo. The man loves his position and can be a bit pomp-ous, but he has a good sense of the region's politics.

However, the captain has grown weary of managing the man's ego. The idea that Lieutenant Colonel Cayetano Justiniani should have to ask for an audience, and that there should be a question as to whether it's granted, is ridiculous. Armijo can be such a pompous ass. If he acts this way to-morrow, Muñoz is going to find it difficult to hide his irritation.

But when the governor greets the commander of the Chi-huahua troops the next day, he's all smiles and graciousness, without a trace of pomposity. He makes a little speech thank-ing Justiniani for arriving so quickly, compliments the condition of his troops and the uniforms of his dragoons, and tells him a proclamation exhorting Santa Fe's citizens to treat the newly arrived men respectfully and fairly is being prepared. "We wouldn't wish prices to suddenly go up now, would we?" he asks jovially.

Justiniani, who's an inch taller than Armijo and half as wide, doesn't blink. "I am quite sure the good people of Santa Fe will meet my men with the same respect my men will extend to them," he says calmly.

"Most certainly!" Armijo says. His hands twitch as if he'd like to rub them together, but then he seems to think better of it. He bows to the lieutenant colonel. "And now let us adjourn to the table. I have a special wine from the vineyards of Bernalillo which I have been saving for just such an occasion as this, although I'm sure it's not equal to that of El Paso del Norte." He gestures toward the next room, ushering them in.

"I'm sure it will be delicious," Justiniani says as he moves forward. "It will give us something to discuss besides politics and battles."

Armijo laughs as if he quite agrees, but before the first course is over, he's launched into an elaborate description of the New Mexican rebels' irrational demands and upstart attitude.

Justiniani makes a quieting gesture. "I do not believe it is necessary to go into all that at this time."

"I only mention it as a preface to expressing my deep desire to avoid further bloodshed," Armijo says. "I wish as soon as possible to inform los insurrectos of the strength of your arms, as well as the military acuteness of yourself and the extensive training and competency of your men. If all goes well, these peones of Río Arriba will return to their

241

senses at the very sound of your name and melt back into the valleys and hills from whence they came."

The lieutenant colonel half smiles at this pretty little speech and raises his drink. "A toast," he says. "To Victory without bloodshed."

Armijo raises his goblet in response. "That it will be so."

Muñoz manages to keep his expression neutral. He's glad Justiniani and the troops are here at last. However, he doubts very much that their arrival will end the insurrection. These rebels aren't so easily quelled. As far as Muñoz can tell, none of their demands have been met, in spite of Armijo's blandishments.

However, Muñoz is thankful he doesn't have to deal directly with Armijo anymore. That's the lieutenant colonel's responsibility as commanding officer of the Vera Cruz troops. So when the captain returns to his rooms Friday morning after reviewing his newly arrived squadron, he's surprised to find a request to meet Justiniani at the palacio.

When Muñoz gets there, the Vera Cruz commander is positioned just outside the door to the governor's office, gazing at the crowded plaza. The captain snaps a salute and Justiniani returns it, then leads the way inside.

Armijo is standing by the fireplace, talking to a cluster of men. His face brightens when he sees the two officers. He hurries toward Justiniani with both hands out. "Please allow me to extend my gratitude to Your Excellency for responding so quickly to my request for your presence," he says.

Muñoz's eyes narrow. He's never seen the man so obsequious. But Armijo is focused only on the lieutenant colonel. "I believe you have met everyone here, have you not?"

Justiniani glances toward the fireplace and shakes his head.

"Ah, forgive me." The governor turns and begins, each man bowing politely in turn. "Donaciano Vigil, my Secretary of State. Mariano Chávez and his father-in-law, Pedro José de los Dolores Perea. Nuevo México's most illustrious padres, Antonio José Martínez and Juan Felipe Ortiz. And of course, you are already acquainted with our presidio Captain, José Caballero."

The two men exchange a salute, then they all look at Armijo. He moves to his desk, reaches for a crumpled document in the middle of it, and turns back to the others. "There is disturbing news from the north yet again. The insurgents have announced their intention to march on Santa Fe and free their compatriots here. This time they are led, if you can call it that, by El Coyote Vigil."

"I don't understand it," Padre Martínez grumbles. "Taos and Santa Cruz were both calm when I came south two days ago."

Armijo looks at Donaciano Vigil, who steps forward and hands him a long, closely written sheet of paper. Armijo's elaborate signature at the bottom is so large Muñoz can read it from across the room.

The governor flourishes the document. "You see here a copy of my response to the impetuosity of los insurrectos. In this proclamation I order them to disperse immediately and permanently, and to dispatch El Coyote Vigil and the genízaro Gonzales here to Santa Fe to make their submission. If they do not respond within twenty-four hours, the four rebel prisoners will be executed." He flicks the back of a fingernail against the page and one corner of his mouth lifts in what seems to be amusement. "It is my final offer."

Muñoz's jaw tightens. And the man says he doesn't want bloodshed. He and the others look at Justiniani.

Armijo is focused on him, too, but he's not through speaking. The amusement has disappeared. "I warned the insurrectos last fall that further provocation would result in instantaneous retribution!" His eyes shift to Captain Caballero. "We should have taken action then! The delay has only increased their recalcitrance!"

The captain's nostrils flare. He opens his mouth, then seems to think better of it. But his defiant gaze doesn't leave Armijo's face. He clearly doesn't regret his October decision.

"The people of Don Fernando de Taos will not join them this time," Padre Martínez says. "I have exhorted them into submission and they have responded appropriately."

The governor shakes his head. He suddenly looks tired. "Don Fernando has also risen."

Martínez's chin jerks, his eyes blazing. "Those reprobates!" He moves forward. "Consider me your chaplain, sir! Yours is a righteous cause. I will stand beside you as you bring these rebels back to their senses!"

Muñoz glances at Justiniani, who's studying both the general and the priest with hooded eyes. "What of the Indians?" the lieutenant colonel asks.

"Los indios bárbaros will be upon us in an instant if los insurrectos succeed in their quest," Armijo says.

"That's to be expected. But the civilized ones? The pueblos?"

244

"I have already sent word warning them explicitly not to participate in the coming engagement."

Pedro Perea moves slightly forward. "So you believe it will definitely come to a fight?"

Armijo lifts his hands, palms up. "It may be that we can escape bloodshed. However, the rebels must understand that we are prepared and entirely capable of suppressing them if they refuse to desist."

"Or prepared and entirely capable of executing their imprisoned leaders, at any rate," Justiniani says drily.

Armijo turns toward him. "It is my hope that the blood of the four will be sufficient to bring the rest to their senses."

"You are definitely going to execute them?" Padre Ortiz asks.

"The coyote and the genízaro have twenty-four hours," Armijo answers. He can't quite keep the satisfaction from his face. "Then we will know how to proceed."

~ ~ ~ ~

It's a long twenty-four hours. Justiniani and the governor also seem to find it lengthy. They summon Muñoz to the governor's office the next afternoon, but when he arrives he learns that there's still no news from the north. They simply want someone else to talk to. The three men make desultory conversation, the lieutenant colonel and captain seated in front of the desk, Armijo behind it twiddling his thumbs.

They all look up when Donaciano Vigil enters the room. He has a folded paper in his hand. "The rebel answer, Your Excellency," he says in a neutral tone.

Muñoz gives him an amused look. How does the man do it? However, Armijo already has the missive in his hands and is tearing it open. Then he catches himself and leans back in his chair, trying to look nonchalant as he reads.

When he gets to the end he frowns, reads the message through again, then tosses it onto the desk. "You can peruse it if you like," he tells Justiniani, who doesn't lean forward. "Its language is as convoluted as their earlier statements. The only thing clear is that the insurrectos remain recalcitrant and El Coyote and Gonzales have chosen not to submit." He waves a hand toward the paper. "You see what I have to contend with!" There's a note of triumph in his voice.

The lieutenant colonel nods expressionlessly. "And now?"

Armijo slaps the desk with both hands and rises to his feet. "And now it is time to do what ought to have been accomplished in October. These rebellious ones must understand beyond all doubt that I am not a man to be trifled with." He turns to Vigil. "Find Captain Caballero and tell him to undertake to carry out my orders of October." He scowls. "This time there will be no excuses."

A shiver runs up Muñoz's spine. It's one thing to kill in battle, but cold executions have always troubled him. They seem so uncivilized. So calculating.

"The event will occur at nine o'clock tomorrow morning," Armijo continues. His eyes flit over Muñoz, then Justiniani, without seeing them. "However, not on the plaza. That is the people's space and these men do not truly represent the people." He nods to himself, then his eyes return to Vigil. "The inevitable results of their actions will take place in front of the old guardhouse north of town."

Then he straightens and puts one hand on his desk as if giving a judgment. His voice deepens. "Let it be proclaimed throughout the city that the just consequences of the rebel prisoners' offenses will be meted out to them tomorrow morning at nine of the clock. In addition, prepare a formal proclamation to be issued immediately after the event, announcing in the most emphatic terms that the executions have been accomplished and the reasons for which they occurred."

Donaciano Vigil's face is a careful blank. He nods, bows slightly, and leaves the room.

Armijo turns back to the others, rubbing his hands together. Muñoz looks away.

"It may be well to have the men under my command carry out the sentence," Justiniani says. He doesn't wait for Armijo's agreement before he turns to Muñoz. "Captain, you will choose the men and direct the proceedings, if you please."

Muñoz's head jerks toward him, then he nods stiffly. A military man follows orders. The 'if you please' is a mere formality. At least he won't know the men being punished.

But he'll know the people watching.

~ ~ ~ ~

When the captain and the men he's detailed for the task at hand march up to the old guardhouse the next morning, Muñoz is startled by the number of Santa Fe residents already present. Gertrudis Barceló stands beside the road with a cluster of women, one of them young and quite pregnant.

A little further on, Pedro Perea has a young grandson in each hand. A slightly older girl stands next to them, her eyes shining with excitement. Donaciano Vigil is also there, supporting a rebozo-wrapped old woman. At least he didn't bring his children.

Then Muñoz's squad reaches the four waist-high rounds of pale cottonwood chopping blocks that have been placed at intervals in front of the guardhouse. His attention snaps to his duty. He details two men to stand behind each block, then turns to study the crowd.

They've moved out in a kind of semicircle, facing the execution site. They aren't pushing too closely or showing much emotion. They seem more sleepy than anything else. They blink back at him as if they can't quite believe what they're seeing.

He notices Don Pedro has made no effort to place his grandchildren in the front row where they'd have a clear view. He may want them to understand what happens to malefactors, but he's not forcing them to absorb every detail.

Muñoz turns his back to the crowd and faces the execution space. A silence falls. Birds chirp somewhere overhead.

Then there's a shout from the direction of the plaza. Padre Ortiz appears, holding a tall wooden crucifix like an upright sword. Two presidio soldiers are behind him, then the Santa Cruz alcalde, his hands linked to his waist with ropes. He's followed by more soldiers, then the scar-faced El Quemado Vigil, another set of armed men, and the Montoya brothers, bound and guarded in the same way.

Finally, bringing up the rear, Governor Armijo appears. He's in full uniform, his hand on his ceremonial sword, the white plume of his bicorne hat jaunty in the morning air.

The procession halts as it reaches the first of the execution blocks. The guards turn smartly to face the crowd, the prisoners more slowly. Governor Armijo marches past Muñoz and his men to the far end of the crowd, and wheels to face them. His chest puffs as he looks them over, but he doesn't speak. Instead, he nods briskly to Padre Ortiz, who moves toward the prisoners. He steps from one man to the next, speaking words of comfort, making the sign of the cross.

Esquibel lowers his head, moves his bound hands in an awkward attempt to cross himself, and begins to weep. El Quemado's hands jerk as if he'd like to punch the padre in the stomach and he scowls at the crowd.

The younger Montoya is very pale. He sways a little in the morning coolness. As the priest reaches him, his lips move but no sound comes out.

Antonio Abad Montoya leans toward him, his eyes black with pain. "Forgive me," he says.

Desiderio gathers himself, shakes his head, and gives him a watery smile. "It happens in the best of families," he says. Then he focuses on Padre Ortiz.

There's a sympathetic murmur from the crowd. Padre Ortiz makes the sign of the cross over Antonio Abad, then moves away from the prisoners to join Armijo.

Muñoz waits until the priest settles, then glances at the governor. But the man's gaze is lifted toward the stony Sangre de Cristo peaks beyond the guardhouse's sagging flat roof. There will be no last-minute mercy here.

The captain takes a breath, holds it, releases. How he hates executions. Especially public ones. But these men have endangered the community, have led an insurrection that still threatens the land. And he is under orders. Muñoz stiffens himself and gestures to the first sergeant.

The man snaps a salute, then barks an order. A dragoon steps away from the furthest round of cottonwood, moves to the Santa Cruz alcalde, and takes him by the arm. Esquibel startles, then submits to being led across the small, suddenly silent, space. The trooper places a hand on his shoulder and presses down, guiding Esquibel into position beside the wood. He sags against it. Tears stream down his face.

The other prisoners are led to their places, then the first sergeant snaps another command.

Four men come forward with blindfolds. Only Esquibel flinches as they're applied. El Quemado spits into the face of the man tying his. The younger Montoya's lips are moving again. The women in the crowd begin to pray: "Dios te salve, María, llena eres de gracia, El Señor es contigo."

Muñoz turns toward the governor for the order to proceed. Armijo's staring north, not toward the mountains, but his face is still empty of any emotion. His eyes do not stray to the captain's.

Muñoz's lips twist in disgust. The man wants this done, already has the proclamation explaining the reason for it written up, but he can't bring himself to give the command. Muñoz nods to the sergeant, who barks an order.

Four dragoons step from the ranks, carrying machetes. The newly sharpened blades flash in the morning sun. The executioners move into position, one beside each wooden block, and the guards step out of the way.

The women's prayers are suddenly more fervent, supported now by the rumble of male voices. Muñoz looks at the governor, who still stares into space.

But he's ordered this execution and it must be done, the sooner the better. The captain turns to the first sergeant and nods. The man raises his hand. The executioners lift their blades. The hand drops and the steel swings in unison, hissing as they hit flesh.

There's a collective gasp. Someone in the crowd shrieks and is quickly hushed. Muñoz forces his own emotions into stony silence.

Then he hears Pedro Perea's voice saying, "And that is what happens to those who disobey those God has put in authority over them." A child whimpers.

Captain Muñoz bites back the bile rising in his throat and moves toward the insurrectos and their decapitated heads. Blood still spurts. The crowd moves with him. He can feel them at his back, straining to see. He stops, but still they press forward. "So much blood," someone mutters.

He braces himself and starts to turn, raising his hand. But his men have already seen the danger. A dragoon fires a shot into the air and the sergeant yells a warning at the crowd.

Muñoz whirls toward him. "Get the corpses away!" he cries. "Quickly!"

But there's no real need for urgency. The gunfire has done the trick. Or perhaps the finality of the thing has sunk in. The tension seems to drain from the onlookers and they slowly disperse, eyes everywhere but the blood-stained stumps of wood and what lies beside them. By the time the bodies of the executed men have been carried off, only Muñoz and his dragoons remain.

And then the road is empty in the morning light as the blood darkens on the big rounds of cottonwood and slowly sinks into the sandy soil beside them.

~ ~ ~ ~

The town seems stunned by what's happened, especially when word trickles in that the rebels massing in Santa Cruz show no signs of dispersing. Little commerce is transacted in the plaza over the next two days and no one lines the road to wave goodby to the troops as they ride out Friday morning.

Justiniani is in front, between the flag bearers and trumpeter, with Captain Muñoz just behind, between Governor Armijo and Padre Martinez. The captain keeps his eyes straight ahead as he passes the execution site. Armijo glances toward it. His face twists as if he's seeing it for the first time. The blocks of cottonwood are still in place. The stains look almost like black paint now, or tar.

"It was necessary," the governor mutters with white lips. He turns to Donaciano Vigil, who's riding at his left hand, since Caballero has been left behind with a contingent of men to guard the capital. "When we return, those blocks must be destroyed," he says. "Incinerate them."

Vigil nods. "As you say, Excellency."

"I sincerely hope that los insurrectos have received the message and absorbed its meaning, and that doing so will turn them from the path of destruction." He gives Muñoz a sharp look. "That is why I ordered their executions. So that others will not follow in their footsteps."

"You did what was necessary," Padre Martínez says firmly.

Muñoz looks straight ahead. There's no indication that the executions have persuaded any of the rebels to go home. He tries to keep his expression neutral, but inside he's groaning in disgust. As a military man, he knows how to follow orders, that it's not his place to question the rationale for them.

But he's been here too long and seen too much. He's sick to death of Nuevo México and its complications. He takes a deep, solidifying breath, trying to find something else to think about.

The air here is crisp and clear, at any rate, even if it is cold at this time of year. The sky is a luminous blue. The road ahead rises gently, then drops again over a series of rolling hills covered with juniper, their blue-green needles tipped with a light, glittering snow. On his right, the snow-topped mountain peaks blaze in the sun. It's a glorious day, if a man is well wrapped.

Armijo feels it too. His head turns left, then right, with a satisfied smile, as if it all belongs to him. The track bends slightly here and the governor can see the men behind him without much effort. His smile broadens.

Muñoz follows his gaze and his own lips quirk upward in spite of his mood. It is quite a sight. The dragoons are tall on their shining mounts. They look very competent in their black helmets, their red coats, their weapons ready to hand. The presidio soldiers ride behind them, their round, flat-brimmed black hats in neat rows.

"The very sight of them should spark fear and sense into the heart of the rebels," Armijo says with satisfaction.

"I pray it is so," Muñoz says.

"God has blessed us with strong arms and strong minds," Martínez says sententiously. "I am sure it is so."

They camp that night just south of the pueblo of Po-joaque, among sandy hills scattered with more rock than juniper, and wake to more snow. There's less than an inch on the ground, but the breeze that rises with the sun is persistent. It blows bits of snow this way and that, powdering the men and their animals with needles of ice.

The wind follows them north, dashing snow into their faces, then turning and buffeting them from behind. Justiniani leads the way into the Pojoaque river valley and past the turn Donaciano Vigil says heads west to San Ildefonso and the río del Norte—the one Pérez and his men followed early last August.

Muñoz winces. That was also a confrontation in which a Nuevo México governor thought a rebel force could be intimidated into submission. He glances at Armijo, who's still looking pleased with himself, then deliberately turns his mind both from the August events and what might occur today.

They've entered the river bosque and are cutting across it. Even in midwinter, it's a lovely place: the gnarled gray majesty of the cottonwoods, dead leaves rattling in the wind, old grass crunching underfoot. The wind has died a little and the snow sparkles on it all in crystalline joy.

However, Muñoz can't shake an underlying sense of foreboding. The only sound is the creak of saddles, the occasional snort of a horse. There's no movement in the woods. No one collecting downed branches. No boys guarding grazing sheep or goats. Even the water they cross seems subdued.

~ ~ ~ ~

And then they break out of the trees and into the fields beyond. Justiniani jerks to a halt. Muñoz and the others rein in behind him. On the far side of the snow-covered pastures, jagged sandstone cliffs cut off the northern horizon.

The wind lifts. Bits of ice sting Muñoz's face. He squints at the road ahead. It runs straight toward the crags.

The lieutenant colonel turns and beckons to him and the governor. They move forward, Padre Martínez and Sergeant Vigil close behind.

"What is it?" Armijo asks.

Justiniani points across the fields. Muñoz leans forward, trying to see. A burst of snow lifts from a buff-colored outcropping to the right, furthering obscuring his view.

"The cliffs," the lieutenant colonel says impatiently.

"You see before you what is known as Pojoaque Pass," Armijo says, evidently thinking the man wants information. "It is identified as such as a result of its proximity of the pueblo behind us."

Justiniani shakes his head, eyes still fixed on the sandstone barrier. "Look more closely."

The blowing snow lifts slightly, the wind moving it sideways, and the face of the cliff seems to soften, then sharpen, almost as if the great crags are slowly dancing. Muñoz blinks and refocuses. His breath hisses through his teeth. The sandstone is alive with tiny specks—men scrambling up, down, and across its rugged surface, positioning themselves.

"¡Maldición!" Armijo mutters.

Justiniani turns his head, studying the length of the great barrier and the road that leads toward it and on to Santa Cruz. "The only way through is forward," he says thoughtfully.

Armijo doesn't answer. He's peering at the point where the track disappears into a small break in the jagged wall.

Muñoz follows his gaze. Black clusters of insurrectos stain the rocks on either side of the road. "There will be blood shed this day," he says quietly.

"Surely it won't come to that," Armijo mutters. "There should be a delegation. I gave them plenty of time to learn of the executions. And they can see for themselves that the dragoons have arrived from the south." His voice rises. "Surely they'll wish to negotiate!"

"I see no evidence of a desire to parlay." Justiniani's expression is as flat as his voice as he turns to the governor. "With your consent, I believe the most appropriate maneuver is to send men forward while also flanking them." He nods at the cliffs. "The insurrectos have focused on the road. I recommend that small detachments be sent farther down either side to scale the heights behind them while the dragoons charge the center."

Armijo continues to stare at the sandstone crags as he reluctantly nods.

The lieutenant colonel glances at Muñoz, then points toward the stony outcropping in the nearby field. "That's the best vantage point. I will position there. Send me word as necessary." He gives Armijo a small bow. "I leave it in your hands, Excellency. My men are at your command."

Armijo's mouth opens to protest, but Justiniani is already trotting away, Padre Martínez at his heels. On the road behind Muñoz, the dragoons' horses shift expectantly. Their riders watch the governor.

He nudges his horse with his knees, moves a few paces forward, then reins in and stares bleakly at the pass. "Why won't they go home?" he whispers. "Will it never end?"

Muñoz moves forward. "We wait your command, Excellency." He tries to sound respectful, but impatience edges his words. Delay is of no use. Surely the man sees that.

Armijo turns toward him, his face troubled. "I suppose it must be done." Then his mouth twists. "The rabble. How dare they continue to resist!"

That's more like it. However, he still doesn't give the command. Muñoz suppresses a huff of annoyance and leans toward him. "Con su autorización, Excellency," he says. "My little company is enough to roust that rabble."

"Yes," the governor says. "But only with my authorization." A shudder runs across his shoulders. Then his back straightens. "That rabble!" he mutters. He wheels his horse to face the dragoons. The sun glints on their black hats, their solid shoulders. Behind them, the presidio soldiers lean forward on their mounts, watching him.

He beckons to Sergeant Vigil, who trots over. Armijo speaks in a low voice, gestures toward the cliff, and waves left and right.

Vigil nods, wheels, and moves past the dragoons to his men. He gives a series of sharp commands and half the company divides neatly into two parties, and angle in opposite directions across the fields, toward the farther ends of cliffs. The rebels don't respond. They seem unaware of them, focused only on the men still in the road.

Armijo's gaze follows the presidio soldiers, his face still filled with indecision. There's a long moment of silence. Muñoz peers toward the sandstone crags. The presidio men reach their objective, vault from their mounts, and clamber into the rocks. It's time.

Armijo's horse sidesteps in the road. Muñoz glances toward the rocky outcropping where Justiniani is watching, then turns to the governor. "Con su autorización, Excellency," he says again, more urgently this time.

Armijo's face twists again. Then, eyes still on the cliffs, he nods.

Muñoz turns, speaks to his first sergeant, then settles his horse, facing the Pass. He draws his sword and points it into the air. Behind him, his straight-backed troopers sit even straighter and tighten the grip on their horses' reins, a coiled spring ready for his command. He lifts his chin and straightens his sword arm, aiming it toward the cliffs. "Forward, Vera Cruz!" he cries. His voice whips the cold air.

Armijo's mount leaps out of the way as the dragoons sweep past him and pound up the road. The black forms of the insurrectos move toward each other, waiting. They seem oblivious to the presidio men who crouch behind and above.

Muñoz and half a dozen dragoons race through the pass. The rest rush the lower slopes, snow and rock flying under their hooves, forcing the rebels backward toward the waiting soldiers.

Armijo has followed with the rest of the presidio men. Somewhere behind, he cries "Forward! To death or to Víctory!" More dragoons, joined by the presidio contingent, break through the pass and whirl to the sides, hunting along the back of the cliffs for fleeing insurrectos.

And then it's over and Manuel Armijo, Cayetano Justiniani, and Captain Muñoz are sitting their horses at the top of the pass and gazing at the body of El Coyote Vigil. A pale-faced Padre Martínez bends over the corpse, his lips moving. Soldiers and dragoons cluster nearby.

"We should make an example of him," Justiniani says.

"Cut off his head," a presidio man suggests. "Stick it on a pike back there at the crossroads to La Mesilla."

Armijo grimaces. "We aren't barbarians." His eyes narrow. "However, hanging would certainly be appropriate." His lips twist, though it's hard to tell if it's in distaste or humor. "Especially there." He nods toward a small cluster of men. "Take him to the crossroads and hang him from the largest cottonwood you can find." He raises his voice. "Let all who view this rebel's body be reminded forever of the fate which awaits traitors and insurrectos!"

Martínez makes the sign of the cross one more time and straightens. "And the others?" He gestures at the bodies scattered among the rocks. "I have done all I can for these. But those who fled northward—"

Armijo turns to Justiniani. "They may be dispersing," the lieutenant colonel says.

The padre makes the sign of the cross. "I pray it is so."

Armijo glances at the nearby soldiers and reaches down to rub his left thigh. "We must ensure this insurrection is truly over, whatever the cost to ourselves."

Justiniani looks at the sky, now a crystal blue in every direction. "It is still early."

"Let us complete what we have begun and roust any who remain under arms," the governor says. "Until Santa Cruz de la Cañada is under my control, there will still be those who think there is room for revolt in Nuevo México." He turns to Muñoz. "If your men would be so good as to lead the way."

Muñoz doesn't know whether to be bemused or annoyed. Is the governor giving the dragoons a place of honor or using them as a guard against further attack? But now isn't the time for speculating about the man's possible motives. The captain sends his troopers on up the road.

~ ~ ~ ~

Almost four hours later, the snow is gone but not a single insurrecto has been sighted. Muñoz frowns uneasily. Either all the rebels have slipped away or they're regrouping.

He shivers. Gray clouds have crept in from the mountains and are dropping lower by the minute. The cold has sharpened, grown more damp. Even the stalwart Justiniani is pulling the lapels of his uniform up and over his chest. Padre Martinez leans back to his saddle bags, pulls out a striped wool blanket, and wraps it around his shoulders.

Armijo is too proud to add another layer, but he does lean forward and rub his left leg. "This wound always responds with resounding negativity to the winter cold," he says.

"This is certainly a land of contrasts," Muñoz responds, pushing his uneasiness aside. "I understand this upper river area is quite warm during the summer."

Armijo grimaces. "Blazing hot. It's worse here than in Alburquerque."

The padre's eyes twinkle. "It's cooler in Taos."

The others have no time to respond. There's a shout up ahead, then a volley of shots, the shrill scream of a horse. They spur their mounts forward.

The rebels have barricaded themselves in the sparsely wooded hills on either side of the road and are laying down a sharp fire of both bullets and arrows. Sergeant Vigil bellows an order and presidio men swing off the road and gallop toward the far side of the heights and up the slopes, repeating the strategy they'd used earlier in the day. Muñoz's dragoons surge forward in tandem, heading up the road.

He, Armijo, and Martínez follow Justiniani to the top of a small hill, and stare toward the heights, Armijo rubbing his leg and Padre Martínez muttering a prayer.

This confrontation takes longer. The insurrectos have learned from the morning maneuvers. They niche themselves between trees and closely set rocks where mounted men can't get at them, and take up positions on their flank, watching for presidio men. A dragoon tumbles from his horse, which flees wildly down the slope. Another pushes into the trees at the top and is brought down by what seem to be arrows from all directions.

But, although the rebels are fighting hard and well, there are fewer of them this time. Eventually the firing slows, then dies completely, and they begin to trickle down the hill, hands in the air.

As the trickle turns into a stream, Muñoz lets out a breath he hadn't realized he was holding. He turns to Armijo. "It's done."

The governor looks up, still holding his thigh. His face is pinched with pain. "I most certainly hope so." Then he spies a thin short figure below, dragoons on either side. He straightens, his leg forgotten. "Is that Pablo Montoya?"

"Yes, that's him," Martínez says. "Perhaps now he'll listen to what he's told and submit to those in authority over him."

Armijo's eyes lift toward the heights. More rebels step from the trees. "Excelentisimo," he mutters. He rubs his hands together, his wound forgotten. "Most excellent indeed. Now we'll have an end to it at last."

He turns to Justiniani. "We can seek shelter at the Santa Cruz de la Cañada rectory tonight." He grins conspiratorially at Martínez. "I understand the cellars there contain an exceptionally good wine."

~ ~ ~ ~

Not all the insurrectos have surrendered. Small groups of dragoons and presidio men work their way from field to field and casa to casa, gathering them in.

Muñoz's detachment includes Donaciano Vigil. Most of the homeowners submit to the search of their compounds quietly enough, but at the seventh house, they get a different kind of reception.

It's a good-sized hacienda, a sprawling adobe with a small cluster of workers' casitas nearby. Clearly the home of ricos. As Muñoz and the others reach the gate, he notices Sergeant Vigil has stepped back, as if he doesn't want to be seen by these particular residents.

The captain nods to a soldier, who pounds on the closed gate loud enough to be heard inside the house. On the other side of the wall, a dog barks, and a woman yells, "Who is it?"

She doesn't sound nervous. The captain glances at Vigil, who grimaces. "It's the home of Antonio Abad Montoya," he says.

Then the gate swings open and a wild-haired woman faces them. She has an old musket in her hands and fury in her eyes. When her gaze reaches Vigil, her lips pull back, showing her teeth. "Primo," she says contemptuously. Then she shifts to Muñoz. The gun barrel centers on his chest. "You will not enter here."

The captain keeps his voice calm. "We must search your home."

"This piece is primed. I'll shoot the first person who steps through my gate."

"We're looking for rebels. You must submit."

"Submit!" The barrel wobbles a little, then steadies. He steps backward but she moves forward, staying with him. "I have submitted long enough! No more!" She turns toward Vigil. The muzzle goes with her, aiming for his torso. Her voice rises. "There are no rebels here! They're all dead!"

There's sudden movement at the door on the other side of the yard. They all turn toward it. A wide-eyed little girl with unruly braids stares out at them.

"Go back inside!" the woman snaps. She glares at Vigil. "You have left us with nothing!"

"Prima—" He moves forward, a hand out for the weapon's muzzle. She jerks it up, aiming for his face, and he stops.

Then the child moves to one side. A man steps from the shadows. His clothes are tattered, but he bears his bulky form with a strange dignity. "It is I whom you seek," he says quietly.

Silence drops over the courtyard. Donaciano Vigil takes off his hat. "Señor José Angel Gonzales," he says formally. "We meet again."

The former governor smiles wryly. "I had hoped to encounter you under quite different circumstances." He turns to Muñoz. "I believe you are searching for me."

The captain nods mutely. A dragoon appears at his side, proffering a strip of rawhide for the prisoner's hands.

"You will not need that," Gonzales says. He looks at Vigil. "I will go as quietly as you did at La Mesilla." He turns to the captain. "If you will be so kind as to take me to Governor Armijo." He turns to the woman and bows. "Doña Dolores, I thank you for your hospitality."

She frowns as she lowers her weapon. "Be careful. They kill rebel leaders with impunity."

He smiles gently. "Perhaps there is still hope, but it is as God wills."

Her frown deepens, but she steps aside to let him pass. He moves out of the courtyard, ahead of the captain and sergeant. The gate slaps shut behind them and the crossbar scrapes into place as they reach the road.

"Governor Armijo and Lieutenant Colonel Justiniani plan to sleep at the Santa Cruz rectory tonight," Muñoz tells the prisoner.

Gonzales nods, acknowledging the information, but does not speak as he moves up the road between the presidio sergeant and the captain of dragoons. Muñoz studies him out of the corner of his eye. There's something about the bulk of the man and his quiet bearing that demands respect.

They are within sight of the hill that contains the Santa Cruz plaza and church before the rebel leader speaks again. He turns to Donaciano Vigil. "How have you been these past months?" he asks courteously.

The sergeant smiles. "Busier than I expected."

Gonzales' eyes twinkle. "I have noticed that Manuel Armijo is a man who likes to make proclamations."

Vigil chuckles, then sobers. "He wishes peace above all things."

"I hope so."

Muñoz and the sergeant both give him a questioning look, but Gonzales lapses back into silence. They climb the hill to the plaza and the big adobe church on its western edge, then move on to the rectory.

A handful of dragoons rest in the courtyard, while two presidio soldiers stand outside the house door. They stiffen when they see Gonzales. He nods politely and moves forward, but Muñoz puts a hand on his arm. He has a sudden urge to protect the thick-shouldered cibolero. "It may be well if I announce you," he says.

Gonzales looks at him thoughtfully, then nods. "Gracias."

A guard opens the door. The captain steps inside.

Armijo stands on the other side of the room, his wounded leg as close to the adobe fireplace as he can get it without scorching his trousers. His face is filled with irritable pain.

Justiniani sits at a small table in the opposite corner, staring into a goblet of wine. Padre Martínez stands nearby, holding a small calfskin-covered book. They all look up when Muñoz enters.

He focuses on the governor. "I have brought José Angel Gonzales to you, Excellency."

Armijo jerks away from the fire and stares at him. His fingers twitch against his leg.

Muñoz turns toward the door. Gonzales is already in the room, Sergeant Vigil just behind him. The rebel leader strides toward Armijo, his hand out. "Please accept my congratulations on a well-fought campaign, governor," he says politely. "I have come to negotiate our surrender."

Armijo's mouth opens, then closes into a tight line. He glances at Gonzales's hand but doesn't take it. His fingers curl into two fists.

Gonzales doesn't appear to notice. His hand drops to his side. "I can guarantee the immediate peaceful return of my men to their homes and occupations," he says. "In exchange we ask for assurances that our communities will be exempted from the federal sales tax."

Armijo's lips curl. "Your guarantee? There is nothing for you to guarantee. I have today destroyed what is left of the rabble you refer to as your men." He steps forward, almost touching Gonzales' chest with his own, his eyes black slits of anger. "You are in no position to demand concessions from me. I have been appointed constitutional governor and principal commandant of all of Nuevo México. My supreme objective was to establish peace and good order, but you and your unspeakable rabble—"

He pulls back and looks around the room, taking in the onlookers. Justiniani, still at the table. Muñoz halfway to the door, the sergeant just inside. Padre Martínez has closed his book. His eyes dart between Armijo and Gonzales.

The governor's face hardens even more, vindictive as well as angry. "And now I will establish my authority once and for all, and in the most effective and rapid way possible." He jerks his chin at the priest. "Padre Martínez, be so good as to hear this genízaro's confession in preparation for the appropriate recompense for his labors."

Muñoz's head jerks. Surely he doesn't mean to execute Gonzales, too? Hasn't there been enough killing?

Gonzales also seems surprised. He stares at the governor openly. Then his face changes. He peers into Armijo's face

266

as if really seeing him for the first time, then nods calmly and turns to the priest.

Martínez moves forward and leads the cibolero into the far corner. They murmur together for a few minutes, then Gonzales bows his head, the padre makes the sign of the cross over him, and speaks again, slightly louder but still too low for Muñoz to hear.

When they've finished, Gonzales turns back to the room and faces Armijo. Again there's that look, a mixture of contempt and a kind of pity.

The governor glares back at him. His fingers twitch against his leg. Then he shoves his right hand under the left side of his jacket, turns to Muñoz, and waves his other hand toward the prisoner. "Take him."

The captain and the rebel leader consider each other, then turn toward the door and Donaciano Vigil. The sergeant steps back, then sideways toward Justiniani and the table, his face a careful mask.

Armijo huffs with impatience. "Captain!" he snaps.

Muñoz turns.

"Five bullets!" Armijo says. "One for each prisoner he forced me to kill in addition to one for himself!"

Muñoz stares at him for a long minute. Armijo glares back at him. The captain stiffens his spine, nods in acknowledgement, and moves grimly toward the door, Gonzales beside him.

At the threshold, Muñoz glances back. Justiniani is staring into space. Vigil is watching Armijo, whose expression is a mixture of spite, hurt pride, and physical pain. The priest is crossing himself and mumbling a prayer.

Gonzales has also paused. He, too, glances around the room. Then he looks at the captain. "I did what was necessary to ensure that the voices of my people were heard," he says gently. "If this is the result, then so be it. Their cause will not die with me."

Muñoz bows slightly, honoring the man's quiet strength, and follows him outside and across the courtyard. The dragoons who've been resting there rise to meet them, then fall in behind.

THE END

AUTHOR'S NOTE

There are a number of accounts of the events in New Mexico in August 1837 and the following five months. Most of them were written by anglo historians in the late nineteenth and early twentieth centuries and reflect the biases of their time. Many are part of longer histories of New Mexico, and their particular retellings focus on specific portions of the rebellion rather than trying to provide a comprehensive overview. No one seems to have pulled key documents together and tried to tell the entire story from start to finish until 1985, when Janet Lecompte published *Rebellion in Río Arriba 1837*.

Lecompte's work was the backbone of my research process. However, she focused on the sequence of events more than the background to them or the relationships of the individuals involved, things critical to writing a biographical novel. I combed various other sources for this type of detail, and the publications of the New Mexico Genealogical Society were essential to this effort, but of course many of the physical descriptions of the people in these stories and the emotional connections between them are conjecture on my part.

The various other sources I used, including *Old Santa Fe Magazine,* provided fascinating details that I incorporated where I could. I especially enjoyed José Francisco Perea's memories of Santa Fe during the winter of 1837/38, including his description of the plaza and his and Joaquín's schooling in the spring of 1838.

Of course, there were gaps in the historical record that my sources didn't bridge but my story demanded to be filled. This is the fun of writing historical fiction—imagining the details and connections the records don't provide. For example, I don't know that presidio Sergeant Donaciano Vigil was involved in Alcalde Esquibel's arrest, that Esquibel was arrested during the feast at Chimayó, that his wife visited him in jail, or what, if any, emotional experiences he may have had there.

I also don't know that Vigil or Captain Muñoz were responsible for José Angel Gonzales' capture in January 1838 or present during the famous (and possibly apocryphal) interaction between Gonzales and Governor Armijo. As with the Perea family story, I've used the information available to me and attempted to create a plausible chain of events that incorporates that information. Again, this is the fun of writing historical fiction.

One of the most frustrating aspects of writing historical fiction is when the historical record of a major event provides no background for it, no reason for what happened. In this novel, the incident I most struggled with in this regard was the August 1837 deaths of Santiago Abreú and Diego Sáenz in the indigenous community the Spanish called Santo Domingo Pueblo.

All the sources I found focus on the details of the event itself—Abreú's capture, confinement in the stocks, and subsequent death and dismemberment. However, they provide no explanation for why this happened, or for Sáenz's demise. The clear implication of the narratives that have come down to us is that the people at Santo Domingo were uncivilized, treacherous savages capable of the most barbarous and irrational actions and that Abreú and Sáenz just happened to be the men they captured, so were the ones who were killed.

This racist thread of Santo Domingo treachery (at the battle of La Mesilla) and savagery (the use of Pérez's head as a football, as well as Abreú's death) runs through all the published accounts of the 1837 revolt. My initial reaction to this trope was a suspicion that both the anglo and Spanish historians wanted to place the blame for the more gruesome aspects of the rebellion on the Pueblo warriors, thereby metaphorically washing the other participants' hands clean. If this was the case, then I could safely assume that whatever actions they ascribed to the warriors and people of Santo Domingo were, at the very least, greatly exaggerated, and move on.

However, even if exaggerated, there could be some truth to these accounts. After all, though there's some disagreement in the sources about whether only Santo Domingo warriors desecrated Albino Pérez's dismembered head, they're unanimous about how Santiago Abreú and Diego Sáenz died at the pueblo. If this was indeed the case, I needed to explore why these deaths occurred and why they were carried out in the way reported. None of the historical records provide even a trace of an answer to these questions. Again, the idea seems to be that the deaths were a natural result of the Santo Domingo character but not the consequence of any action on Abreú's or Sáenz's part.

As I said earlier, I enjoy bridging the gaps in the historical record. However, no information at all is a very large gap. I began to explore further, moving back in time and broadening my scope. In that process, I learned that, aside from long-simmering tensions between the Spanish/Mexican conquerors and New Mexico's First Peoples, an incident during Santiago Abreú's 1832-33 term as Governor could explain what happened at Santo Domingo in August 1837.

During that period, a man named José Francisco Ortiz, or "El Sonoreño", was granted the right to mine in what is now known as the Ortiz Mountains, east of the pueblo of Santo Domingo. This cluster of peaks includes Mount Chalchihuitl, a location important to First Nations people across the region as a source of turquoise, the opaque blue-green stone which was, and still is, revered for its healing and protective properties.

This handover to Ortiz must have been deeply disturbing to the land's traditional users, especially those who lived as close to it as the people of Santo Domingo. Not only was Ortiz of Spanish ancestry, he was from Sonora. Since he hadn't been born and raised in New Mexico, it's unlikely he would have understood or felt any empathy with its First Peoples or their concerns.

In addition, New Mexico's historical record indicates that Ortiz may not have been the most savory of men. His first appearance in the archives is in September 1805 as the defendant on a charge of vagrancy, theft, and sedition.

However, Ortiz was apparently a versatile man able to make friends in high places. In late 1809, he acted as agent for Santa Fe presidio Captain Manrique to receive his semi-annual salary at Chihuahua. However, Ortiz was also involved in some slippery mercantile dealings. In June 1820, he was sued for 11,000 pesos when he neglected to pay for merchandise received in Chihuahua in a timely manner. And then there's the report that after Ortiz and two associates were given the mining grant, he had officials invoke a seldom-enforced law that forced one of his partners out of the operation, leaving more for himself.

These incidents lead me to suspect that Ortiz's relationship with the traditional users of the mountains he was mining wouldn't have been a pleasant one. He gained the right to mine during Santiago Abreú's term as governor. This and the long-standing conflict between the Spanish and Pueblo peoples seems to me to provide a plausible explanation for the August 1837 events at Santo Domingo.

As I pointed out earlier, I suspect racism is at the bottom of the lack of historical explanation regarding why Abreú and Sáenz died. In this case, the record was simply silent. In other cases, this bent in the historians' attitudes is more evident. For example, half-anglo author Benjamin M. Read happened to be a good friend of the adult Demetrio Pérez, son of Albino Pérez and Trinidad Trujillo. According to Read, the 1837/38 rebels were a bunch of illiterate dark-skinned peasants who refused to listen to their betters and killed off the cream of New Mexico society.

Except for Donaciano Vigil, of course, who Read also seems to have known. I suspect it's not a coincidence that Vigil happened to have pale skin. Read treated him with respect, even though at least one later historian asserted that he aided and abetted the rebels.

Those suspicions may have been well-founded. Vigil did, after all, act as José Angel Gonzales's Secretary of State. In January 1838, he was court-martialed for his actions in 1837, a trial I don't cover in this novel.

Vigil was exonerated and went on to hold key positions not only in Armijo's administration, but under the Americans after they arrived in 1846, a fact which may account for Read's respectful treatment. After all, American approval clearly meant Vigil was a man of substance who could be trusted. Vigil's reputation has held over the years. He's still described by New Mexico historians as an example of a respected nineteenth century New Mexican statesman.

Manuel Armijo's reputation did not hold up so well. Ralph Emerson Twitchell, writing in 1912, accused Armijo of fomenting the 1837 rebellion in order to regain his position as governor. Other historians went so far as to claim that Armijo ordered the January 1838 executions of the Montoya brothers, Alcalde Esquibel, and El Quemado Vigil in order to suppress information about his own involvement in the rebel coup.

I can find no basis for these accusations, which I suspect reflect the historical discomfort with Armijo's apparent 1846 betrayal of New Mexico into the hands of the Americans rather than what occurred in 1837/38.

Ironically, Armijo's ascension to power in late 1837 meant one of the rebels' complaints would be addressed. Instead of naming yet another outsider as New Mexico's governor, the Central Government appointed Armijo, a man from an old New Mexico family. In March 1838, another insurrecto concern was addressed when Mexico City formally exempted New Mexico from the hated sales tax.

Would these events have occurred if the men from Santa Cruz de la Cañada and other Río Arriba communities hadn't revolted? More importantly, would the insurrectos have risen if their concerns had been addressed in a timely manner in the first place? It's hard to say, but these are certainly questions worth considering. The answers may be relevant even today.

CHARACTER BIOGRAPHIES

Abreú, Francisco de Paula Luis y Onsaga (1831–1930) Son of José Ramón Abreú and María Pelegrina Domíngues. Francisco grew up to be a businessman in Santa Fe, where he operated a small mercantile store. He served as a Union officer during the Civil War and rose to the rank of Colonel. Because of the other Francisco's in this book, I've chosen to call him Luis.

Abreú, José Ramón (1806–1837) Prefect of northern New Mexico who was killed August 9, 1837 at the rebel camp west of the Santa Fe plaza. The middle Abreú brother, he was married to María Pelegrina Domíngues, with whom he had a son, Francisco de Paula Luis y Onsaga Abreú.

Abreú, Marcelino (circa 1808–1837) Schoolteacher at Tomé who happened to be in Santa Fe in early August 1837. The youngest of the Abreú brothers, he died with them during the uprising. He was married to María Brigída Olona (1813–?), with whom he had four children.

Abreú, Santiago (circa 1797–1837) Oldest son of a family which arrived in New Mexico in the late 1790s, so were considered relative newcomers. Santiago was governor of New Mexico in 1832–1833 and a District Judge from 1835 until his death on August 10, 1837. He was married to María Josefa del Refugio Baca (September 1805–?), with whom he had four children.

Aponte, Manuel (?–?) Brevet Lieutenant Colonel of the government troops at La Mesilla on August 8, 1837. Aponte was badly wounded there during hand-to-hand combat with Juan

"El Quemado" Vigil. He fled with Pérez to Santa Fe and was subsequently captured by the rebels, but is believed to have survived.

Aragón, Juan (?–?) Magistrate at Don Fernando de Taos whose intervention saved Padre Martínez from a rebel mob in late 1837.

Armijo, Manuel (1790–1853) Only person to serve as New Mexico Governor three times: 1827–1829, late 1837–1844, and 1845–1846. Although Armijo's reputation is tarnished by the fact that he relinquished New Mexico to the invading Americans in 1846 without a fight, in 1837/38 he does seem to have kept the region from going up in flames.

Barceló, María Gertrudis "Doña Tules" (circa 1800–1852) Entrepreneur who owned a gambling salon in Santa Fe and loaned money to influential men. She raised several adoptive or foster daughters, including María Petra Gutierrez and María del Refugio Sisneros.

Bernal, María Ramona (1798–after 1840) Widow from the Santa Cruz de la Cañada area who was José Angel Gonzales' third wife. She may have had as many as three children when they married in 1836, one by José María Gutierrez, whom she'd wed in late 1829, and two other sons whose baptism records list their fathers as "unknown."

Caballero, José (circa 1773–?) Captain of the Santa Fe presidio troops during late 1837. His son Esquipula would marry Santiago Abreú's daughter Soledad in August 1839.

Chacón, José Albino (1806–after 1859) Santa Fe's assistant assistant, or third, alcalde in August 1837. Chacón was responsible for Albino Pérez's burial, although Petra Gutierrez said years later that she and the other women identified in Chapter 6 were also involved. Chacón was an alcalde at Santa Fe off and on until 1846, when he and his family moved to the Taos Valley.

Chávez, Antonito (?–?) Leader of a group of Albuquerque militia who, on August 9, 1837, refused to assist Governor Albino Pérez against the rebels.

Chávez, José Francisco (1833–1904) The son of José Francisco Perea's paternal aunt, María Dolores Lavinia Perea and maternal uncle, Mariano Chávez. As an adult, Chávez served as Lieutenant Colonel of the 1st New Mexico infantry during the Civil War. In 1864, he defeated José Francisco Perea in the contest to serve as New Mexico's representative to the U.S. Congress.

Chávez, José Mariano de Jesús (1802–?) José Francisco Perea's maternal uncle. At the September 8, 1837 meeting at Tomé, he nominated Manuel Armijo as commander of the combined loyalist militia/presidio troops and was subsequently named second in command. He was married to Perea's aunt, María Dolores Lavinia Perea, and was José Francisco Chávez's father.

Chávez, Josefa Mercedes (1812–1865) José Francisco Perea's mother. The daughter of Francisco Xavier Durán y Cháves II and Ana María del Carmen Alvarez del Castillo, she married Juan Dolores Perea around 1826. José Francisco Perea was their oldest son.

Chávez, María Dolores Longina (1826–1887) Youngest sister of José Francisco Perea's mother, Josefa Mercedes Chávez. She may have gone by "Dolores" rather than "Longina," but I've used the latter name in this book to differentiate her from the other women named Dolores. She married José Leandro Perea, the younger brother of José Francisco's father, around 1843.

Domíngues, María Pelegrina (circa 1808–?) José Ramón Abreú's wife. They married in May 1827 and had one child, Francisco de Paula Luis y Onsaga Abreú.

Esquibel, Juan José (1788–1838) The alcalde of Santa Cruz de la Cañada in 1837. His jailing and subsequent "release" marked the beginning of the rebellion. Esquibel's wife, María Rafaela Martín, had eighteen siblings, most of whom lived in the Santa Cruz area, which meant her husband was related to many of the local residents. They had seven children together.

Giddings, James Madison (1813–1890) American trader who was in and out of Santa Fe throughout the 1830s. He and Petra Gutierrez married in May 1842. The evidence that he was the father of her first child is inconclusive.

Gonzales, José Angel (1799–1838) A buffalo hunter, or cibolero, from the Taos area. Twice widowed, Gonzales married María Ramona Bernal at Santa Cruz de la Cañada in December 1835. He had two sons by his first wife and may have brought them to the joint household. Gonzales directed the rebel forces at La Mesilla and was named governor by them after the battle. His heritage included Taos Pueblo and possibly a Plains tribe.

Gutierrez, María Petra (1823–after 1865) Gertrudis Barceló's foster daughter. In February 1838, Petra gave birth to María Consuelo de los Rayos "Rayitos" Gutierrez, whose father may have been James M. Giddings. María Petra and Giddings married in 1842 and went on to have at least ten children together. Gertrudis Barceló raised Rayitos and provided for her in her will.

Herrero, Dolores (circa 1783–after 1841) Gertrudis Barceló's mother, who arrived in Santa Fe to live with her around 1832 and died there some time after 1841.

Hurtado, Joaquín (?–?) Governor Albino Pérez's aide in Fall 1837. The historical record about the revolt provides no real information about this man. In fact, there isn't even agreement about his first name, which may have been José, Joaquín, Manuel, or some combination of the three.

Justiniani, Cayetano (1800–1863) Lieutenant Colonel and Commander at El Paso in late 1837. He led the dragoons and artillery from Chihuahua to Santa Fe in December 1837/January 1838 but seems to have taken little active role in the final battle at Pojoaque Pass.

Lucero, María de la Luz (1812–after 1856) Wife of José Santiago Martínez. They had at least four living children at the time of this novel: three boys and a girl. María de la Luz's pregnancy that winter resulted in another girl, María Francisca, in early March 1838.

Martín, José María Tomás (1808–1845) Corporal in the Santa Fe presidio troop in 1837 and Salvador Martín's youngest son. José María Tomás was captured by the rebels in August 1837 but returned to Santa Fe later that fall. Family baptism, marriage, and census records identify their last name as both Martín and Martínez. For the purposes of this novel, I've chosen to use the shorter version.

Martín, María Rafaela (1788–?) Juan José Esquibel's wife. Born and raised in Santa Cruz de la Cañada, she married Juan José Esquibel in late 1810, when she was almost 23 and he had just turned 22. They had seven children together.

Martín, Salvador (1763–after 1837) The man outside whose home Governor Pérez was killed on August 10, 1837. Martín, known as "Tío Salvadorito," and his wife María Antonia Chávez y Armijo had nine adult children in 1837, most of whom lived with their families in the Santa Fe/Agua Fría area.

Martínez, Antonio José (1793–1867) Member of a prominent Taos Valley family and the Catholic priest there from 1826 to 1857. By 1837, he was also a member of New Mexico's Legislative Council. A strong personality from a wealthy family, Martínez was in almost constant conflict with the rebels. He would remain active in New Mexico politics until the 1850s.

Martínez, José María de Jesús (circa 1800–circa 1867) The oldest of Padre Martínez's three younger brothers.

Martínez, José Santiago (1804–after 1880) Younger brother of Antonio José Martínez and the subprefect of the Taos District in 1837/1838. He was married to María de la Luz Lucero, with whom he had four children and another on the way at the time of this novel.

Montoya, Antonio Abad (1813–1838) A leader in New Mexico's August 1837 revolt. The oldest of four. In 1830, he and his sister María Catarina married the siblings María Dolores and José Ramón Vigil. Antonio Abad and María Dolores had one child, María Ygnacia. He and his brother Desiderio were executed in Santa Fe three days before the January 1838 battle at Pojoaque Pass.

Montoya, Desiderio (1816–1838) Younger brother of Antonio Abad Montoya, who was jailed with him in Fall 1837 as a leader of the revolt. They escaped execution in October that year only to die on January 24, 1838, eight days after Desiderio's 22nd birthday.

Montoya, José Pablo (circa 1791–1847) Leader of the September 1837 rebel attempt on Santa Fe. Born in Abiquiu, José Pablo had settled in the Taos area by 1824 and returned there after the rebellion failed. Nine years later, he was involved in the early 1847 uprising against the American takeover.

Montoya, María Catarina (1819–after 1866) Antonio Abad and Desiderio Montoya's oldest sister. She married José Ramón Vigil, the brother of Antonio's wife, in August 1830. In late 1836, when María Catarina appears in the novel, they had one child, a little boy named José Francisco.

Montoya, María Ygnacia (circa 1830–after 1845) Daughter of Antonio Abad Montoya and María Dolores Vigil. She married Juan Pedro Martínez in 1845.

Muñoz, Pedro José (?–?) Mexican captain of the Vera Cruz dragoons who participated in the final battle against the rebels. Muñoz was in New Mexico by early October 1837, arriving well ahead of his men, but seems to have returned home with them the following year. He would reappear in New Mexico in late 1841, when he led a detachment of dragoons from Chihuahua to assist Armijo against the threatened Texan invasion. He and his dragoons remained in Santa Fe at least until Fall 1845.

Ortiz, José Francisco "El Sonoreño" (?–1848) 1833 grantee of the mining rights to the mountains east of Santo Domingo Pueblo. For details, see the Author's Note.

Ortiz, Juan Felipe (1797–1858) Red-headed priest at Santa Fe and vicar-general of New Mexico from the 1830s until his death in January 1858. Ortiz was from a wealthy family and was active in New Mexico politics during most of his career.

Perea, Joaquín (1832–?) José Francisco Perea's younger brother. The two boys attended school together in Santa Fe in early 1838 while their family were refugees in Santa Fe.

Perea, José Francisco (1830–1913) Scion of the wealthy Perea family of Bernalillo which had intermarried with the rico Chávez clan. José Francisco was the oldest son of Juan Dolores Perea and Josefa Mercedes Chávez. He left memories of the winter of 1837/38 behind in an article published by W.H.H. Allison in the 1914-15 edition of *Old Santa Fe Magazine.*

Perea, José Leandro (1822–1883) José Francisco Perea's uncle who, by the time he died, was reputed to be the richest man in the region and was commonly known as the Sheep King of New Mexico. He and María Dolores Longina Chávez married around 1843.

Perea, José Ynes (1837–1910) Youngest member of the Fall 1837 Perea family party to Santa Fe. In 1869, José Ynes would become the first Hispanic Presbyterian pastor in New Mexico.

Perea, Juan Dolores (circa 1807–1864) José Francisco Perea's father. He and Josefa Chávez married around 1826 and may have had as many as 18 children before her death in 1865.

Perea, María Dolores Lavinia (circa 1810–after 1854) José Francisco Perea's paternal aunt, who was married to his mother's brother, Mariano Chávez. After Mariano's death circa 1847, she married Henry Connelly, the American trader who became governor of New Mexico in 1861. She seems to have been commonly called "Dolores" but, given the other women with that name in this novel, I've chosen to use "Lavinia" for her instead.

Perea, María Petra (circa 1829–1865) José Francisco Perea's older sister. She married Juan Montoya in 1846 and had ten children with him.

Perea, Pedro José de los Dolores (1782–after 1837) José Francisco Perea's grandfather and a member of New Mexico's Council in the late 1830s. In 1801, he married Barbarita Romero de Perea (1784–after 1827) and had thirteen children with her. At least three of their offspring married into the Chávez family.

Perea, Rufina (1828–1855) José Francisco Perea's oldest sister. She would marry Silverio Castro shortly before her death in 1855.

Pérez, Albino (?–1837) Governor of New Mexico from April 1835 to August 1837, when he was killed during what is popularly called the Chimayó rebellion. He is said to have left behind a wife in Mexico City and a child in Santa Fe, the son of his housekeeper, Trinidad Trujillo.

Pino, Juan Esteban (1782–?) New Mexican official who held posts ranging from inspector-auditor to lieutenant colonel of rural militia and member of New Mexico's governing body. During the period covered by this novel, he was both a member of the Council and a District Judge. He was married to María Nicolosa Troncoso, with whom he had four children.

Prada, Juana (circa 1812–?) One of the women who went to the rebel camp the night of August 9, 1837 to try to find out what had happened to the governor and his officials. She also assisted with Pérez's burial.

Sáenz, Diego (?–1837) Aide to former governor Santiago Abreú, who died with him at Santo Domingo Pueblo on August 10, 1837.

Sánchez, José Víctor (1802–after 1875) Taos-area merchant who in early 1837 complained to the Santa Cruz de la Cañada alcalde, and then Governor Pérez, that two men from Santa Cruz hadn't paid the 100 pesos they owed him. There's no evidence Sánchez ever received his money. Sánchez and his wife Ana María de Jesús Servé had lost their only child in 1834. They would have another son, Juan Nepomuseno, in May 1840.

Sarracino, Francisco Antonio José Félix (1790–after 1850) Governor of New Mexico from 1833 to 1835. He was replaced by Albino Pérez, who then named him subcomisario, or treasurer. In April 1836 Sarracino was charged with malfeasance and temporarily removed from office, and Manuel Armijo was appointed acting treasurer. Sarracino was reinstated in late July 1837. He was wounded at the battle of La Mesilla and briefly captured. He escaped to his home in Pajarito and stayed there until late September, when he put in a claim for the large gilded mirrors Pérez had borrowed from him.

Servé, Ana María de Jesús (Nov. 22, 1818–before 1863) Víctor Sánchez's wife. They had lost their only child, a little boy, in 1834 and would not have another, Juan Nepomuseno, until 1840.

Sisneros, María del Refugio (1826–?) Gertrudis Barceló's adopted daughter. María del Refugio was 11 years old in late 1837 when I imagine her meeting the Perea boys. She married merchant Santiago Flores in 1841.

Trujillo, Trinidad (?–?) Albino Pérez's housekeeper and mistress from 1835 to Fall 1837. She bore him a son, Demetrio Pérez, in December 1836. According to Demetrio,

Trinidad's grandfather was Bartolomo Fernández, who arrived in New Mexico in the early 1700s.

Vigil, Donaciano (1802–1877) Presidio sergeant who was captured at the battle of La Mesilla and served as Secretary of State under both rebel governor José Angel Gonzales and Manuel Armijo. Tall, well-spoken, and educated, Vigil held various New Mexico government positions under both the Mexican and American administrations, most notably as civil governor following Charles Bent's death in 1847. He was married to María del Refugio Sánchez, with whom he had at least eight children.

Vigil, José Ramón (1805–after 1866) María Catarina Montoya's husband. They had six children together and raised them on a ranch in what is now downtown Española, New Mexico.

Vigil, Juan "El Quemado" (?–?) Rebel who wounded Manuel Aponte at the battle of La Mesilla. Some historians believe his nickname means he came from the village of Quemado, near Chimayó. However, "quemado" is Spanish for "burnt, angry, or irritated." For this reason, I've imagined him as having a burn scar that earned him the label "El Quemado." I've also chosen to identify him as a cousin of Antonio Abad Montoya's wife, Dolores Vigil. Given the number of Vigils in the Santa Cruz area, this is plausible but by no means certain.

Vigil, Juan Antonio "El Coyote" (?–1838) Rebel leader from Truchas, a mountain village east of Santa Cruz de la Cañada. Given his nickname, there's a strong possibility El Coyote wasn't of pure Spanish ancestry. He was active in the Taos area and reportedly threatened Padre Martínez's life if the priest didn't stop preaching against the revolt. Vigil co-led the final uprising and was killed at the battle of Pojoaque Pass.

Vigil, María Dolores (circa 1813–?) Wife of Antonio Abad Montoya. They had one daughter, María Ygnacia, who was born circa 1830. María Dolores was the sister of José Ramón Vigil, the man who married Antonio Abad's sister María Catarina. She and her brother were distant cousins of Donaciano Vigil.

VOCABULARY

abuelo – grandfather (Spanish)

acequia – drain, irrigation ditch (Spanish)

Alburquerque – Original spelling of today's Albuquerque, New Mexico. The town was named for the then-Viceroy of New Spain, the Spanish Duke of Alburquerque. It's unclear when the first 'r' was dropped and the spelling changed to Albuquerque. Twitchell uses the old form consistently in *Leading Facts, Vol. 2* and I have chosen to use it throughout this book. (Spanish)

alcalde – a magistrate who served as both local justice of the peace and head of the municipal council (Spanish)

alma mía – dearest, darling. Literally, "my soul." (Spanish)

americano/americana – any non-Spanish speaking white person in New Mexico (Spanish)

amigo/amiga – friend (Spanish)

anglo – term applied in the American Southwest to anyone with some non-Spanish European blood, especially of an English-speaking white person coming to the Southwest from the Eastern or Midwestern U.S. (Spanish)

arroyo – intermittent streambed, a creek (Spanish)

banco – adobe bench built as part of an interior wall, usually beside a fireplace (Spanish)

bicorne – two-cornered cocked hat (English)

bizcochito – rolled and cut cookie flavored with anise and cinnamon (Spanish)

bosque – wooded area on the edge of a body of water (Spanish)

bueno – very well, all right (Spanish)

buenos días – good day, good morning (Spanish)

bulto – carved statue of a holy person, usually made of wood (Spanish)

calabozo – jail, cell, dungeon (Spanish)

Camino Real de Tierra Adentro – Royal Road of the Interior Land, the highway that ran from Mexico City to Taos. It was renamed the Camino Nacional following independence, but is still commonly referred to as El Camino Real. (Spanish)

camisas – shirts (Spanish)

carreta – two-wheeled wooden cart pulled by ox or donkey (Spanish)

casa – house, dwelling (Spanish)

casita – small house, cabin (Spanish)

cepo del reo – pillory, stocks (Spanish)

chamacos – kids (Spanish)

chamiso – a type of large sagebrush (Spanish)

cibolero – buffalo hunter (Spanish)

corrida del gallo – rooster race (Spanish)

coyote – person of Spanish and New Mexico Indian ancestry, or someone with an anglo father and a mother who was either Spanish or Indian (Spanish)

Don – mister, sir. Used only before a man's first name (Spanish)

Don Fernando de Taos – Today's town of Taos. Through the centuries, this community has been called Don Fernando de Taos, San Fernando de Taos, San Fernandez de Taos, and Taos. Because Taos Pueblo, 3 miles northeast, was also referred to as Taos during this period, I use Don

Fernando de Taos or (short form) Don Fernando in this
novel. (Spanish)

Doña – lady, ma'am, madam, mistress. Used only before a
woman's first name (Spanish)

el cerro de Chimayó – village of Chimayó, literally, "the
hill of Chimayó" (Spanish)

el Niño Jesús – the baby Jesus (Spanish)

español/españoles – Spanish (Spanish)

Estados Unidos Mexicanos – United Mexican States, the
official term for Mexico's federation of thirty-two states
(Spanish)

genízaro – a member of the non-Pueblo First Peoples who
was "rescued" by Spanish settlers, or a child or descendant of one of these captives (Spanish)

gracias – thanks, thank you (Spanish)

hacienda – farm, plantation, the main house on such an estate (Spanish)

hermano – brother (Spanish)

hijos – sons (Spanish)

indios bárbaros – unacculterated or "wild" First Peoples
tribes. This usually meant the Navajo, Apache, and Comanche but could also refer to other groups (Ute, Kiowa,
etc.) who—unlike the Pueblo Indians—weren't Christian-
ized. (Spanish)

jefe – boss, chief, leader (Spanish)

La Bajada –In northern New Mexico, the black basalt escarpment south of Santa Fe en route to Alburquerque.
Literally "the descent, the slope". (Spanish)

la Ciudad de México – Mexico City (Spanish)

La Guadalupana – the Virgin of Guadalupe (Spanish)

la mandona – the bossy one (Spanish)

league – a unit of distance, about three miles (English)

lo siento – I'm sorry (Spanish)

Los Padillas – community south of Albuquerque near the pueblo of Isleta. A prosperous farming area, the Mariano Chávez family was still living there in 1846, when Susan Magoffin visited them.

maíz – corn (Spanish)

maldición – damnation (Spanish)

matanza – act of slaughtering, also the feast that follows the slaughter (Spanish)

me llamo – I am named (Spanish)

mi querido – my love (Spanish)

monte – gambling game in which players bet which card will match the suit in the next one drawn. Gertrudis Barceló was known for her skill as a monte dealer. (Spanish)

niña – little girl (Spanish)

nombre – name (Spanish)

ojos – eyes (Spanish)

olé – bravo (Spanish)

padre – priest. Literally, "father." (Spanish)

paisanos – country men (Spanish)

palacio – the palace. In New Mexico, the building on the north side of the Santa Fe plaza that once served as the governor's residence and offices. During the 1830s, it also included at least one prison cell. (Spanish)

pendejos – inept, clumsy, and/or stupid people (Spanish)

peones – farm workers, unskilled laborers, people of low social status (Spanish)

piloncillo – small pylon-shaped cone of brown sugar (Spanish)

por favor – please, literally "if you will" (Spanish)

portal – covered porch or portico (Spanish)

prefect – a regional administrator and justice of the peace (Spanish)

presidio – military garrison (Spanish)

primo/prima – cousin, close friend (Spanish)

qué – what (Spanish)

rebozo – a long woven shawl (Spanish)

río – river (Spanish)

Río Arriba – upriver district of New Mexico north of Santa Fe (Spanish)

río del Norte –the major waterway in New Mexico along which the primary Spanish settlements and many pueblos were established. Now known as the río Grande (Spanish)

sala – living room, parlor, hall, large room (Spanish)

señor – mister, sir (Spanish)

señora – lady, mistress, madam, gentlewoman, married woman (Spanish)

sí – yes (Spanish)

tía – aunt (Spanish)

tío – uncle (Spanish)

vamos – go on (Spanish)

vecinos – citizens, friends, neighbors (Spanish)

ventisca – blizzard, storm (Spanish)

vigas – ceiling beams (Spanish)

SHORT BIBLIOGRAPHY

Abbink, Emily. *New Mexico's Palace of the Governors.* Santa Fe: Museum of New Mexico Press, 2007.

Allison, W. H. H. "Santa Fe During the Winter of 1837-1838." *Old Santa Fe Magazine.* Santa Fe: Old Santa Fe Press, 1914-1915: 170-183.

Bloom, Lansing. "Barreiro's Ojeada Sobre Nuevo Mexico." *New Mexico Historical Review.* Santa Fe: Historical Society of New Mexico, 3:73-95.

Chartrand, René. *Santa Anna's Mexican Army, 1821-48.* Oxford: Osprey Publishing, 2004.

Chávez, Fray Angélico. *But Time and Chance: The Story of Padre Martínez of Taos, 1793-1867.* Santa Fe: Sunstone Press, 1981.

Cobos, Rubén. *Refranes, Southwestern Spanish Proverbs.* Santa Fe: Museum of New Mexico Press, 1985.

———. *A Dictionary of New Mexico and Southern Colorado Spanish.* Santa Fe: Museum of New Mexico Press, 2003.

Kraemer, Paul. *An Alternative View of New Mexico's 1837 Rebellion.* Los Alamos: Los Alamos Historical Society, 2009.

Lecompte, Janet. *Rebellion in Río Arriba 1837.* Albuquerque: University of New Mexico Press, 1985.

May, Ella Louise, Virginia L. Olmstead, Margaret Leonard Windham, and Evelyn Lujan Baca. *New Mexico Baptisms of Santa Fe, Parish of Saint Francis of Assisi, Vol. III.* Albuquerque: New Mexico Genealogical Society, 2002.

Read, Benjamin M. *Illustrated History of New Mexico.* Santa Fe: New Mexican Printing Company, 1912.

Sánchez Rau, Patricia and Henrietta Martínez Christmas. *Santa Cruz Marriages, 1826-1849 and Roots, Ltd, Addendum.* Albuquerque: New Mexico Genealogical Society, 2013.

Stanley, F. *Giant in Lilliput: The Story of Donaciano Vigil.* Pampa: Pampa Printing, 1963.

Twitchell, Ralph Emerson. *The Leading Facts of New Mexican History, Vol. 2.* Cedar Rapids: Torch Press, 1912.

Weber, David J. *The Mexican Frontier, 1821-1846: The American Southwest Under Mexico.* Albuquerque: University of New Mexico Press, 1982.

Will, Martina E. "The Abominable Stench of Rotting Corpses: Protecting Public Health by Exiling New Mexico's Dead, 1804-1850." *La Crónica de Nuevo México.* Santa Fe: Historical Society of New Mexico, August 2000: 2-5.

Made in the USA
Middletown, DE
17 September 2023

38581884R10172